PAX BRITANNIA

TIME'S ARROW

ULYSSES GAVE IN to the waves of exhaustion threatening to overwhelm him, allowing his body to sag. He took a deep breath.

Where had the Sphere brought him to? Was he back in his own time?

Slowly, Ulysses turned his stupefied gaze to the object gripped tightly in his right hand.

It was a knife, its hilt and blade slick with blood, as was the palm of his hand.

He swore, letting the knife fall from his fingers.

A thunderous banging from what sounded like several storeys below had him leaping to his feet, despite the pulsing pain of the gunshot wound.

The furious knocking subsided and a gruff voice shouted, "*C'est les gendarmes! Ouvrez la porte!*"

"Oh, boy," he said with a heartfelt sigh. "Not again."

Ulysses Quicksilver adventures
Unnatural History
Leviathan Rising
Human Nature
Evolution Expects
Blood Royal
Dark Side
Anno Frankenstein
Time's Arrow

Other novels from the world of *Pax Britannia*
El Sombra
Gods of Manhattan
Pax Omega

PAX BRITANNIA

TIME'S ARROW

By
Jonathan Green

Abaddon
Books

WWW.ABADDONBOOKS.COM

An Abaddon Books™ Publication
www.abaddonbooks.com
abaddon@rebellion.co.uk

First published in 2012 by Abaddon Books™,
Rebellion Intellectual Property Limited,
Riverside House, Osney Mead, Oxford, OX2 0ES, UK.

10 9 8 7 6 5 4 3 2 1

Editors: Jonathan Oliver & David Moore
Cover Art: Pye Parr
Internal Illustration: Pye Parr
Design: Simon Parr & Luke Preece
Marketing and PR: Michael Molcher
Creative Director and CEO: Jason Kingsley
Chief Technical Officer: Chris Kingsley
Pax Britannia™ created by Jonathan Green

UK ISBN: 978-1-78108-064-1
US ISBN: 978-1-78108-063-4

Printed in the US

For Isaac Jeffrey Zitron – one day.

And for Eliot Ray Fullarton Taylor – not long after that.

Once I, Chang Chou, dreamed that I was a butterfly and was happy as a butterfly. I was conscious that I was quite pleased with myself but I did not know that I was Chou. Suddenly I awoke and there I was, visibly Chou. I do not know whether it was Chou dreaming that he was a butterfly or the butterfly dreaming that it was Chou.

– Chang Tzu, c.369-286 BC

Killing one butterfly couldn't be that important! Could it?

– Ray Bradbury, 'A Sound of Thunder,' 1952

PROLOGUE

Past Imperfect

ULYSSES QUICKSILVER OPENED his one remaining eye. All he could see was a blur of black shadows and ice-white light. He felt cold all over, and yet sweat was beading on his brow.

He had been shot enough times in his life to know that now was one of those times. He felt sick with pain; a dull, throbbing ache in his right shoulder.

He blinked, trying to banish the grey patches from his clouded vision. He blinked again and only then realised that the lingering haziness was caused by the clouds of dust settling around him.

He sat up carefully, feeling woozy.

There in front of him, where the exit from the sepulchre should be, was a pile of rock debris as high as the chamber's vaulted ceiling. He found himself wondering how much of the ancient fortress must have collapsed in the cave-in to create such a mountain of rubble.

Ulysses felt the insistent throb in his bones and knew that danger hadn't done with him yet.

He turned to the source of the pulsing, ice-white light. The Sphere was still active, opening a tunnel through time and space, creating a hole in the skin of the world that should never have existed.

Combined with the damage already caused by the Iron Eagle's crash-landing, the eldritch energies so unleashed were worrying at the very fabric of the Schloss Adlerhorst, at a molecular level. They were tearing the ancient castle apart. This had already resulted in the devastation Ulysses could see before him, and he suspected that, if what he had witnessed on the Moon more than fifty years into the future was anything to go by, it was only a matter of time before the rest of the Alpine stronghold came down on top of them, burying them beneath innumerable tons of rock and rubble.

Groggily getting to his feet, Ulysses took in the rest of the sepulchral cavern. Any doors or other access points there might once have been were buried behind the landslide, with no chance of Ulysses ever uncovering them in time. There was only one way out of here now.

His left hand clamped over the bullet wound in his shoulder, Ulysses began to pace across the debris-strewn, stone-flagged floor. He moved from looming pillar to looming pillar. The cyclopean columns were all that was holding the roof up. All the while he kept his eye on the figure standing next to the time-transmat device.

The warped freak that had once been Daniel Dashwood was busy atop the steel dais, silhouetted against the glare of the Sphere's nimbus of searing white light. His face was still covered by the ion mask and he was pulling on an over-sized glove over his left hand. And he was utterly ignorant of Ulysses' presence.

Suddenly the universe had turned and he had been given a second chance.

Judging by his behaviour, Dashwood must have recklessly assumed that Ulysses was already dead – or as good as. But where was he planning on going this time? Was it further back into the past, to try to put right all that had gone wrong at Schloss Adlerhorst? Did he intend to travel to somewhere else in 1943 to escape the imminent destruction of the castle? Or was he heading back to the future – back to what Ulysses still thought of as the present – eighteen months or so from the end of the twentieth century?

Ulysses doubted Dashwood could hear his approaching footsteps, what with the droning whine of the device and the seismic rumbling of the mountain peak as it slowly shook itself apart. Besides, he was talking to himself; although from the tone of his voice, it sounded more like he was berating himself.

Another voice – Germanic, feminine and synthesised – rang out over the throbbing hum of the machine and the ice-floe crack of the weakening walls. "Coordinates set. Launching in one minute."

Ulysses watched as Daniel Dashwood made an adjustment to one of the controls built into the thick vulcanised rubber glove and prepared to step into the temporal vortex.

Flexing his back and straightening his body, Ulysses focused his mind on dispelling the numbness that was threatening to leech away the last of his strength. He concentrated on one thing and one thing only – the pulsing glow of the Sphere.

Dashwood didn't know anything about his approach until Ulysses was right behind him.

Something having alerted him – a sound perhaps, a barely perceptible change in air pressure, some heightened sixth sense – Dashwood spun round.

"Thirty seconds," the tinny female voice of the Enigma engine intoned, as it commenced the final countdown. The logic engine was a monolith of black metal and glittering components on the other side of the platform, glimpsed between the hurtling gyroscopic bands of the Sphere.

Ulysses threw himself at the villain, all his anger and passion rising like a volcanic tide within him. His fury gave him the strength he needed, enabling him to blot out the throbbing ache of the gunshot wound.

He slammed the traitorous Dashwood into the zone of the Sphere's influence and the two of them were immediately assailed by unfathomable forces. Tendrils of light, like fingers of incorporeal mist, whirled about them, while their faces were buffeted by hurricane winds.

"You!" Dashwood hissed from behind the ion mask as Ulysses landed on top of him and they came nose to nose.

"Yes, me," Ulysses snarled, kneeling across Dashwood's body and pulling him up by the front of his robe.

"I thought you were dead." Dashwood spat, clawing at Ulysses' hands with ragged fingernails. "Twice."

"You thought wrong," Ulysses replied.

Letting go with his right hand, he pulled the mask from Dashwood's face, casting it aside.

His one eye widened in momentary surprise. It was like looking at an anatomist's model of a human head, made from layer upon layer of translucent material. There was Dashwood's arrogantly handsome face, and beneath that, layers of moving muscle; a network of blood vessels and capillaries. He could see the man's eyeballs quite clearly, as well as the thread of the optic nerve behind each one. Behind transparent lips he could see Dashwood's teeth, set within the gums covering the jaw that was just as clearly visible beneath. He even fancied he could see right down to the skull, the layers of flesh and subcutaneous fat seeming to peel away under his close scrutiny.

Forming his hand into a fist, he dealt Dashwood a resounding blow and winced. The transparent flesh and bone felt as solid as that of any other man.

"Twenty seconds," the Enigma engine tolled.

The pronouncement was accompanied by a crack like a thunderclap from the roof of the chamber.

Ulysses froze and looked up. He saw the treacherous tracery of the black fissure opening above him, crazing like a crack in the splintering ice of a winter pond.

It was all the distraction Dashwood needed.

His punch caught Ulysses in the stomach, putting his diaphragm into spasm and forcing the air from his lungs.

Ulysses doubled up. Dashwood grabbed hold of him with both hands and, with startling strength, threw him off. Ulysses landed on the other side of the platform, outside of the Sphere's influence.

"Fifteen seconds," the Enigma engine's voice echoed from the walls of the collapsing crypt.

Leaving Ulysses curled up in agony – wracked with pain from his shoulder wound as much as the punch to the stomach – Dashwood scrambled into the cradle at the heart of the transmat device.

"Come on, come on!" he hissed through clenched teeth. His whole body trembled as he waited for the machine to launch him through the hole it had opened in time and space.

There was another apocalyptic crash and then a moment of eerie silence. It was followed only a few seconds later by the thunderous noise of a piece of masonry hitting the dais not five feet from Ulysses.

"Ten seconds."

The threat of being crushed by another cave-in spurred him on, giving him the resolve to draw on every last scrap of strength he had. Forcing himself up onto his feet one last time, Ulysses turned towards the whirling Sphere. Flashes of actinic lightning were erupting from it now. The figure of Dashwood at the heart of the machine was nothing more than a blur.

"Five seconds."

Ulysses leapt, but not at Dashwood. Instead he grabbed hold of one of the static rings that generated the energy lattice. It was that lattice that held the unimaginable forces of the temporal vortex at bay – effectively creating its own microcosm of time and space, separate from the rest of reality. Ulysses cried out as his exertions tore at his injured shoulder. But he held on.

"Four."

His own momentum carrying him forwards, he brought his knees up to his chest and kicked out at Dashwood.

The man shouted in alarm as Ulysses planted both feet firmly in the middle of his chest, the force of the blow sending him tumbling backwards out of the machine.

"Three."

His shoulder's own scream of pain silencing him, Ulysses let go.

He landed, sprawled in the cradle, and felt another hand grab hold of his and hang on. A hand encased inside vulcanised rubber.

Ulysses stared down through the lattice of the cradle as Dashwood's death's-head leer peered up at him, their faces separated by the rippling heat-haze distortion of the temporal field between them.

The glove's wrist-mounted controls thumped against one of the support rings of the Sphere; Ulysses heard the keys rattling.

"Course change confirmed."

"One."

"Launch."

The body blow Dashwood had dealt him was as nothing compared to the forces that assailed Ulysses now as every atom of his being was blasted into the black oblivion of null-space.

LIQUID LIGHT SWAM like mercury around him, cocooning him within a ball of shimmering silver. Time and space lost all meaning as reality unravelled.

The present melted away into the past, as the past became the future, the skeins of fate unravelling into eternity.

And as time unwound, so did consciousness.

A melange of memories assaulted his mind in a torrent – recollections of events yet to happen – all there in his past.

And then recollection became reality and he was re-living the moments that had made him the man he was today, whenever that might be...

...ANOTHER BLOCK OF mooncrete crashed to the ground, shattering upon contact with the platform and denting a handrail. That had been too close for comfort.

With fumbling fingers, Ulysses finally managed to undo the knots that bound Emilia to the chair and pull the gag free of her mouth.

As her father helped her up, Ulysses pushed them both along the walkway towards the exit from the domed chamber.

A figure stood in the thick of the swarming Selenites, and yet remained untouched.

Ulysses felt he should recognise the man, even though he could barely see him between the milling alien ants.

Emilia looked up at him with desperate eyes. Her hair was a mess, hanging in ruffled tangles around her shoulders. Tears streaked her face.

"Go!" Ulysses implored her. "You have to get out of here now!"

"But what about you?" she said, grasping him by the shoulders.

"I'll catch you up."

"You're going after Daniel, aren't you?"

"I have to. I can't let him get away again. The consequences would be too terrible to contemplate."

Emilia's own anxious expression sagged.

"Will I ever see you again?"

Ulysses smiled weakly. "Oh, I'm like a bad penny, me. You don't get rid of me that easily."

"As if I'd want to."

Ulysses looked across the chamber, trying to get a good look at the man hiding in the shadows.

There was something about him, something Ulysses couldn't put his finger on, but without understanding why he felt that he could trust the man.

"Go," he urged Emilia and her father, sending them on their way. "I'll be back, I promise."

The domed chamber at the heart of the moonbase reverberated with the insectoid clacking of the Selenites' mandibles, the furious screams of Dashwood's transmat clones and the ever-present white noise of the glowing Sphere.

"Sir!" Nimrod called from the other end of the curving walkway. "They're getting away."

Ulysses turned from his manservant to Emilia, to suddenly find her lips on his. Taken aback, he gave in to the moment.

Emilia broke contact and whispered, "And make sure you keep your promise this time."

With a crash of metal and mooncrete, another piece of the fractured dome came down on the walkway, dragging a steel girder down with it. Ulysses only just pulled himself back in time before the debris hit, tearing through the walkway and slamming into the fractured floor of the chamber.

"Now go!" Ulysses shouted, blowing Emilia one last kiss, before turning and running for the dais.

Shielding his eyes against the glare of the light pulsing from the whirling rings, Ulysses tensed.

The power of the machine thrummed through his body. It felt as if the vibrations would unravel the very fibres of his being.

This was it; there was no escaping his fate now. He had seen what repeated use of the Sphere had done to Dashwood – in both body and mind – but, as Nimrod had said, they had passed the point of no return.

Ulysses glanced back down the buckled staircase. Waves of light rippled throughout the chamber as myriad fractures split the walls of the dome. It surely couldn't be long before the structure gave way altogether.

His eyes found Nimrod standing in front of the Babbage engine's control console. And Nimrod's gaze of steely resolve found his.

"Go, sir!" he yelled, his voice barely audible over the thrumming whine of the Sphere.

"I'm coming back for you!" Ulysses shouted, the tears streaming down his face. "I'll come back, I promise!"

And then through the waves of light, the tears, the smoke and the dust, Ulysses glimpsed movement on the far side of the chamber. The man standing at the entrance to the chamber had his hand outstretched towards Nimrod.

And then there was no more time for reminiscing about what might have been. Time had caught up with him.

Ulysses turned, and with a mumbled "Here goes nothing!" threw himself into the retina-searing sphere of light...

...HE WAS FALLING through time again, the past, the present, the future...

A myriad possibilities...

An infinite number of potential realities...

He saw the fingerprints of the Creator across eternity...

A ball of incandescent heat, like a captured sun, fell through the years. The chronosphere left a trail of unresolved potentialities in its wake, whilst he lay curled at its centre, shivering as impossible fractal patterns of frost etched their way across his exposed skin.

The furious heat of the tamed sun evaporated, the shell of the chronosphere melting away like ice on a magma floe...

*　　*　　*

...THE LIGHT FADED and Ulysses Quicksilver was plunged into darkness. His body felt uncomfortably hot.

His nose wrinkled in response to the distinctly unpleasant smell of burnt hair and scorched fabric.

Slowly, he stood up.

He felt vitrified soil beneath him, as hard and smooth as glass. It splintered and cracked with every move he made.

He peered bewilderedly about him, not knowing where – or even *when* – he was.

The cold gust of wind took him by surprise.

He took a deep breath, sniffing the air as he did so.

He looked up, the all-enveloping darkness that had first met his gaze softening to midnight blue.

As he blinked the last of the grey patches from before his eyes, he made out pinpricks of light in the heavens above. The luminous white ball of the moon gazed down at him from behind the shadows of clouds.

He took a wary step forward, the earth beneath his feet snapping like sugar glass.

Wisps of smoke rose from his suit. Running a hand through his scorched hair, he realised that it was standing on end.

He took several deep breaths, keen to clear the stink of burnt hair from his nostrils.

He was able to make out other scents now. The resinous aroma of pine needles. A dampness on the air. Leaf mould.

And then the night lit up all around him as half a dozen torch-beams pierced the darkness. Somewhere nearby an engine roared and he was caught in the searing glare of sodium headlights.

"*Halt!*" a harsh voice shouted over the sudden revving and the clatter of rifles taking aim.

The voice was speaking German.

"Stop, in the name of the Führer! Raise your hands where I can see them and do not move if you value your life. You are now a prisoner of the Third Reich. *Sieg heil!*"

Slowly, obligingly, Ulysses did as he was told...

...HE CAME TO, to find himself being slapped repeatedly across the face.

Blearily he opened his eyes, struggling to focus on the person in front of him. There was the impression of an armoured helm.

Losing the battle with consciousness, he phased out again for a moment.

"Wake up!" a voice snapped. It sounded like it was coming from another room.

Ulysses struggled to open his eyes but his eyelids felt as heavy as lead.

"I said wake up!" the voice came again, louder this time. It was accompanied by a mighty blow across the face that snapped his head round, shocking him into opening his eyes.

The chair he had been tied to rocked on its legs, threatening to tip over.

There was blood in his mouth. Mustering what strength he could, he spat a great gobbet onto the stone-flagged floor. Probing at the inside of his cheeks with the tip of his tongue, he felt a molar give and wondered how many more blows it would take before the tooth came out altogether.

A claw-like hand grabbed hold of his chin, and he winced. All he could see of his gravel-voiced interrogator, under the glare of the lamps, was the silhouette of a hooded figure. It appeared almost monastic.

Blinking against the intensity of the arc-lights Ulysses concentrated on the shaded face in front of him.

It was metal; he was sure of it.

"What's your plan, eh?" the helmed figure demanded.

Ulysses stared at the metal mask in confusion. Try as he might he was struggling to recall who his interrogator was, where he was, what he was doing there, and why he was being interrogated at all.

And then he remembered.

Peering up through eyes blackened and swollen from the beatings he had received he saw the metallic faceplate more clearly now.

He saw the thin slit in imitation of a mouth, through which the desperate man's rasping words came. He saw the rectangles that had been cut for his eyes. They were lit from within by an eerie ice-blue glow as the ion mask laboured to

18

stabilise the cellular structure of the man's face, and prevent it from collapsing altogether.

"Daniel Dashwood," Ulysses said with a chuckle...

...ULYSSES GASPED FOR breath. He felt a chill on his brow from the evaporating beads of sweat.

He looked around himself anxiously, and soon realised he was only seeing through his left eye. The right seemed to be covered by something. He tried to blink, but his right eye stubbornly refused to respond.

He was in some kind of laboratory, that much was plain. Flickering, inconstant sparks of blue-white light lit the chamber, revealing bare stone walls, banks of primitive Babbage-esque engines, and workbenches supporting a plethora of glass tanks. The tanks were full of a soupy yellow-green fluid, and suspended within that murky miasma...

A host of hideous memories – or were they hallucinations? – abruptly assailed his waking mind...

Masked surgeons. Glinting, razor-edged scalpels. The glare of arc-lamps. Fingers probing where fingers were never supposed to go...

Ulysses gasped in shock and tried to sit up, but he was prevented from doing so by the leather harness that had been used to secure him to the operating table.

He could move his head, but that was all.

He started to panic. He had been somewhere like this before. More memories...

An operating theatre, its tiled walls crusted with dried bloodstains...

His heart quickened, his breathing nothing more than shallow panting gasps.

It was said that after it was gone, a man did not remember the pain he had once had to endure. And it was a good thing too, otherwise Ulysses would have gone mad, he was sure of it.

However, he was aware of a dull ache in his face. It was his eye. He went to rub it, before remembering that he couldn't move his hands.

Tensing his arm, Ulysses tried once more to extricate himself.

He gritted his teeth as the leather cuff rubbed the sparse flesh of his wrist raw. It was no good; no matter how hard he tried, he wasn't going to be able to free himself that way.

He stopped and tried to relax, hoping to clear his mind so that he might come up with a way out of the fix he was in.

As he lay there, pondering his predicament, the sounds of the lab filtered through to his conscious mind.

There was the rising hum of electrical capacitors, the crackle of discharging energy, and the wheezing hiss of a bellows, the rattle of an Enigma engine processing streams of data, and the *glub-glub* of air bubbles in a tank of fluid. Lastly there was the clatter of surgical instruments in a kidney dish and a murmur of voices. It took Ulysses a moment to register that they were speaking German.

"He's awake, Doktor."

A voice; young, male and subservient. It sounded strangely familiar.

"Is he now?" came another voice. This one was more thickly accented and cracked with age, or with insanity.

There was a metallic crash as something was dropped into a pan. It was followed by the sound of footsteps ringing from the floor of the laboratory.

Moments later Ulysses found himself staring up at an emaciated spectre in a blood-stained surgical gown, the splatters glistening wetly in the crackling lightning bursts.

"Ah, so he is," the scarecrow-like creature said in its broken voice. Various magnifying lenses were mounted on a metal clamp around the creature's head.

Pulling away its surgeon's mask, the freak regarded him with a disquieting death's head leer. The demonic doctor was smiling at him.

"Good evening. And how are you feeling?"

Ulysses stared at the gaunt face in abject horror. How was he feeling? What kind of a question was that?

"But how rude of me. I have not yet introduced myself," the deathly surgeon fretted. "I am Doktor Folter of the Frankenstein Corps, and I shall be your surgeon for the duration of this procedure."

Ulysses swallowed hard. "Procedure?"

"But of course. It is a long time since we have had any spare parts of such quality to work with, even despite the injuries you have sustained since being brought here. But thankfully, most of that is only superficial damage. Your left arm especially," he said almost hungrily. "Such strong and supple flesh. So young and fresh."

"My eye," Ulysses mumbled. "What's happened to my eye?"

"This eye, you mean?" Folter said casually, holding up a pair of forceps. Gripped within its metal teeth was a glistening ball of white jelly, shreds of fine muscle still attached...

...ULYSSES STEPPED OVER the body of the guard. The soldier had been unconscious ever since Victor Frankenstein's creation had smashed the man's head into the wall hard enough to knock his eyeballs out of his skull. Past this first obstacle, Ulysses squeezed past the hulking giant, which brought him to the threshold of the cell. There he froze.

He opened his mouth to speak, but no words came.

The young man standing in the middle of the room gave him an appraising look and then, smiling, took a step forward. He offered Ulysses his hand.

Ulysses stared at him dumbly.

He had seen the young man's photograph a thousand times – with his instantly recognisable bushy moustache and strong jaw-line. Then there was the painting that had once hung on the wall behind his desk, back in his study at his home in Mayfair. And most importantly, his own memories of the man.

He had never looked this young, of course, but the man was still, unmistakeably, his father.

"Quicksilver," the young man said, Ulysses dumbly taking the proffered hand and shaking it. "Hercules Quicksilver."

Ulysses mouthed the words as his father spoke them, continuing to stare at the haggard-looking man in stunned amazement.

"And you are?"

"What?" Ulysses mumbled, coming out of his catatonic stupor.

"Your name; what is it?"

Ulysses' mind raced as he tried to think of what to say.

"Shelley," he suddenly blurted out.

"I can honestly say that I am *very* pleased to meet you," Hercules said, shaking the older man firmly by the hand. The older man who was, in reality, the son he did not yet know he would have.

Ulysses continued to stare at him, tongue-tied and open mouthed.

"Now, if you'll pardon me for saying so," Hercules said, taking charge, "if this is a rescue, shouldn't we be about escaping?"

"This way," said Katarina Kharkova, the blonde-haired vampire appearing within the devastated doorway.

"Excuse me," Hercules said, giving the looming giant a wary glance as he squeezed past.

Still in a state of shock, Ulysses turned to follow...

...HIS PULSE QUICKENING, he strode between the pillars supporting the castle sepulchre's vaulted ceiling, heading in the direction of the clinging shadows and spasmodic bursts of lightning. Half-hidden by the colossal columns was something Ulysses had never thought to see again.

The broken concentric rings of the gyroscope had gone, replaced by two interlocking rings joined perpendicular to one another. The gleaming steel rings bristled with connectors and electrodes. From these the barely contained energies harnessed by the device dissipated into the atmosphere. Despite looking quite different from its last iteration, it was still unquestionably the same machine that had landed him in all this trouble in the first place.

But now, as he stood before the Sphere, bathed in its crackling glow, to Ulysses it appeared as nothing less than a beacon of hope; the means to his salvation. A second chance.

A way home.

The device was already running up to speed. Someone was planning on teleporting out of there; that much was clear. To Ulysses' mind it could only be one person.

Darting anxious glances about him, Ulysses' knuckles whitened around the butt of the gun in his hand. Pressed flat against a pillar, he searched for his quarry, his heart playing his ribcage like a xylophone.

The horrifically-disfigured and molecularly-unstable sociopath Nazi collaborator Daniel Dashwood was here, Ulysses was sure of it. With the Icarus Cannon destroyed and Schloss Adlerhorst succumbing to the Iron Eagle's attack, the traitor was clearly planning on cutting his losses and getting out of there while he still could.

But then he hadn't counted on Ulysses Quicksilver catching up with him.

"Ten minutes and counting," came the dulcet synthesised tones of the Enigma machine on the other side of the crypt.

Ten minutes. More than enough time to bring Dashwood's audacious scheme to an end. Perhaps even enough time to make his own escape back to the future.

Warily, Ulysses peered around the column.

He was immediately transfixed by the object resting atop its own specially fashioned iron dais. He stared at the whirling rings of the device as it powered up to launch speed.

It truly was a wonder of German engineering. With all the resources of the Third Reich at his disposal, Dashwood had achieved in a matter of months what had taken Alexander Oddfellow several years.

Taking a calming breath, tightening his grip on the pistol, Ulysses stepped out from behind the pillar. He ducked behind it again immediately as the screech of unoiled hinges carried across the vault. It had come from the other side of the sepulchral chamber.

Ulysses froze. His heart was pounding so hard he was sure that whoever else was there in the chamber could hear it echoing off the walls.

And then, over the thrumming whirr of the energising Sphere, there came a scrabbling sound from somewhere behind him.

A booming *clang* echoed across the chamber as the protesting hinges gave and the steel door banged open. It was followed by the *tap-tap-tap* of running footsteps and then a familiar voice exclaimed, "Damn! What the hell is that?"

"I don't know," came a young woman's voice in response to Hercules Quicksilver's enquiry.

Panic-stricken, Ulysses risked another glance from behind the pillar. Hercules and his companion had no idea of the danger they were walking into.

For a moment he considered calling out to them, warning them that they were not alone. But Dashwood – and he was certain that it was Dashwood lurking in the shadows at the back of the crypt – already knew they were here. He was doubtless moving to deal with the threat they posed at that very moment. If Ulysses called out to them, the only person who would benefit would be Dashwood. The villain would be alerted to the fact that Ulysses was there too, and the precious element of surprise would be gone.

Creeping around the crumbling column, Ulysses made his way ever closer to the Sphere platform. He glimpsed movement at the periphery of his vision, and ducked out of sight once more. His back to another pillar now, he peered to his right across the chamber.

And then he saw them, still making their way towards the Sphere. Hercules was leading the way, his female companion – the one called Cat – padding along behind him. She was moving as quietly as her feline codename suggested.

"Nine minutes and counting," came the Valkyrie voice of the Enigma engine.

In the time it took to blink, a shadow detached itself from the darkness and then Dashwood was there, seizing Cat from behind, his right arm around her neck. The woman gave a startled cry that quickly became a choking wheeze.

Ulysses stared in appalled horror at the man, the same man who had stolen fire from heaven. It was he who had brought the future crashing so catastrophically into the past and had tortured Ulysses to the very edge of sanity.

Even as Hercules made to go to the girl's aid, Dashwood – the ion mask still hiding his face – raised the gun in his right hand and put it to the woman's head.

Before Hercules realised what was going on, Ulysses was already breaking into a sprint.

"Not so fast!" the masked man said as Hercules turned to confront him. "I have your woman, so I wouldn't try anything clever if I were you. Or anything stupid, for that matter..."

The villain's voice trailed off. There was confusion in the man's eerily-lit eyes.

"Dashwood!" Hercules exclaimed.

"Wait a minute," the other spluttered. "You're not Quicksilver." His arm went limp and the gun slipped from his captive's temple.

"Oh but I am," Hercules snarled and sprang at the man.

In that split second, Dashwood's strength of purpose returned.

Without a moment's hesitation he pointed the gun at Hercules and fired –

– just as Ulysses collided with his father.

...ULYSSES QUICKSILVER OPENED his one remaining eye. All he could see was a blur of black shadows and ice-white light. He felt cold all over, even though there was sweat beading on his brow.

He had been shot. He felt sick with pain; a dull, throbbing ache in his right shoulder.

He blinked, trying to clear his clouded vision, and sat up, feeling woozy.

There in front of him was a mound of rocks and rubble as high as the vaulted ceiling of the chamber.

He felt the insistent throbbing in his bones and knew that he wasn't out of danger yet.

He turned to the source of the pulsing light. The Sphere was still active, tearing a hole through time and space that should never have existed.

The eldritch energies unleashed by the Sphere were steadily shaking the weakened stronghold apart. It was only a matter of time before the rest of Schloss Adlerhorst came crashing down on top them, burying them all – the good and the bad.

Ulysses groggily got to his feet. Surveying the sepulchral cavern, it was clear that there was only one way out now.

His left hand clamped over the bullet wound in his shoulder, Ulysses hurried between the last looming pillars still holding up the roof, his eye on the figure atop the steel dais.

He had been shot, he was losing blood, and he was still cruelly visually impaired, but suddenly the universe had turned, and life had given him a second chance.

The warped freak that had once been Daniel Dashwood was occupied, pulling on a single, oversized glove. And he was utterly ignorant of Ulysses' presence.

A second chance...

"...THREE," THE ENIGMA engine intoned.

His shoulder's scream of pain silencing him, Ulysses let go of the generator ring and landed, sprawled in the cradle. He felt another gloved hand grab hold of his and hang on.

Ulysses stared through the rippling heat-haze distortion of the temporal field and into Daniel Dashwood's grim death's-head leer.

The glove's wrist-mounted controls thumped against one of the support rings of the Sphere; Ulysses heard the keys rattling.

"Course change confirmed."

"One."

"Launch."

The body blow Dashwood had dealt him was as nothing compared to the forces that assailed Ulysses as he was blasted into the black oblivion of null-space...

...ULYSSES BLINKED, HIS vision swimming.

The whirling Sphere had gone, to be replaced by a molten ball of liquid silver light that spun and swirled like mercury on water.

Ulysses winced in pain. His nemesis's hand was still gripped tight about his. The esoteric mechanisms of the control gauntlet crackled and hummed. Everything below the elbow lay outside the sphere of whirling, silvered light.

Dashwood hung in the void, the howling winds of the temporal vortex taking their toll on his flesh, devouring his body with the raw hunger of the void.

As Ulysses watched, his own face slack with horror, Dashwood's flesh withered, his skin falling away in a whirl of grey flakes. The muscle beneath atrophied and blackened until that too was nothing more than dust, cascading like sand through an egg-timer into the void.

The madman's staring eyeballs collapsed inwards, melting like wax inside their orbits. In a moment there was nothing left of them but dark stains in the sockets of Dashwood's age-bleached skull.

His mouth open in a silent scream, the traitor's tongue shrivelled. The layers of flesh peeled away and the man's blood evaporated in a fine red mist.

Just as Ulysses was beginning to wonder whether his terrifying journey through time would ever end, the eternal darkness exploded in a nanosecond burst of light as brilliant as a supernova.

PART ONE

Red-Handed

Time is a brisk wind, for each hour it brings something new... but who can understand and measure its sharp breath, its mystery and its design?

– Paracelsus

CHAPTER ONE

The Scene of the Crime

ULYSSES LANDED HARD, flat on his face, on what felt like rough floorboards. Fresh waves of nausea pulsed through him with the pain from his shoulder and he blinked as the supernova brilliance faded to a murky grey twilight.

Something hit the floor beside him with a hollow clatter.

He felt uncomfortably hot and his skin was clammy. There was the coppery tang of blood on his tongue.

The unpleasantly familiar stink of scorched human hair – his own, he assumed – merged with the charcoal smell of roasted timbers.

His whole body shaking, he pushed himself up onto his hands and knees. Leaning back onto his heels, he pulled off his smouldering jacket, wincing again as his right arm came free.

He was kneeling at the centre of a perfect circle of blackened floorboards. The burn-marks ended abruptly; the bare boards beyond remained completely untouched.

The next shocking sight to greet him was Daniel Dashwood's skeleton. Steam was rising gently from the bones lying to Ulysses' left, half-in and half-out of the circle.

Ulysses started. He dropped Dashwood's hand – still encased

within the control glove – and put out an arm to stop himself falling backwards.

His hand came down in something warm and sticky.

He pulled it back in surprise, his fingers brushing against something cold and hard that shifted at his touch. His hand had closed around the object and he raised it to his face for a closer look. As he did so, he turned to see the handprint he had left in the pool of dark blood creeping out from under the body.

He could not stifle his gasp of surprise. The body was face-down on the floor, but just from the sheer amount of blood oozing away between the floorboards, and the waxy pallor of what little flesh he could see, Ulysses was certain that the poor wretch was dead – whoever he might have been in life.

He looked from the corpse to the room.

There was more ceiling than walls, the sloping sides meeting at the apex of the roof above him, and it was sparsely furnished. The body was lying beside a filthy, unmade bed that looked old enough to have been an antique.

There was a draught blowing in under the door of the mouldering attic room. Opposite it, a cracked mirror had been hung on the only wall tall enough to accommodate one. Beneath the mirror, on a rickety table, sat a cracked porcelain bowl bearing a crazed-glaze painting of flowers. A mismatched earthenware jug with a chipped rim sat within it.

The only other piece of furniture in the room was a small writing desk, positioned beneath a shuttered dormer window. The fallen chair before it had once been painted cream, but was now worn and chipped.

Ulysses gave in to the waves of exhaustion threatening to overwhelm him, allowing his body to sag. He took a deep breath.

Where had the Sphere brought him to? Was he back in his own time?

Slowly, Ulysses turned his stupefied gaze to the object gripped tightly in his right hand.

It was a knife, its hilt and blade slick with blood, as was the palm of his hand.

He swore, letting the knife fall from his fingers.

A thunderous banging from what sounded like several

storeys below had him leaping to his feet, despite the pulsing pain of the gunshot wound.

The furious knocking subsided and a gruff voice shouted, "*C'est les gendarmes! Ouvrez la porte!*"

"Oh, boy," he said with a heartfelt sigh. "Not again."

"*Ouvrez la porte!*" the angry voice came again from downstairs.

Ulysses was either in France or in a place where French was the native tongue. Happily, he had an ear for the language. After all, he was - as many a young debutante could testify - a cunning linguist.

He did not know the intricacies of the Sphere's operation, but he suspected Daniel Dashwood had not intended on taking a vacation to France. But if the course alteration had only been a minor one, and if he had actually been intending to flee to Germany or even back to England, it seemed perfectly plausible that the Sphere could have sent him to France instead. He wouldn't know for sure until he had been able to get his bearings properly, or had the chance to speak to someone. Someone with fewer anger issues than whoever it was hammering on the door downstairs.

But right now what Ulysses was even less sure about was when in time he was. That would take some investigating, too.

The thunderous hammering came again, the voice growing more impatient and irate.

"This is your last chance! This is the police! Open the door or I'll have it broken down!" There was a tremendous crash from somewhere at street level. The owner of the voice was making good on his promise.

Staggering to his feet, Ulysses scoured the room for anything that might enable him to escape.

There were only two ways out of the garret room – through the door, or through the window.

For the briefest moment Ulysses wondered whether he should simply open the door and wait for the gendarmes to find him, and then worry about trying to explain to them how he came to be there, alongside a dead body.

But then what was he thinking? Who was going to believe that he had travelled through space and time to end up here? And what would they make of the scorch-marks on the floorboards, let alone the corpse lying in a pool of its own congealing blood?

He took a step backwards and caught his reflection in the cracked glass above the wash bowl.

He was in a worse state than the room. He was still wearing the scruffy suit he had purloined from Castle Frankenstein. His right hand was wet with blood, as were the knees of his trousers. The eye-patch and a few days growth of stubble didn't help either.

He no longer looked like the bachelor once voted 'Best Dressed Man of the Decade' by *The Strand* magazine. If *he* had been a French policeman and had walked into the attic and found a stranger looking like that – with a dead man's blood on his hands and the victim lying next to him – he would have pronounced him guilty as soon as the next man.

Worst case? The gendarmes would shoot first and ask questions later.

He looked at the door, noticing the key in the lock for the first time. Stumbling over, he tried the handle.

The door was locked.

Had he been set up? But surely that wasn't possible. His arrival at this time and place had been pure fluke, hadn't it?

No, Ulysses decided, the best he could hope for was that he would be arrested and interrogated by the police. Normally, he would have thought he could talk himself out of pretty much anything, but he doubted that even his undisputed charm and silver tongue could help him this time.

Never mind the fact that he was inside a locked room with two dead bodies; how was he supposed to explain away the presence of the steaming skeleton? Frankly any explanation he gave would make him sound like nothing less than a certifiable nutcase – or, at worst, a total psychopath. The best he could hope for, then, was to be checked into a room for one at the local sanatorium; the one with the special rubber wallpaper and the jacket that buckled up at the back.

There was no way he was going to be able to talk his way out of this one, and he wasn't going to be able to fight his way out either. Certainly not in his current condition, and with the full weight of the French police on his case.

Ulysses hastily dropped the incriminating knife, as if it was suddenly too hot to handle, and wiped the sticky blood from his hand onto his already ruined trousers. After being caught up in a crash-landing, and a cave-in, and hurled through time, a little blood wasn't going to make a lot of difference to the state of his apparel.

The man could not have been dead more than a matter of minutes. His true killer could not be far away.

In the stillness of the room something banged behind him.

Ulysses froze.

The killer surely couldn't still be in the room, could he?

Ulysses looked anxiously around the room, but there was – as he had at first thought – no one else there. He relaxed and breathed again.

A second loud *bang* drew his attention to the dormer window, which appeared to be open and swinging in the breeze. Whoever had killed the poor unfortunate lying on the floor of the garret room had apparently left this way.

Ulysses' head suddenly swam, and he took a stumbling step back, putting his hand to the exposed laths of a wall to keep upright.

The gunshot wound had not been as bad as it might have been, but it was beginning to take its toll on him nonetheless, not helped by the fact that his mind was still reeling from the impossible journey he had taken only a matter of minutes before.

There came another splintering crash from downstairs, accompanied by a shout of, "We're coming in!"

The crash was the impetus Ulysses needed to marshal his thoughts and push aside all feelings of doubt and physical incapability. He moved to the door again, his hand on the key in the lock, but then stopped.

He was weak. The police were coming up the stairs. If he left through the door what were the chances that he would be able to avoid them and get away? Not knowing the layout of the building, he decided that the odds weren't good enough.

Stumbling away from the door again, Ulysses circumnavigated the patch of burnt boards and pooling blood. His foot caught the prone skeleton as he crossed the draughty attic space to the writing desk. The bones they fell apart with a clatter at his touch. Leaning across the desk, he pushed the window fully open with the heel of his hand. The putty of the sill of the garret room window had been deformed by a number of gouged ridges.

His eye fell on the sprawl of papers covering the desk, which fluttered and shifted in the breeze, making a noise like nesting birds in a dovecot.

A piece of manuscript paper protruded from the pile of newspapers and ink-stained blotters. A bottle of ink had tipped over, spilling its blue-black contents across the desk and much of the paper covering it.

Intrigued, he gave the corner of thick, yellow parchment a tug, pulling it free. A few bars of musical notation had been written upon it before being crossed out so vigorously that the nib of the pen had torn through the paper in several places. And at the top of the piece of sheet music, written in a hurried scrawl, was what he took to be a title:

Black Swan

The crisp morning sunlight painted bright bars of light across the desk, drawing his attention to the curled copy of *Le Monde* lying there.

Roughly folding the musical manuscript paper in half, he stuffed it into a jacket pocket, concentrating on the revelation the broadsheet held for him.

Ignoring the headline – something about a new production by the Paris Opera – Ulysses focused instead on the date.

Jeudi 7 Mai 1998

It looked like it could well be several days old, but the newspaper hadn't begun to yellow in the sun yet. So, Ulysses concluded, it couldn't be *that* old. It was some time after the seventh of May.

Ulysses hesitated as he set the chair on its feet again in front of the desk.

The seventh of May 1998.

Could it be as much as a month after the seventh of May?

He studied the paper again and came to the conclusion that it was most unlikely. But even if it was as late as June, then the implications were still the same.

Hard as it was to reconcile, it seemed that Ulysses had arrived back in 1998, some weeks before he had originally left for the Moon in pursuit of his ne'er-do-well brother Barty.

Ulysses' mind reeled. For some reason, that truth seemed even more incredible and harder to accept than the idea of travelling back to the Second Great European War, although meeting his father – who, at that time, was younger than Ulysses – had been a tough one to come to terms with. To think that there was another Ulysses Quicksilver, living his life in London, making plans to travel to the Moon, with no idea of the horrors that awaited him there and beyond...

Ulysses absent-mindedly put a quivering hand to the scars under his eye-patch, where his right eye should have been...

"Poor bastard has no idea what he's got coming," Ulysses said, staring at his reflection in the mirror once more.

It was still hard to believe that the dishevelled wretch he was looking at was actually him. He still thought of himself as looking as he had done before his second trip to the Moon – at about this time, in May 1998, as it happened.

Staring into the grizzled face, with its lean, unshaven chops and sinister eye-patch, he then stared through it, seeing the younger, handsome man he had once been.

And seeing that other, happier and more youthful man in his mind's eye, he also saw a woman standing at his side, her arm through his, a smile on her lips and love in her contented gaze.

Emilia Oddfellow – the woman he loved and the woman to whom he had once been engaged years before. The woman he had been forced to leave behind on the Moon when he leapt into the whirling time tunnel created by her father's teleportation device.

The pounding of heavy boots on the bare boards of the stairs shook him into action again.

"How could you have been so stupid?" he chided himself as he climbed up onto the desk and out through the window, a manic smile finding its way onto his face.

CHAPTER TWO

Déjà Vu

ULYSSES CLUNG ONTO the window frame with both hands, steadying himself on the sloped roof outside the garret room. A chill breeze gusted into his face. The sunlight was sharp and bright in his one good eye. He winced and blinked against its sudden intensity, tightening his grip on the splintered frame as a wave of dizziness threatened to pitch him off the edge of the roof.

He closed his eye, letting the sounds of the metropolis wash over him as he concentrated on regaining mastery of his reeling senses. He could hear the distant sound of car horns and costermongers announcing their wares in Parisian French.

From the room beneath him, he could hear pounding footfalls, underscored by breathless grunting and grumbling voices. From the sounds of them they would like as not give short shrift to anyone they found waiting for them there.

Ulysses opened his eye again, his swimming gaze ranging over the vista of rooftops bristling with aerials, as the latest wave of vertigo mercifully passed.

It wasn't only vertigo; it was exhaustion too. After all that he had been through, it was hardly surprising that fatigue was finally catching up with him.

To the left, some streets away, he caught sight of what looked like the sails of a windmill. They were crimson in the stark sunlight. He cautiously turned his head to the right, not wanting to make any too hasty movements and bring on another bout of nausea. He gasped.

A spear of cast iron rose above the skyline some miles to the south-west.

The sudden crash from the room behind him, as the gendarmes smashed open the door of the garret, shook him into action once more.

It didn't matter that he felt fit to drop. It didn't even matter that he had already been shot. What was the expression? *You can rest when you're dead.*

Ulysses eased himself out across the sloping roof, fighting to maintain his balance as the soles of his shoes slipped on the steep tiles. Using the dormer window to aid him, Ulysses scrambled up the roof to its crest, gasping a sharp intake of breath as his exertions tugged at his right shoulder.

"You're getting too old for this," he muttered under his breath. Here, at the apex of the roof, thankfully the verdigrised copper tiles flattened out, forming a narrow rat-run across the top of the rundown tenement.

Keeping his eye on the path ahead of him, hearing the appalled shouts of the gendarmes coming from within the garret, and praying that his vertigo wouldn't choose this moment to take charge again, Ulysses jogged along the ridgeline of the roof.

The enraged voices of the French policemen became more distinct as one of them leaned out of the window. Ulysses didn't pause. Any hesitation now could be fatal. He picked up the pace again.

"There he is!"

Ulysses started to run, his heels ringing from the discoloured copper. He was far too used to daring rooftops pursuits, but he wasn't usually the one being pursued. Only a few yards ahead of him, the roof ended abruptly. And beyond that, on the other side of a yawning six-foot-wide void, another building and another rooftop ridge.

Ulysses put on an extra burst of speed as he sprinted for the edge, kicking off at the last possible moment, arms windmilling as he hurtled through the air. He crashed down on top of the adjoining roof, feet slipping from underneath him momentarily, then somehow managed to get his half-falling, half-stumbling legs under control again and jogged on, gasping with the pulsing pain that every step brought with it.

Ulysses was suddenly thankful for the town planners, whose efforts – or perhaps the lack of them – had resulted in the tenements here being crammed together so tightly. He wasn't certain he could have cleared a wider gap, given his current condition.

But then, if he had been able to clear the gap, so could the policemen whose footsteps he could hear coming after him. He only hoped they weren't armed, or if they were that their haphazard pursuit of him would keep them from turning their guns on him too soon.

He looked around himself; to the left, the roof sloped down and dropped to the street below. To his right, it formed one side of an enclosed courtyard. Ulysses didn't fancy either option as an escape route, but the footprint of the building that he could now see from above gave him an idea.

A little further along, the roof turned sharply right; the brickwork of a chimney stack reared up behind the ridge. Leaping across the right angle, Ulysses slid and scrambled down the slope beyond and was only arrested by the obstacle formed by the sturdy brickwork.

The crack of a pistol confirmed his worst fears as brick chips flew from the stack just above his head.

Ulysses pulled himself around and behind the chimney, his gaze falling on the shadowy gulf that yawned between this building and the next. Clinging tightly to the brickwork, Ulysses tensed as he felt the vertigo threaten to overcome him again.

He took a deep breath and waited for the insufferable giddiness to pass. Every second he remained here was another second closer to capture. But if he were to continue in this vein it would very likely be the end of him.

Ulysses heard a break in the tapping footfalls and then a loud crash, followed by another. Two men had followed him across the gulf. He opened his eye. His sense of balance restored, it was time to move again.

He left his hiding place and set off at a run.

There was a shout from a gendarme. The policemen were still atop the roof ridge, but Ulysses was relying on the fact that their precarious position would have put a stop to their pistol-toting antics – for the time being, at least.

At the next corner a flagpole hung out over the road. But before that there was a sturdy aerial, bolted to the roof and projecting straight up.

Putting everything he had into his desperate run, Ulysses made it up the slope of the roof to the aerial ahead of the policeman, grabbed hold with both hands, and swung himself around the pole as the sprinting gendarme caught up with him.

Ulysses' feet caught the policeman in the ribs, causing him to lose his balance and slip from his precarious position on the roof ridge. Both gendarmes cried in alarm as the man hit the tiles and slid down the roof, feet kicking futilely, and his comrade broke off pursuit to go to his aid.

Ulysses hurried on.

He was nearing the edge of the roof again, and caught a glimpse of the cramped cul-de-sac beyond. It might be narrow, but it was still several yards to the far side of the street, and Ulysses didn't think he'd be able to make a jump like that. His own desperate flight faltered as he looked for alternatives.

There was still the flagpole to his left, and he could now see the frontages of the buildings beyond. The next tenement along sported balconies right across its façade, as did the houses in front of him, on the opposite side of the street. He could use the pole to swing over to one of those and put some more distance between him and the policemen. He didn't know where he'd be able to go from there, but he was sure to be able to lose them once he had ducked indoors.

"Stop!" came a scream from behind him, accompanied by the crack and *spang* of a bullet ricocheting from a roof tile.

Ulysses risked a glance back over his shoulder. The gendarme he had almost booted off the roof was back on his feet and pounding towards Ulysses, incandescent rage turning his face the colour of the Moulin Rouge windmill. He held a smoking gun in his hand.

There was nothing else for it.

Ulysses sprinted for the end of the ridge. Reaching it he didn't slow his desperate flight for a second, long strides carrying him, half-falling and half-running, down the slope of the roof.

With every iota of strength left in him, Ulysses hurled himself across the street. Arms and legs flailing, his leap of desperation became a wailing, floundering fall, and he dropped towards the cobbled street six storeys below.

And then the wrought ironwork of a jutting balcony was rising to meet him. The first flew past his eye like a cruel jest, but he crashed onto the one below.

He hurtled through the closed French doors beyond, entering the room in a shower of glass splinters and broken wooden staves, rolled to a halt, feeling the softness of the carpet under him as well as the stabbing points of broken glass sticking into him.

He lay there for a moment, lungs heaving, thigh muscles on fire, ankles throbbing. His face stung; he assumed it had been cut in a dozen places by the whickering glass shards.

He heard the echoing crack of a pistol again and the muffled impact of the bullet burying itself in the carpeted floor beside him.

Ulysses rolled onto his hands and knees, dragging himself upright with the aid of a porcelain-bedecked sideboard. And then he was barrelling through the door out of the dusty, mote-shot drawing room and into the room beyond.

Slamming the door shut behind him, he heard the report of two more pistol shots and felt the impacts of the rounds embedding themselves in the door frame.

Panting, Ulysses exited the apartment as quickly as he could.

Reaching the landing in the stairwell that ran the entire height of the tenement building, he glanced up and down over the edge of the railed balustrade. He could not see or hear any sign of another living soul, and so gave himself a moment to catch his breath and work out what to do next.

In all likelihood, Paris's finest would soon be entering the apartment building from street level in their determination to capture the suspected murderer.

Ulysses set off up the stairs, using the balustrade to help pull himself up.

He might be beyond exhaustion, and he suspected that there was still a bullet lodged somewhere in his shoulder, but, perversely, he hadn't felt this alive in a long time. But then again, a small part of his mind wondered, perhaps that was euphoria brought on by blood loss.

Following the turn of the stairs he came to another landing, barely pausing for breath as he commenced his climb of the next flight. At the top of the second flight he came to a featureless door which opened, at a kick, and led him out onto the roof of the apartment block. Back in the open air, he could hear shrill whistles from a street away, over the honking of distant car horns and even the occasional shout of "Stop! Murder!"

Ulysses immediately threw himself back into hiding beside the rooftop exit. Peering around the edge of the flimsy structure, he could see the two policemen who had pursued him this far retreating across the roof of the building opposite as they struggled to find a way off the tenement.

The roof Ulysses now found himself on was flat, as were those of the buildings adjoining it. Following a course that led him as far away from the direction he had come as possible, Ulysses set off again, navigating the roofscape with care as he advanced even further into this neglected region of Paris.

It was clear even from the roof that he was in one of the more lugubrious areas of the city. He had visited Paris years ago, before commencing the Paris-to-Dakar rally, but on that occasion he had only taken in the tourist sights – the Eiffel Tower, Notre Dame and the Paris Opera.

But looking about him now, orienting himself by the Eiffel Tower, Sacre Coeur and the red windmill of the Moulin Rouge, he guessed that he was somewhere within the artists' quarter of Montmartre. Perhaps even somewhere within the vicinity of the Rue Morgue.

The whistles and shouts were getting louder. The police must have entered the adjacent street.

Scrambling over a low wall that delineated the border between one building and the next, Ulysses picked up the pace again. Alone among the forests of aerials, without armed police directly at his back, he was able to take time to think and plot a course by which he could lose himself in the labyrinthine slums without ever having to set foot on the ground. Fire escapes led to rooftop terraces, rusted iron bridges spanned six-storey chasms, and wall-mounted ladders gave access to yet more balconies and other rooftop ridges.

The whistles began to recede, the voices becoming scattered, as the police were forced to split up to continue their search for the fugitive. And gradually Ulysses left one street after another behind him, without ever having to descend to ground level.

If it hadn't been for the fact that he was fleeing for his life from the Parisian police, Ulysses might have actually enjoyed himself. There was barely a cloud in the sky, the late spring sun raising a heat-haze from the warm copper roofs. The weather could almost have been described as balmy.

Gasping for breath, Ulysses took a moment to wipe away the sweat that had collected in the hollow behind his eye-patch.

And that was when he saw it.

It was emerging from the fourth floor window of a building at the end of the shadowed cul-de-sac. Eight feet tall, with arms like great sides of beef covered in thick black hair, it swung from the open window with startling grace and agility, launching itself towards a fire escape another floor up, and reaching it with ease. From there the beast swung itself up onto the roof.

The massive ape landed not ten feet from him, its sledgehammer fists sending clouds of dust rising.

Ulysses froze.

The beast snorted, and its beady black stare fell on the exhausted, injured man, the atmosphere thickening between them. Ulysses' heart thumped against the cage of his ribs, the bullet wound pulsing in unkind sympathy.

He had seen gorillas before at London Zoo, but he had never seen a silverback so big. And he had never seen one with thick steel electrodes sticking out of its skull like a crown of thorns – or arms bound with cables, its forearms sheathed in metal vambraces, and its knuckles riveted with steel pins. Its flesh was scored by myriad, crude scars where it had been stitched together around the electrical and mechanical implants. Each of its major joints bore a heavy industrial screw to strengthen it.

Its fists crushing the concrete, the giant ape craned its head forward, lips curling back to expose a mouth crammed with what looked like enamel chisels.

Ulysses met the beast's furious stare with his one remaining eye, his hands automatically going for his sword-stick and his gun, although he had neither with him, and hadn't since being taken captive in Castle Falkenstein. Slowly, instinctively, Ulysses began to back away from the augmented monster. He had battled ape-men, dinosaurs, sea monsters, hybrid vivisects, mutated giant insects, werewolves, vampires, and even Nazis in his time – but he had never faced off against anything quite like this before.

A guttural growl rose from within the brute's huge barrel chest as it slowly knuckled towards Ulysses.

Ulysses caught sight of something else as the beast advanced. Bolted to the back of its neck was a box of blinking lights that looked like a transmitter of some kind. Red LEDs winked on and off as the beast moved towards him. The transmitter was connected to the electrodes sunk into the beast's skull via bundles of twisted cabling.

Ulysses came to an abrupt halt as he stumbled against the edge of a steepled skylight.

Rising up on its hindquarters, the gorilla pounded its chest with its massive, augmented fists, giving an animal bellow that rang out over the rooftops of Paris. It seemed to Ulysses as if the roar silenced the other sounds of the city for a moment, as if the city was holding its breath in anticipation.

This was it; Ulysses' time was up. He was a dead man unless he did something fast.

He looked around, desperately searching for anything he could improvise as a weapon.

He caught sight of the porcelain bowl out of the corner of his eye: a broken toilet, discarded with all manner of other detritus atop the tenement building.

Grabbing hold of the ceramic cistern cover with both hands, he swung it like a cricket bat as the gorilla came for him.

The porcelain connected with the brute's forearm, and shattered. Ulysses threw his arms across his face to protect himself from the ceramic shrapnel.

The ape howled as a piece of the broken cistern lid cut into the meat of a bulging bicep and another sliced across its back, connecting with the transmitter bolted between its shoulder blades.

The beast retaliated with a swipe of its arm that lifted Ulysses off his feet and sent him hurtling through the air to come down hard on the slope of another raised roof light. Cracks crazed the glass at his impact. Ulysses lay stunned, his back and shoulders aching, the air forced from his lungs by the ape's assault.

He was unaware of the primate abruptly breaking off its attack and bounding away across the rooftops of the Rue Morgue.

But he *was* aware of the sharp *crick-crack* of the roof light under him. Blinking hard as he forced himself to come to his senses, his head reeling, wanting nothing more than to give in to the blissful oblivion of unconsciousness, Ulysses tried to sit up.

The movement was accompanied by another crystal-sharp crack. He stopped and tried shifting his weight to the left.

Crack!

Ulysses froze, not daring to move a muscle, seeing the ape bounding away across the rooftop and into the distance. And then, with one final splintering *snap,* the roof light gave way under him and he was falling once more, with no way of saving himself.

CHAPTER THREE

Les Miserables

"Madame Sandrine," Reynard said, casting his eyes to the floor, a touch of colour at his cheeks. "I did not mean to intrude."

Sandrine gasped, feeling her heart swell and flutter like a butterfly within her breast, pulling her gown close about her shoulders.

"You are not intruding," she replied, tilting her head to peer up at him coyly, feeling the blood rushing to her cheeks.

"That is well, then," the burly gardener replied. He stood with his hands behind his back, his muscular arms tensed. She marvelled at the swell of his biceps beneath his shirt sleeves. She caught a glimpse of the curls of dark hair covering his taut chest, the firm pectorals visible under the sweat-stained linen.

Reynard said nothing more but remained within the doorway, at the threshold to her chamber.

"Did you want something?" Sandrine asked, taking a cautious step towards him, letting her hand fall from the gown. The chiffon parted to reveal the bodice of her tightly-laced whalebone corset, her bosom rising as she caught her breath again.

"Yes, I... I only wanted to tell you that..."

"Go on," Sandrine said. "There's no need to be shy. You don't need to feel embarrassed."

"It's the rose, ma'am."

The butterflies danced from her stomach to her heart. "The white rose I planted in memory of my late husband's passing?"

"Yes, ma'am."

A sudden doubt seized her mind, setting the butterflies into a fluttering frenzy. She turned to the window, gazing through it to the carefully tended gardens below. "Is everything alright? Nothing's happened to the white rose, has it?"

"No, ma'am, it's fine."

"Then what?"

Slowly he brought his right hand around from behind his back. "It's come into bloom, milady."

He was holding a stem of thorns topped by the curled ivory petals of a luxurious bloom.

"Oh, Reynard," Sandrine gasped, hurrying from the window to the young man. "It's beautiful."

"Like you, milady," the gardener said, offering her the rose.

"Reynard," she chided, a smile on her lips, her neck flushed crimson. As she took the cut stem from him, her fingertips caressed his rough, callused hands. Sandrine's entire being thrilled at the contact.

She felt like a girl of sixteen again, embarking upon her first love affair. She was not old, by any means, widowed and childless at twenty-five, but she had known marriage and men before.

"Reynard," she said, taking a step closer to him, her pale fingers tracing the buttons of his shirt. "Would you do something for me?"

"If it is within my power," the youth replied, meeting her gaze for the first time, causing her heart to skip a beat. She could have drowned in those chestnut eyes of his.

"Oh, I am sure it is," she said and, standing on tiptoe, raised her mouth to his, and planted a kiss on his trembling lips. But the kiss was not returned.

She took a step back. "I'm sorry, I went too far. I am too bold."

"No, lady, you are not," he said then, suddenly more assured in his tone and his movements than she had ever known him.

Taking a step towards her, so that there was not a hair's breadth between them, he took her in his arms and –

THE SPLINTERING CRASH tore Josephine away from the romantic world in which she had lost herself in an instant. She dropped the book with a startled cry, and spun around on the stool in front of the dressing table. She saw the man plummet from the shattered roof light and onto her bed, accompanied by a rain of splintered wood and shattered glass.

She jumped from her seat, sending it tumbling to the floor, and covered herself up as best she could with the negligee she was wearing.

The man on the bed wasn't moving. Was he dead or just stunned? And what had he been doing up on the roof of Madame Marguerite's Boarding House?

She took in the man's torn and scorched suit, the stubble, the waxy pallor of his cheeks and the eye-patch, but underneath all that she could also make out his patrician features and the fine bone structure of his face. He might look like a vagabond and a wastrel on the surface, but such exquisite bone structure spoke of a nobler heritage.

Josephine caught her breath as her heart skipped a beat. This was just like *The Garden of Love*; not so much the part where the handsome stranger had fallen from the roof and landed on her bed, but other than that…

He was like the hero, Count Christos, in *The Gilded Lily*; the dispossessed noble who had to masquerade as a lowly ostler until he could prove his identity and reclaim his one true love from the unscrupulous cousin who had denied him his birthright.

Her imagination awhirl with possibilities, Josephine warily approached the bed.

She cleared her throat. "Are you alright?"

The man gave no response; he continued to lie where he had landed, seemingly stunned.

She took another step closer. "Um, I said, are you alright?"

The man suddenly jerked upright, his one eye flicking open, and Josephine screamed again.

* * *

Ulysses blinked several times rapidly, his blurred vision slowly coming into focus. His body ached, the uncomfortable throbbing of the gunshot wound joined now by nagging pains in his back and belly. His breath came in short, ragged gasps.

Something had shocked him into sudden alertness. Flopping back onto the pile of blankets and quilts beneath him, he craned his head to see where he was, steadily taking in the details of the room.

There was a dressing table with an ornate oval mirror above it, although the gold-paint was flaking from the cracked wood, and the chamber was bedecked with a variety of dusty drapes and chiffon veils. They might once have been splendid and luxurious but now they were nothing but a tattered testament to better times. The room looked more like a tart's boudoir than the bedchamber of a royal courtesan.

But the bed itself – even in spite of the glass fragments and splinters sticking into his back – felt as comfortable as clouds. And at that moment all Ulysses really wanted to do was give in to the oblivion of exhaustion and pain that was threatening to overwhelm him.

He shifted and tried to sit up. Pain lanced through his back, but all he could manage was a feeble cry. A frozen numbness was steadily spreading from the wound in his shoulder that brought with it a blissful, morphine-like release.

He blinked tears of pain from his eye and caught sight of the girl for the first time. She was pretty, in an uncomplicated kind of way, her dyed red hair fashioned into extravagant ringlets, and she was wearing much too much make-up for Ulysses' liking.

His vision began to swim again.

"Help me!" he gasped.

The girl looked at him in bewilderment. He had made his plea for assistance in English.

Focusing his mind once more he tried again, this time in French. "Please, help me."

And then he could fight it no longer, the room fading into premature darkness as unconsciousness took him.

*   *   *

Josephine gave a sharp intake of breath. The handsome stranger had – in the moments before he blacked out – asked *her* for help. Her heart fluttered inside her chest.

It was so romantic. A handsome stranger falling into her bedchamber and asking her for help, no doubt having just fought some noble duel –

– on the roof.

Josephine peered again at the broken window, but there was no sign of anyone else up there; at least not as far as she could tell. She had no idea what was going on other than that the last thing this dishevelled hero had done, before blacking out in pain, was to beg her for her help. And at that moment Josephine determined that she would do all that she could for him.

The door to her bedchamber flew open and Madame Marguerite stormed into the room, followed by Oscar, her burly son.

Where the owner of the boarding house was short and stocky, her son was tall and muscular – not unlike how Josephine imagined the gardener Reynard from *The Garden of Love* looked.

"What is it, child?" Madame Marguerite gasped, clearly out of breath after having to drag herself upstairs from the parlour on the ground floor. "We heard a crash and you screaming, and I knew you weren't with a customer, so I grabbed Oscar and we came as fast as we could!"

It was then that Madame Marguerite's eyes fell upon the unconscious man lying on the bed for the first time.

"Saints preserve us! What's going on here?" She turned to the girl. "Are you entertaining customers behind my back?"

"Hardly!"

"Then what's he doing here?"

"He came in through the window."

The madame peered up at the broken roof light. "Well, that's going to have to come out of your wages, for a start."

Josephine turned on the madame, her mouth open wide in an 'O' of indignant outrage.

"Is he dead? Oscar, check if he's still breathing."

Oscar did as he was told, putting two fingers to the man's neck and watching for the slight rise and fall of his chest.

"He's alive, alright. But his pulse is weak. He's not in a good way."

"So what's he doing here?"

"I don't know," Josephine admitted. "He didn't say."

"He spoke to you?"

"He looked at me and said 'Help me,'" Josephine replied, a dreamy look in her eyes.

Madame Marguerite stared at Josephine, utterly flabbergasted.

"He asked you to help him?"

"I think he's English."

"And what's that got to do with anything? He still came in through the roof and besides, he looks a mess!"

"But we *have* to help him."

"We have to help him, do we?" Madame Marguerite grunted like a disgruntled sow. "Well answer me this, my girl. Why? Because of some foolish romantic notion you've got stuck in your head? Has he got any money? Have you checked his pockets?"

Josephine's face had become a florid crimson. "No, of course not!"

"Well, then, you haven't thought this through, have you? He looks like he's in a bad way; if he stays here we'll have to send for Doctor Cossard, and he doesn't make house calls out of the goodness of his heart, as you well know."

Josephine's cheeks blushed beyond crimson to beetroot. She knew of Doctor Cossard from bitter personal experience. Many of the Madame Marguerite's girls did. It was Doctor Cossard they went to see when they were – how did Madame Marguerite put it? When they were 'inconvenienced.'

And then a thought flashed through her mind.

"He *might* have money. He might be loaded, for all we know. His family might pay us handsomely if we were to nurse him back to health and return him to them." An expression of desperate hope lit up her face.

"What kind of a family must he belong to, to end up falling through the roof of your bedchamber looking like that?"

The middle-aged dowager took a step nearer the bed and inspected the prone figure. The unconscious man was breathing deeply as if fast asleep.

"But he has a trustworthy face, I'll give you that; except for the eye-patch. I suppose he might even be considered handsome, under the dirt and the stubble."

"So you'll help him?"

"I thought he asked *you* to help him."

"But you'll call Doctor Cossard?"

The older woman turned to her son, who was waiting, respectfully silent, at the edge of the room. "Oscar, go and get Doctor Cossard."

"Oh, thank you, Madame Marguerite!" Josephine exclaimed, catching the woman up in her arms and squeezing her tight. "Thank you!"

"Steady on, girl!" the madame gasped, pushing herself clear of the girl's enthusiastic embrace. "His bill's going to have to come out of your earnings. And you'll probably have to work double shifts for a week to earn enough, too."

"I don't care," Josephine said, although the monetary consequences of her actions making her somewhat more subdued.

But in her heart, she was still ready to believe that he was some forgotten hero and that it was her destiny to aid him in his hour of need, that he might complete his gallant mission. And knowing that was enough.

CHAPTER FOUR

Detective Dupin Investigates

THEY SAID THAT when the telephone rings at two in the morning it's never good news. Well, in Auguste Dupin's experience, a call that interrupted lunch at the Escargot didn't bode well for the rest of the day either.

The police-cab eased its way past the throng of curious onlookers that had gathered in the Rue Morgue like vultures around a dead zebra. There were so many of them that great-coated constables had been employed simply to hold the crowds back rather than carry out any actual police work. In Magna Britannia, and in its capital Londinium Maximum in particular, Dupin knew that the Metropolitan Police Force was bolstered by a veritable army of automaton robo-Bobbies. But in France they preferred to do things the old way. The robot revolution was yet to take hold within the City of Light; one revolution in France had been enough.

Detective Inspector Dupin had barely managed to open the cab door before a keen detective sergeant was at his side, his trench coat flapping about his legs like the wings of a flustered bat.

"So," Dupin said, interrupting the eager youth before the

sergeant opened his mouth to speak, "there's been a murder in the Rue Morgue."

"Er, yes, sir."

"How ironic."

"Sir?" The sergeant clearly didn't see the irony himself.

"Doesn't matter," Dupin said with a dismissive wave of his hand.

The entrance to the crumbling tenement, and the immediate section of street in front of it, was still in the process of being taped off and secured. The door into the building was wide open, the police having previously kicked it off its hinges.

The two men passed through into the murky gloom beyond.

"Nice place," Dupin muttered. He paused at the bottom of a flight of stairs. "Up there, is it?" He craned his head, taking in the full height of the stairwell.

"Yes, sir. At the top."

"Now there's a surprise."

"Sir?"

His withering sarcasm was obviously wasted on the sergeant.

Taking a deep breath and putting a hand to the banister, with a "Here goes, then," Dupin set off up the stairs.

He had been like the sergeant once, full of youthful optimism. But twenty years on the streets had knocked any such idiot eagerness out of him. He wasn't so old that he was ready to be pensioned off, but he understood now that the fight against crime was a war of attrition that slowly but surely wore you down. Every victory, no matter how small, was to be savoured like a bitter glass of absinthe while you could still appreciate what had been achieved.

Generally, policing was all about maintaining a balance – the status quo. There were villains in all strata of society but it paid to know which were on your side, show due respect to those that were your betters, and do all you could to eradicate the nutjobs, the psychopaths and the nonces along the way.

The murder of a poet, or musician, or whatever the constable who had disturbed his meal had said the victim was, fell firmly within the purview of the latter type of crime. It was an anomaly.

A rabid killer had struck in the Rue Morgue, without sense or reason, and had to be captured and eradicated, put down like the rabid dog he – or she – was before killing again. There was no sign of theft, and from his initial impression of the man's address, Dupin thought it unlikely he had possessed anything worth stealing.

So, first impressions were that the dead man hadn't been the victim of a robbery gone wrong, and from what Dupin's subordinates had discovered so far it seemed unlikely that this had been a family feud or a lover's spat. And then there was the fact that there were two bodies – after a fashion.

"How long ago was it that Sergeant Lecoq and his men failed to apprehend the suspect?"

"An hour, sir."

Dupin set off up the next flight of stairs. "And Sergeant Lecoq ran all the way up here, did he?"

"I don't believe he ran, sir," the detective sergeant said. "He certainly wasn't the first on the scene."

"Who was then?"

"Er…" The sergeant hesitated, checking his notepad as they continued to climb. "Constables Bâcler and Cochon."

"Lucky them."

Dupin said nothing more, saving his breath for the final flight. Reaching the top at last, the detective paused in the doorway of the dead man's attic room as he caught his breath.

Although the room's single dormer window was open, the air was still thick with the coppery tang of blood and the abattoir stink of organs that should never have been exposed to the air.

No matter how many murders he might have investigated over the course of the last twenty years, no matter how many mutilated corpses he had stumbled across in that time, Dupin had never become entirely inured to the brutality of one human being taking of the life of another.

Dupin sniffed. There was another familiar, acrid smell hanging in the corrupted air of the garret; the smell of burning.

The body was lying face down on the floor next to a filthy, unmade bed. A pool of dark, half-congealed blood covered the rough floorboards surrounding the pallid corpse, but despite the blood obscuring much of the floor beside the bed, the perfectly circular burn mark was clearly visible.

The dead man's garb matched the less than salubrious

surroundings Dupin found himself in. He looked like so many of the other artist types who populated this part of town, surviving on little more than hopes and dreams and absinthe.

Dupin acknowledged the crimson footprints and the bloody smears beyond the pooling circle with a grunt of annoyance. Clearly, for those first on the scene and keen to apprehend their murder suspect, preservation of the crime scene had not been uppermost in their minds.

The fact that there was a bloodless corpse in the middle of the room was troubling enough. The inexplicable burning was something else altogether.

And then there was the scatter of bones at the edge of the charcoal-black circle. There wasn't a scrap of flesh on them. In fact, they looked like they had been boiled clean.

Even without Doctor Cadavre and his forensics team having finished running over the crime scene, it was already quite clear in Dupin's mind what must have happened here.

The man's feet were the vital clue in untangling the order of events. The soles of the dead man's shoes had crisped, as if under a burst of intense heat. So, the man had died first, the burning had occurred after he was dead – or at least dying – and the bones had turned up last of all.

"Apart from uniforms' footprints being all over the place, this is how the body was when Sergeant Lecoq and his men arrived on the scene," Dupin said.

"That's right, sir," the detective sergeant confirmed.

"And nothing's been moved?"

"No, sir," said one of the constables present in the room.

Dupin took in the bones again, the body, the blood, the burn marks, the bed. Then he eyes strayed to the square of light coming in through the dormer window, and the rickety desk standing beneath it.

"And these papers were all over the floor like this when you arrived, too, were they?" Dupin asked, addressing the constable.

"Yes, sir, although I wasn't the first here, of course."

"So you're not Bâcler or – Cochon? You weren't one of those who gave pursuit?"

"No, sir," the constable said. Seeing the look forming on the detective inspector's face, and feeling quite happy about passing the buck to his colleagues, he nodded towards a lanky constable standing on the other side of the room.

The shamed gendarme raised a hand in wary acknowledge. "I'm Bâcler, sir."

The man's uniform was in disarray and drying sweat had stuck his hair to his forehead.

"Was this" – Dupin took in the spill of papers with a wave of his hand – "like *this* when you got here?"

Bâcler looked at the fallen papers nervously. "No. Not quite bad as that."

"How do you mean 'not quite as bad'?"

The constable swallowed nervously. "Some of the papers were on the desk."

Dupin breathed in sharply through his teeth, cursing under his breath.

"The fugitive set the avalanche off, sir," the constable went on, in a valiant attempt at damage limitation.

"And you finished the job in your eagerness to apprehend the suspect." Dupin cast a needling stare about the room. "And where is the fugitive now?"

For a moment nobody said anything.

In the end, it was Constable Bâcler who broke the awkward silence. "Still at large, sir."

"Still. At. Large." Dupin pointedly emphasised each damning word in turn. "And what has been done to rectify that most regrettable situation?"

"Sergeant Lecoq did send out patrols to continue the pursuit at street level but…" The constable trailed off.

"Let me guess, you lost him."

Bâcler looked down at his feet, unable to meet the inspector's gaze any longer.

"And where is Sergeant Lecoq now?"

"He's gone back to the station, I believe," the lanky constable said. "Way I heard it, he twisted his ankle at the bottom of the stairs, whilst giving chase himself."

The look on Bâcler's face made it clear that he didn't believe the excuse for the Sergeant's absence any more than Dupin did.

"Well, I'm going to give you the chance to redeem yourselves," the detective said.

The constables looked at each other warily, fearing that they already knew what was coming next.

"I want you to conduct a house-to-house search of this entire area, starting with this very street."

The detective's pronouncement was met by a chorus of groans and muttered complaints.

"Come on, Sergeant," he said, turning to the eager youth, "get it sorted. We've given the rogue enough time to get away as it is. Let's not give him any more."

"Reports are that he was injured," the detective sergeant added.

"Before our boys gave chase, you mean?"

"Yes, sir."

"Well there you go," he announced to the room. "Chances are he won't have got far, so get moving!"

As the two constables headed for the stairs, Dupin turned his attention to the murder victims once more.

"Right then," he said, unenthusiastically. "Let's take a closer look at this poor sod, shall we?" He gestured to Doctor Cadavre and his forensics team with a wave of his hand. "Are you happy if we get the body turned over now?"

"If you insist," Cadavre said grumpily.

"I insist," Dupin countered.

The pathologist nodded at his subordinates, who proceeded to do as the inspector had requested.

"Any sign of a murder weapon?" Dupin asked.

"Already bagged and tagged," Cadavre said, as another member of his team passed a sealed evidence bag to the inspector.

The handle was covered with crimson gore, but from the shape and size of it, it looked like the kind of knife an artist or scribe might use to sharpen a blunt pencil or to cut a quill. It did not look like the kind of weapon a killer would select to make an assassination. So the possibility of it being an impulse crime remained... Dupin crouched down, taking a moment to study the body more closely, without actually touching it. It looked like the knife had gone in under the man's ribs, probably puncturing his heart, or at least slicing open a major vein or artery. The detective took in the sodden cloth of his shirt, his trousers, the way the blood had congealed across one side of his face.

Dupin's eyes widened as he caught sight of the livid purple bruising around the man's neck. The collar of his shirt and the way he had been lying on the floor had obscured the tell-tale marks up until that moment.

The detective rocked back on his heels and stood up again.

"What do you make of that?" he asked the detective sergeant, a sparkle entering his eyes as he gestured at the corpse and the blue-black bruises.

"He was strangled," the other murmured in horror.

"Certainly looks like it to me."

Doctor Cadavre was there now, bustling between them to get a closer look at the body.

"But what killed him? Being throttled or being knifed?"

"I'll need to study the body more closely before I can determine the precise cause of death," Cadavre said dourly, peering at Dupin over the top of his half-moon spectacles.

"You can't hazard a guess for me now, doctor?" Dupin pressed, a wry smile forming on his lips.

"Well, if I *had* to hazard a guess, I'd say that he was strangled before he was stabbed, but that he was probably still alive – although not necessarily conscious – when the knife went in."

"Thank you, doctor," Dupin laughed, slapping the disgruntled Cadavre on the back. "That's good enough for me for now."

Dupin saw the expression of confusion in the detective sergeant's face.

"Your thoughts on the suspect, sergeant?"

The young man looked at him, his mouth open like a goldfish, and with about as many ideas to offer. All he finally managed was a "But…"

"The question you should be asking yourself is, why strangle somebody if you're already carrying a knife?"

"That's just what I was thinking," the sergeant confessed, his look of bewilderment deepening.

"Don't worry, sergeant, I'm not reading your mind," Dupin said. "It's not a parlour trick. But that aside, the answer's simple. You wouldn't."

"Sorry?"

"You wouldn't throttle someone if you were armed with a knife."

"So who had –"

"The knife?" Dupin interrupted. "Isn't it obvious? There was only one other person in the room – if you discount our bony friend over there."

"The victim?"

"Precisely."

From the sergeant's expression it looked like it might take him a while piece together the jigsaw for himself.

"Our friend here," he said of the body at their feet, and then broke off, before changing tack. "By the way, do we have a name for the deceased?"

The detective sergeant looked at him blankly.

"Never mind; it's not important at the moment. So, our friend here, finding himself under attack, picked up the nearest thing to him approximating a weapon with which to defend himself."

"Then how did it end up in *him*?" the sergeant asked.

"Judging by the entry wound, I reckon it would be a fair assumption to say that he fell on it during the struggle, most likely after his attacker had finished strangling him, when he was already unconscious, if not actually dead."

Realising the implications of what he was saying Dupin looked to the window again, his expression darkening.

"You say the gendarmes chased a man from here?"

"Yes, sir. Um…" the detective sergeant stalled, checking his notes again. "Six feet tall, brown hair, Caucasian, unshaven. Had an eye-patch over his… right eye, I believe."

"An eye-patch?"

"Yes, sir."

"So you couldn't miss him if you ran into him in the street."

"No, sir."

Dupin looked at the body once more.

"Any other distinguishing features?" Doctor Cadavre asked. "Anything about the size of his hands, for example?"

The sergeant checked his notebook again.

"No. Why?"

Cadavre lent down and traced the shapes formed by the bruising on the dead man's neck. Four fingers as fat as prime butcher's sausages and one thick thumb. The man's attacker had throttled him using only one hand. "Only I've never met anyone with hands that big before, have you?" The sergeant stared in shock at the body, his goldfish expression returning.

"So either our prime suspect has enormous hands or he didn't kill our friend here," Dupin said, "which leaves us with three questions. Who was it the gendarmes were chasing? And who killed this poor sod? And who the hell was *that*?" He pointed at the bones.

That was surely the biggest mystery of them all.

"Doctor Cadavre," he went on, "I want to know everything there is no know about our second murder victim here. Anything your forensics techniques can tell us about the owner of that skeleton – anything at all. Age, height, cause of death… I don't know, but anything there is to know. Do you understand?"

Cadavre nodded. "It'll take some time," he began.

"I thought it might," Dupin interrupted him. "And while you're at it, analyse these burn marks on the floor. What caused them, how they come to be here… You get the idea."

The detective felt a thrill of adrenalin pulse through him. The job hadn't given him a buzz like this for a long time, but Auguste Dupin felt more alive now than he had done in years.

The chase was on.

CHAPTER FIVE

Wanted

DOCTOR COSSARD WAS called and duly came, at Madame Marguerite's behest. Josephine, aided by Oscar, had done her best to remove the shards of broken glass and splinters of wood from under him, but Cossard was still unable to hide the surprise on his face when he saw the rough-looking man lying on the courtesan's bed.

The small, rotund surgeon huffed and puffed as, with Josephine's assistance, and Madame Marguerite and her son looking on, he removed the man's ruined jacket and shirt, uncovering the gunshot wound in his shoulder.

As he worked, he started sweating; he even went so far as to take off his jacket, his jowls and chins wobbling.

The patient didn't awaken once during the procedure, thankfully for him, although he did moan faintly as the doctor probed the wound with forceps and fingers.

Finally, over an hour later, the surgeon was done. The bullet had been extracted, the wound had been cleaned, stitched, dressed and his shoulder bound to keep everything covered up. Doctor Cossard packed his bag, put on his jacket, demanded his fee there and then, and then went on his way, leaving the long-term residents of Madame Marguerite's Boarding House just as curious as they had been before arrival, and wondering if Josephine's handsome stranger would even make it through the night.

MASKED SURGEONS...
Glinting razor-edged scalpels...
The glare of arc-lamps...
Fingers probing where fingers were never supposed to go...

THE NIGHTMARISH IMPRESSIONS faded and Ulysses Quicksilver opened his eyes. It took him a moment to work out where he was as his memory sluggishly woke too.

He was lying in bed and there was someone sitting at its foot, their face turned towards him.

Her face.

She was young, possessed of a simple beauty, although she wore too much make-up and her dyed red hair had been carefully positioned around her head in fussy ringlets. He was sure he had seen her before.

She appeared to be dressed in little more than her lacy petticoats and a whalebone corset. It seemed as though he had interrupted her part way through the business of getting ready to go out for the night. Either that, or she was preparing to entertain a gentleman caller in her boudoir. There were ribbons and scrags of a lacy material tied into her hair as well. She looked tired.

Ulysses regarded her closely. He still wasn't used to the fact that his right eye was gone. It felt like it should still be there, that the lid was gummed merely shut and that it might yet open of its own accord, if only he tried hard enough.

He looked from the girl to the boudoir and its tired décor, then back to the girl again. He doubted she was even out of her teens yet.

The effort of looking around made his body shake. He relaxed, allowing his head to sink back into the pillows.

He stared at the ceiling high above him. Crisp daylight

spilled in between and around the boards nailed across the roof light...

And he suddenly remembered falling...

"Where am I?" he asked the girl.

"Pardon, monsieur?"

He blushed, despite himself. Drawing saliva into his mouth, he swallowed, trying to relieve the dryness of his throat. He asked the question again, this time in French.

"You are in Paris," the girl said, her voice soft, her tone one of gentle patience.

Ulysses tried swallowing again. "Water," he managed.

Putting one hand behind his neck, helping him raise his head, the girl put a cup to his lips.

It was warm and had a curious aftertaste, but he could have been supping the cool waters of an Alpine meadow stream. Two grateful sips became several thirst-quenching gulps.

His nurse placed the empty cup back on the bedside table, and did her best to plump up his pillows with her spare hand. As she did so her face came close to his, and his nostrils were suddenly filled with the sweet rosewater scent of her. Her eyes were as captivating as a summer sunset.

"Paris?" he repeated.

"Montmartre."

"Montmartre."

"At Madame Marguerite's Boarding House."

Ulysses' brows knotted. "Would that be a..." There was no need for him to finish the sentence.

Now it was the girl's turn to blush.

"How is your arm?" she asked, quickly changing the subject.

"My arm?"

"Sorry, your shoulder. I meant your shoulder." She sounded flustered.

Ulysses tried moving his right arm. He winced, gritting his teeth with a sharp intake of breath.

"I'm sorry," the girl said, the skin at her throat and breast turning a prickly pink. "I should leave you to rest."

She stood up.

Gently relaxing his arm and shoulder again, Ulysses turned his head to follow her.

"Why are you doing this?" he asked.

The girl stopped. "What do you mean?"

"Why are you helping me?" he repeated, and the girl blushed anew. "I mean, I don't even know your name, and yet here you are... doing all this for me. How did I even come to be here?"

His memory was slowly returning but in such a jumbled fashion that the resulting mish-mash made little sense.

"What day is it?" Ulysses asked.

"What day? Why, Thursday."

"I mean what's the date?"

"The fourteenth of May."

"May. You're sure about that?"

"Yes, I'm sure."

"May." Slowly another memory emerged from the sludge of his unconscious.

"Yes. May. May the fourteenth."

A sparkle entered Ulysses' single uncovered eye.

"And we're in Montmartre in Paris."

"Yes."

"So I *am* in time!" he said with a delighted sigh.

His first assumption had been correct. Emilia and Old Man Oddfellow wouldn't even have left for the Heathrow spaceport yet, never mind boarded the doomed passenger liner *Apollo XIII*. If Ulysses acted quickly enough, he could see no reason why he couldn't become Time's arrow and step in at the pertinent moment to save Emilia from the fate he had witnessed befall her.

And then there was the other Ulysses Quicksilver gallivanting about the place on the other side of the Channel; a happier, less damaged individual. To save the woman who he now realised was the love of his life – and her father – would be one thing, but could he dare to believe that he could save himself into the bargain?

He blinked and a single tear ran from the corner of his eye.

"Are you alright?" the girl asked, taking a seat at the foot of the bed again, a comforting hand finding him through the sheets and blankets beneath which he lay. "Is it the pain? Doctor Cossard wasn't even sure you'd last the night, but I had faith."

"Doctor Cossard?"

"Yes. It was Doctor Cossard who removed the bullet and stitched you up again afterwards."

His eyes narrowed in suspicion. "Why are you doing this? Why are you helping me?"

Hearing a creak, he turned his head sharply to the left, catching his breath as the action pulled at his shoulder.

The door to the bedchamber opened and a dumpy, overdressed woman entered, putting him in mind of a puffed-up peacock.

"Ah, so our patient is awake."

"Who are you?" Ulysses asked through clenched teeth.

"Who am I?" the matriarchal figure said. "I could ask you the same thing." She was followed into the room by a grim-faced youth with the build of a farm hand.

Ulysses tensed. Surely this couldn't be part of some elaborate trap, could it? There was no way this could have been planned by Dashwood, or anyone else, was there?

Ulysses caught himself; that way madness lay.

He looked from the girl to the wrap of bandage binding his shoulder wound.

"Why are you helping me?"

"That's gratitude for you," the older woman grunted. "She's nursed you all through the night and you can't even manage a simple 'thank you'?"

Ulysses tried to sit up. He clenched his teeth against the pain but managed to shuffle himself into a sitting position.

"As to why we're bothering to help you? Right now I have no idea. If it hadn't been for Josephine, I would have had Oscar here cast you out into the street with the rest of the crap."

"Not now, Madame Marguerite," the girl countered hastily.

Ulysses looked to the girl, seeing her blush again, but in his mind's eye he saw the ape once more, its massive fists raised, thick steel vambraces enclosing its forearms, the crown of crackling electrodes protruding from its skull.

If this was some kind of a trap, it was beyond his comprehension.

"So, I think it's about time you showed us some trust in return for our help, don't you? It cost me a hundred francs to have Doctor Cossard stitch you up."

Ulysses looked from the girl to her employer. Was the matron's interest driven by a mother's concern for the girl or was she just worried about protecting her investment?

"It's complicated," he said.

"Well I didn't think you were the postman," the madame said candidly. "You're British, for a start, aren't you? English?"

"Yes," Ulysses admitted with a sigh, "although I've been told my French is very good."

"And who told you that? You know your vocabulary, I'll give you that, but you speak French like you learnt it at boarding school."

"And how would you know what that sounds like?"

"You learn a lot in this business, I'll tell you that for nothing."

As the woman continued her tirade, Ulysses became aware of a distant banging sound, like someone pounding on a door.

"Who's that?" he demanded.

"It's just someone at the door downstairs," Madame Marguerite said, affronted at being interrupted. "What does it matter?"

There was an insistent quality to the banging. Ulysses had heard banging like that recently. It was the same sound he had heard upon arriving at the house of the murdered man.

"Because I can't imagine you receive all that much trade in the early afternoon."

The brothel-keeper looked from Ulysses to the towering youth at her back.

"Oscar," she said, an anxious urgency underlying her words, "go and see who that is, would you?"

The youth departed Josephine's bedchamber

"It's them," Ulysses muttered almost under his breath.

"Who?" the girl asked, glancing at the door.

"The police."

"Are they looking for you?" Madame Marguerite said, her voice rising in a tone of appalled horror.

There was no point denying the truth. "Yes."

"So who are you?"

"You have to help me," Ulysses hissed, trying to get out of bed, gasps of pain punctuating his words and hindering his progress. "I have to get back to London!"

Londinium Maximum suddenly seemed a very long way away. At that moment he would have done anything to hear the ever-present clatter of the Overground as it rattled on its interminable way above the city. He missed the streets that he had walked for so many years, the worn pavements he had trod, with a fierce longing.

He had been away for – what? – two months by his own reckoning, even though he hadn't actually left yet, if that made any sense at all. He missed its familiar vistas, its landmarks, its noise, its bustle, its people. In his mind's eye he pictured it as it had been before the Wormwood Catastrophe: St Paul's not yet overrun by Locust swarms, London Zoo not yet devastated by a train wreck.

As a child he had enjoyed regular visits to the Challenger Enclosure along with Nanny McKenzie and his brother Barty. But they were both gone now – as were the dinosaurs – and he missed them.

He missed his home in Mayfair too. But he would have happily never returned there if it had meant he could be with Emilia again. "Who are you," the woman repeated, more forcefully this time, "and what have you done?"

Ulysses listened. The banging had stopped. He felt the first tentative stirrings of relief deep inside. Perhaps it hadn't been the police after all. Or perhaps they had simply gone on their way.

It was then that he heard the thud of hobnailed boots on bare floorboards somewhere below.

"They're coming upstairs!" Josephine squeaked, putting a shaking hand to her throat.

Ulysses met Madame Marguerite's stare as the brothel-keeper glared at him.

"Alright, alright," he said, wilting under the woman's intense glare. "My name is Ulysses Quicksilver. I am an agent of the British government, and I'm here in Paris working undercover."

Josephine gasped and Ulysses caught the fleeting look of romantic delight in her eyes. Madame Marguerite looked less convinced.

"But if the police find me here my mission is over and a dangerous felon will escape justice."

For a moment, nobody said anything. The thud of footsteps on the stairs was drawing closer with every passing second.

"Oh, what the hell," the middle-aged madame grumbled, bustling over to the side of the bed. "But you're still in no fit state to make any kind of daring rooftop escape, or whatever it is you're planning. They're bound to look under the beds, so we'll have to find somewhere else for you to hide."

"Madame Marguerite!" the girl suddenly interjected. Her gaze lingered on the clothes rack in the corner of the room. "I've got an idea."

CHAPTER SIX

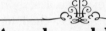

Angels and Insects

THE WARBLING VIBRATO of the soprano's voice crackling from the gramophone player reverberated from the brick walls of the tunnels and secret chambers of the labyrinthine cellars. Puccini's unmistakeable melody was everywhere; the distant spark and hum of electricity and the ticking of the clock on the wall of the study were the only other sounds.

The lepidopterist paused in his work for a moment as the music surged through and around him. Hands poised delicately in the air, he conducted with the tweezers held between his fingers.

And then, as the melody moved on, he resumed his meticulous work. For somebody whose sole aim in life – or so he claimed – was to create chaos, in the microcosm of his own private world he liked things to be fastidiously organised.

The bookcase in the corner, filled with such philosophical texts as the Englishman Hobbes' *Leviathan*, and Poincaré and Hadamard's writings on chaos theory; the rich red leather-upholstered wingback armchair beside it, angled at an exact forty-five degrees; the framed, mounted specimens on the brick wall above the desk where he worked; all was just so.

The specimen cases filled almost every inch of bare brick wall, like some immaculately completed jigsaw puzzle. Most contained butterflies and moths, but some contained exotic jewel-like beetles or dragonflies with iridescent stained-glass wings.

With the Red Admiral in place on the right-hand side of the frame, there was space for two more specimens. Downing tools for a moment, he took up his cup of tea, sat on its own die-cut paper doily on the desk in front of him. It had to be said, for all their crass, over-domineering Imperial bombast, there were some things that the British did very well. And there was a place for bombast in the Great Scheme of Things, as Giacomo Puccini had known so well. As did the butterfly collector himself.

He closed his eyes as he sipped his tea, savouring the tepid infusion along with the soaring musical phrases. The aria was one of his favourite pieces of music. The soprano's pining for a lost love had touched him, even as a child. In fact, it had made a huge impact on him, when he had lived at the Opera with his mother, who had worked there as a seamstress.

It had been too long since Puccini's masterpiece had last been performed on the stage of the Paris Opera. Once upon a time he would have done something about that, but there was little point now. There was only one performance that mattered now and that would be the Opera's last.

The music washed over him, bringing with it a sense of enduring, meditative calm. Just as the lepidoptery did; his art. For that was what he was, at heart - an - artist, although the canvases he sometimes worked upon were on a much larger scale. And none was larger than the city of Paris itself.

Opening his eyes again, blinking at the glare of the lights set within the Tiffany stained-glass lampshades, the collector returned to his work.

The work suited him, its subject matter as much as the meticulous precision it demanded of him. Many thought little of butterflies and moths, beyond what they brought to the world in terms of their natural, symmetrical beauty. Few understood the true power they held within their gossamer-light wings.

Even fewer would have suspected that this mild-mannered, well-manicured, Opera-loving collector was the same man who was spoken of in hushed whispers in the palaces of power, at newspaper offices across the country and behind the closed doors of police stations through the city.

For it was no coincidence that to the wider world he was known as Le Papillon. And yet Le Papillon was more akin to a fictional villain from some penny dreadful, a masked terrorist who brought chaos into the lives of all those whom he chose in an apparently arbitrary manner.

To his victims – the families he ruined, the investments wiped out by his schemes, the property his actions destroyed – there seemed little method to his madness. But then they, with their limited, blinkered mind-sets, could not see the bigger picture.

The very fact that his targets were so random in terms of the people he selected, and the manner of their undoing, was precisely his method. To bring chaos where before there was order, to have the rest of the world live in fear that they could be next, to be an agent of anarchy – that was precisely his *raison d'être*!

He had had a name once, and for those times when he was forced to go out and about in the real world, it was still useful. But it was only a name. Le Papillon was an *identity*. It told the world what he was about, even if the world did not realise it.

As the warbling echoes of *Madame Butterfly* continued to wash over him, Le Papillon selected a Large White from the specimen tray in front of him. It was a male, its wing-tips shaded charcoal grey, but missing the black spots that the female of the species sported on its wings. Spots would have spoiled the look he was trying to create with the piece.

The Large White was another import from across the other side of La Manche.

He manipulated the butterfly into place with his tweezers, only pinning it when he was entirely happy with its positioning.

A bestial howl echoed throughout the vaulted spaces of the extensive cellars.

The man's jaw tensed as the primate roar, although distant, interrupted the diva's divine rendition of Puccini's classic.

His hands froze. He would let nothing disturb his delicate work.

He breathed in through his nose and then out again slowly, his hands still immobile over the mounting board as he listened to the dying echoes of the animal's savage cry. It was either angry or in pain. Most likely both.

He disliked having to let the doctor join him in his lair, but it was a means to an end. And the end justified the means; that was his mantra, after all.

Besides he would not have to put up with his house guest for much longer. Months, the scientist had been carrying out his experiments, continuing his noted ancestor's work – although Dr Montague Moreau had taken it along a different path, utilising alternative branches of science.

At another primate bellow, Le Papillon looked up from his work, glancing back over his shoulder towards the depths of the cellar where the doctor had constructed his caged operating-theatre-cum-laboratory.

Actinic blue flashes of lightning illuminated the shadows, throwing primal shadows across the crumbling brickwork. When the discharges ceased, so did the gorilla's animalistic screams. The last of the crackling bursts of blue fire left a lingering negative image of the howling beast on his retinas. Then, slowly it seemed, the warm glow of the house lamps returned, briefly drawing the man's attention to the organ, half-buried within its arched brick alcove.

It was what one might call a family heirloom. It had, after all, been his great-grandfather's once upon a time. It was whilst sitting at that very instrument that his great-grandfather had been unmasked by his great-grandmother. And yet, in many important ways, it most definitely wasn't the same instrument anymore. The engineer Pierre Courriel Pascal had seen to that.

It still had the multiple keyboards, sculpted brass pipes and intricately carved console, with its protruding, ivory-handled stops, but several significant additions had been made at the behest of its current owner.

Spools of trunked cabling now sprouted from the organ, as if the device's mechanical intestines had ruptured and burst from its teak and brass body. Then there were the appendages that looked like ear trumpets, strange Bakelite blossoms connected to yet more snaking wires. And then, of course, there was the Babbage engine unit itself, that had been built into the organ above its tiers of ebony- and ivory-inlaid keyboard registers.

As the crackling discharges abated and the monstrous shadows faded, the bestial bellows became breathless grunts and the soaring melodies and otherworldly musical phrasing of *Madame Butterfly* calmed his irritated mood once more.

He did not like interruptions. His work demanded precision and care. In fact everything he did demanded precision and care, especially bringing chaos and confusion to the world. For anarchy to be effectively created, it had to be meticulously planned.

The Large White specimen poised over the mounting board, the butterfly collector now pinned it carefully in place. The tempered steel point punctured the fragile, black-furred body of the insect, miniscule desiccated internal organs compressed as pressure was applied.

In fact, through his desk-mounted magnifying lens, the honed point of the pin looked more like the tip of a javelin, as if he was spearing the body of some monstrous insect. Such things were rumoured to have taken over whole swathes of the British capital, while there was talk that moths had been created by the Japanese, in the wake of their experimentation in new forms of power, with wingspans of over two hundred feet. What he wouldn't do to have one of those specimens mounted on his study wall...

The Large White placed in the middle of the board, he looked to his collecting tray for another suitable specimen to complete the piece.

You had to have patience in his game. To create chaos required a great deal of waiting. For an attack to have the greatest impact it had to be executed at the most propitious time. Waiting for the good doctor to complete his work was part of that. Waiting for the Opera orchestra to have time to rehearse was another. The organ – his ancestral heirloom – now *that* was ready to go.

The acoustician had made the necessary alterations to the organ buried in the basement of the Opera House, and soon he, too, just like the composer and the ordinateur-auteur, would meet his maker. Then Le Papillon would be one step closer to pulling off the greatest act of anarchy the world had ever known – greater even than the attacks suffered by

Londinium Maximum, as orchestrated by Magna Britannia's former Prime Minister of good standing, Uriah Wormwood.

The pieces were slowly coming together and fitting snugly into place. Time was counting down to the moment when Le Papillon would unleash a catastrophe upon the world such as it had never known. But for the time being there was nothing he could do but wait.

He paused in his selection of another specimen and leaned back in his creaking chair, taking in the array of collections already on display in the study. They had all been created whilst waiting for various plans to come to fruition. And each one was a flawless demonstration of the crystalline patience he possessed and employed in everything he did.

Butterflies were truly wondrous creatures, and had captured the imaginations of the ancients. And yet, in this modern age of iron and information, so much had been forgotten, the majority of people knowing next to nothing about them.

The various species of *Lepidoptera* had long been associated with the divine in man, that undying part of him that lingered after a body had become the food of worms and bacteria. It was a remarkable example of the universality of animal symbolism, found in cultures on practically every continent. The ancients observed how a butterfly or moth would hover for a time in one place or fly in a fleeting, hesitant manner, and saw this as a reflection of the soul, reluctant to move on to the next world.

The transformation of caterpillar into butterfly provided the ultimate model for human ideas of death, burial, and resurrection. The scattering of flowers at funerals was an ancient custom; the flowers attracted butterflies, which then appeared to have emerged from a corpse. Some even believed that the chrysalis inspired the splendour of many coffins in antiquity. In fact the Greek word 'psyche' meant soul, but could also designate a butterfly or moth, while the Latin 'anima' had the same duality of meaning.

Of all God's creations, surely the jewel-like blue morpho was one of His finest. The specimen in Le Papillon's collection testified to that fact, with its crimpled wing-tips, the stained glass cerulean blue of the minute scales that covered its wings and the dark kohl-shading where they joined the butterfly's body.

An expert knowledge of insect anatomy was required to manipulate the specimen so that it looked like the butterfly had only alighted on the canvas for a moment, and that it might take off again at any second. The careful positioning of an antenna, pulling the wings fully open, whilst avoiding tearing the delicate membrane at the same time.

It had taken him some time to do that, having spent a day collecting specimens in the poppy meadows near Argenteuil, before starting on the composition of this particular piece which, he now realised, was taking on a particularly patriotic tone. Ironic, considering what he had planned for the City of Lights.

Happy with the positioning of the blue morpho, the butterfly collector carefully pinned it in place, trapping it forever upon the board beside the Large White and the Red Admiral.

Puccini was disturbed a second time by the shrill ringing of the Bakelite-and-mother-of-pearl telephone sitting at the corner of his desk. The man's jaw tensed again.

The ringing disturbed the diva's sublime singing, but Le Papillon didn't rush. He laid his tools down on the desk and carefully picked up the handset.

"Yes?" he said.

The electronically-distorted voice at the other end had an English accent. "Le Papillon?"

"But of course," Le Papillon replied, in English.

"How is the work progressing?" There were no conversational niceties, no social pleasantries. The speaker cut straight to the chase.

"The work is progressing as anticipated."

"Meaning?" The voice had a hard edge to it.

"Meaning everything is – as you would put it – going according to plan."

"Explain."

The man snorted. "Excuse me, perhaps I misunderstood the terms of our agreement, but didn't you engage me so that you would not need to know the details of any plan? What was it you called it? Plausible deniability?"

For a moment the voice said nothing. Then it came again, a growl of distorted static.

"Zero hour is set for Saturday, is it not?"

"But of course. That was the date I said I would work towards when you first engaged me."

The voice at the other end of the line remained silent.

"So if I might be permitted to continue with my preparations...?"

"Saturday, then."

"Saturday. There is no need for doubt, everything is in order. Nothing can stand in the way of the plan, quite simply because nobody knows what is coming.

"And when I fulfil my part of the bargain..." He left that particular thought hanging.

There was a click and the line went dead.

Le Papillon smiled and hung the handset back in its cradle.

"Huh. Very patriotic," Moreau grunted, peering nosily over the collector's shoulder.

Le Papillon had heard the other's approach but had chosen to ignore him until now. He turned in his chair, the smile becoming a frozen leer.

"My dear Doctor Moreau," he said. "How goes it?"

"Bloody mess, that's what it is."

The man smelt of sour breath and potent body odour. The butterfly collector had to make a conscious effort not to physically recoil at the noxious smell.

"What is?"

"The transmitter," the doctor grumbled. "Don't know how the bastard managed to damage it, but he did. He should be dead by now, like the other two, but somehow he did a right number on it. Bastard!"

"And this is why you called it back, was it?" Le Papillon said, the smile still fixed on his face.

"It needs sorting. I can't risk having that thing running loose out there and not be able to call it back. That would screw up everything."

The butterfly collector's jaw tensed. The smile remained. "That's one way of putting it, I suppose."

"Bodes well for future missions. After all, for what was really little more than a glorified test run, I wasn't really necessarily expecting to get two hits completed in one go."

"You weren't?"

"No, I was amazed it worked, actually."

"But I thought you said…"

His house guest blushed. "Oh, you know how it is. You say anything to get a gig, don't you?"

"But you assured me. You said you could interpret and extrapolate your ancestor's working notes."

"But it *did* work, that's the most important thing, isn't it?"

At that moment Le Papillon would have quite happily rammed his tweezers up the doctor's nose and into his brain, but the plan had progressed too far to take him out of the equation now – at least, for the time being.

Le Papillon's expertise did not lie in primate psycho-surgery and cybernetics. His acquaintance with the young Doctor Moreau had taken months to cultivate, in case the circumstances arose when he might need the other man's particular skills to help him achieve his own aims.

Besides, only Doctor Moreau knew the intricate workings of the cyber-gorilla. Just as the first man to make a Babbage engine had been the only one able to interpret its internal workings, so only Doctor Montague Moreau knew how the transmitter and electrodes worked and what alterations or repairs would need to be made. A team of surgeons and cogitator specialists might well be able to work out what he had done, but only after completely taking the gorilla apart and re-building it again.

It had to be said, for all his oafish mannerisms and seat-of-the-pants approach to engineering problems, Doctor Moreau did have a very particular talent, and one which was currently vital to the successful completion of Le Papillon's plan.

"So," Le Papillon said through clenched teeth, the porcelain smile still on his face, but only just, "the damage the uplift sustained can be repaired?"

"Oh yes. Just bloody annoying, that's all."

"There is still the acoustician to be eliminated," the anarchist pointed out. "Your pet's targets totalled three. I made that very clear. The composer, the Babbage-engineer and the acoustic scientist."

"And he will be, don't fret so."

"I am not fretting," the man said, his jaw clenching, "but I thought I had made it very clear that all three were to be eliminated as soon after one another as was humanly possible; or inhumanly, if you prefer. It will only be a matter of time before the gendarmes discover the two it has already killed."

"So what?" Moreau said, almost laughing in scorn. "They won't even begin to be able to work out what it was that carried out the killings, let alone trace it to here."

"You're sure about that?"

"Sure I'm sure. I'll have it patched up and back to mission fitness in no time at all."

"No time at all?"

"Alright, first thing tomorrow. I've only got to fix up the transmitter; and then I'll have to fit it with some sort of shield or something, of course, to stop any more accidents like the last one fouling things up. Have no fear, my friend" – Le Papillon hated it when Moreau dared call him 'friend' – "project Black Swan will proceed as planned."

And soon all Paris will understand what happens when Le Papillon beats his wings, the collector considered, keeping his thoughts to himself.

He turned his chair to fully face the noisome doctor now.

"Your pet's 'little accident' – wasn't that what you called it?" Le Papillon goaded.

Moreau shifted from one foot to the other in obvious embarrassment at being reminded of the incident.

"Tell me more about this unarmed, one-eyed man who was able to fend off half a ton of technologically-enhanced adult silverback?"

CHAPTER SEVEN

The Scarlet Pimpernel Returns

"I CAN'T BELIEVE that ruse actually worked," Ulysses said, as he heard the door downstairs close after the departing policemen.

Josephine took both his hands in hers, a delighted smile playing about her rosebud lips.

"I mean, if I'm honest, I've always had a bit of a thing for taffeta, and I've been known to slap on the greasepaint once or twice in the past, you know, a little eye shadow in my student days for the Am-Dram club, but I never knew I could make such a convincing woman."

Josephine laughed.

"And whilst wearing an eye-patch too," Ulysses went on. "Are all Parisian police so short-sighted?"

"A well-placed veil can hide a multitude of sins," Madame Marguerite said.

"I know," Ulysses said, sniggering himself. "And who would've thought I'd look so good in a wedding dress? Do people often get married here?"

"Oh, you'd be surprised," Madame Marguerite chuckled throatily. "But you'd best take it off now. We've got Monsieur

Vicieux coming in at three – he's one of Amelie's regulars – and he always likes her to play the innocent."

The dandy was suddenly filled with a rising sense of euphoria. On a whim, as their joint laughter rose to fill the room, Ulysses took Josephine in his arms and began to waltz her around the room, breaking into song.

"They seek him here, they seek him there, those Frenchies seek him everywhere!" Ulysses sang as he spun the girl about her bedchamber, Madame Marguerite clapping along in time.

Still weak from the surgery and all that had happened to him of late, Ulysses stumbled, gave Josephine one last spin, and collapsed onto the bed. The moment was past.

"Are you alright, Ulysses?" the girl asked anxiously.

"I'm alright," he puffed. "Just feeling a little light-headed, that's all, what with all the excitement…"

Josephine held his hands in hers again, but said nothing more, the look in her eyes saying it all.

"You need to rest," Madame Marguerite said. "But you need to get out of that dress first. I don't want you pulling your stitching."

Ulysses was slightly taken aback. "I didn't know you cared," he said, blushing.

"It's not that. I don't want you getting blood on the dress. It's a bugger to get the stains out."

"So," ULYSSES SAID, with heartfelt purpose, as he surveyed the array of newspapers and pages of his own notes spread out on the bedspread in front of him, "where to begin? On the day I arrive in Paris, two murders are committed, within less than half an hour of each other, and both in the vicinity of the Rue Morgue."

Another day had passed since the police had called at Madame Marguerite's. Two days of recuperating at the brothel and he was feeling better than he had felt in a long time – fifty-five years, in fact, after a manner of speaking. The mysterious Doctor Cossard clearly had some talent.

Ulysses was sitting at the head of Josephine's bed, his right leg folded under him. The courtesan herself had spent last night sleeping on top of the bed beside him, never once making the move to join him under the covers, which had surprised him.

His right arm was back in its sling, and that – combined with the painkillers Madame Marguerite had provided him with from the brothel's surprisingly well-stocked medicine cabinet – had meant he could at least now sit up and move his arm without feeling like white-hot needles were being plunged into his shoulder every time he did so.

The sling did make it difficult for him to make notes, however, seeing as how he was right-handed, but simply being able to bounce ideas off Josephine as he thought things through made all the difference.

As he spoke, he shuffled the pages before him, rearranging his thoughts as he set his mind to the matter in hand.

After all, being top of France's Most Wanted list – rather like the original Scarlet Pimpernel – would seriously restrict his movements around the city and beyond. In his current condition, if he were ever to escape back to England – that he might not only help his lover and her father, but also save his brother from the cruel end fate had in store for him – then he needed to make sure he was no longer wanted by the French police.

The photo-fit didn't help, of course. He was looking at it now, as reproduced inside that morning's edition of *Le Monde*. It was surprisingly good, Ulysses thought to his chagrin, even if it did make him look like a pirate.

An inspector by the name of Dupin had gone public about the murders, the house-to-house search conducted by the police having failed to uncover the suspect, and so his face was now one of the most widely recognised and despised in the country.

And so the best way for him to be about his business, and ensure that the French Police would no longer be hunting him, was to solve the mystery of the Rue Morgue murders for them. But then he had one huge advantage over the detective and the gendarmes; he had come face to face with the true killer himself.

"It looks nothing like you," the girl said.

Looking up he caught the look in her eyes. The skin at the curve of her neck was flushed bright pink. "I mean, you're much more handsome."

"It's the eye-patch, isn't it?" Ulysses said, the corners of his mouth curling upwards. "Girls can't resist a pirate's rakish charm."

Josephine's blush deepened still further and she broke eye-contact.

"Anyway, back to the case in hand. As we now know, there were actually two men who died on Wednesday."

He extracted two rustling sheets from the piles in front of him, internal pages from two different newspapers. One bore a poor quality reproduction of a photograph, of a thin man with a face like a knife. The other – which might have been from the passport records office, by the look of things – was of a swarthy man with a mane of dark hair.

Ulysses' gaze lingered on the grainy image of the sharp-featured individual. "First there's this man, the penniless composer Carmine Roussel." *Who I had my own unfortunate encounter with*, he thought to himself. "And then, what could have only been thirty minutes later at most, this man" – his eyes moved to the picture of the swarthy man – "the ordinateur engineer Pierre Courriel Pascal also met his untimely end."

The dandy regarded the two articles he had torn from that morning's papers.

The two deaths had been unconnected by those who had reported them.

The first was the murder of the celebrated, yet destitute, composer, which was described as both 'brutal' and 'savage' – depending on the particular report one was reading at the time. Having stumbled upon this crime scene himself, Ulysses would have been more inclined to describe the manner of the man's passing using the adjectives 'badly-timed' and 'irritating,' seeing as how he was the one currently taking the blame for the murder.

The write-up in the paper was accompanied by an artist's impression of the man police were hunting in connection with the crime, one which made Ulysses look like some kind of Mexican bandit, emphasising his stubble and adding a scar to enhance the appearance of wanton criminality.

The second article concerned the suicide of Pierre Courriel Pascal, expert Lovelace algorithm coder and apparently something of a pioneer when it came to Babbage engine design, although he was virtually unknown to the public at large. According to the reporter's write-up, the poor wretch had thrown himself out the window of his fourth floor apartment, located only a few minutes' walk away in.

With the savage murder in the Rue Morgue occurring on the same day only a few streets away, the cogitator engineer's suicide had received little coverage, worthy only of a few column inches in one paper, as far as Ulysses could see – the capital-centric *Le Journal*.

Ulysses noted with interest that the police had clearly rationed the information they had fed to the press. There was no mention anywhere of the curious burn marks in the composer's garret, or of Dashwood's skeleton.

But two pertinent facts that the press and the authorities were both aware of and yet had failed to connect was the proximity of the two deaths and their timing. They had occurred within half an hour of each other, by Ulysses' reckoning.

It would not have taken the killer long to get from one apartment to the other, even on foot. By a similar rooftop path to that which Ulysses had taken during his flight from the gendarmes, he could have got there even quicker.

And then there was another fact of which the press, the police and everyone else was blithely unaware. Ulysses had witnessed an eight-foot tall gorilla climb out a fourth-floor apartment on the very street where Pierre Courriel Pascal had died.

All things considered, it seemed highly likely – at least as far as Ulysses was concerned – that it had been the very same apartment.

Suddenly, Ulysses wasn't so sure that the poor programming pioneer Pascal had decided to end it all by taking a leap into the unknown from the fourth floor.

"So," he said, "on the one hand, we have a penniless composer knifed in his apartment, the door locked from the inside, the killer entering and leaving by an attic window, and on the other we have a pioneering Babbage engine inventor like as not thrown from the fourth-floor of his apartment building thirty minutes later, if not sooner."

"You think there's a connection?" Josephine asked, hanging on his every word.

Ulysses nodded. "I do."

Josephine kept her gaze fixed on him, a mixture of astonishment and delight in her eyes. "But what could it possibly be?"

He thought back to the gouged ridges in the putty of the sill of the garret room window, marks that – now he thought about it – had looked like they could have been made by something with massive, man-like hands.

"How about a half a ton of angry, cybernetically-enhanced gorilla?"

"A what?"

"Its forearms strapped in metal and electrodes like cattle-prods plugged into its skull," Ulysses went on.

"You're joking," Madame Marguerite boomed. "Such a thing doesn't exist!"

"You remember when I first awoke after the operation and you asked me how I came to be here," Ulysses said, "and I couldn't remember? Well now I do."

Josephine and the brothel-keeper exchanged disbelieving glances, their mouths agape.

"So what did this gorilla do to you, exactly?" Madame Marguerite said. "Hurled you through Josephine's roof-light, I suppose?"

"Pretty much. After I disturbed it leaving Pascal's apartment."

"Are you sure?" Josephine asked, flabbergasted.

"No, but it seems likely. And besides, it's the best lead I have right now."

Josephine blanched. "But the reports all say that Carmine Roussel was stabbed and that one about the engineer's suicide said he jumped."

"I know," Ulysses admitted, his brows knitting in consternation.

His gaze wandered distractedly around the room for a moment.

"But bear with me here for a minute. Let's assume that Pascal was pushed. And suppose that Roussel wasn't stabbed, or at least wasn't supposed to have been... I know it sounds crazy; I haven't completely worked that bit out yet... But just suppose..." Ulysses trailed off as he struggled to get his thoughts in order.

"But even if the two men were both killed by this half-ton

gorilla of yours," Madame Marguerite piped up, "why? What possible reason could there be?"

"You're forgetting *who*," Ulysses said sagely, a slow smile forming on his face, delighted as he was at the prospect of such an intriguing challenge.

"Who?" the woman echoed.

"The cyber-gorilla was a weapon – just like a knife, a gun or a bomb. I have a feeling the victims' relationship with the ape was irrelevant. We shouldn't be asking *why* they were killed, but *who* wanted them dead. Who would want a composer and a Babbage engine engineer dead?"

The women were silent for several long seconds.

"You think your best bet for getting out of Paris and away from France is by finding the answers to this question?" Madame Marguerite said at last.

Ulysses smiled. "Indeed."

"Are you sure it wouldn't be easier to simply swim the Channel?"

"HERE, WHAT'S THIS?" Ulysses said, turning a page of the paper he was currently perusing. Below a piece about a highly decorated general of the USSA – one General Matt Zitron, Ulysses noted – and the ever-present 'German Problem,' there was a headline that had triggered another recent memory.

"Pardon?" Josephine said.

"Hang on," Ulysses said, remembering to speak in French again, for his companion's benefit.

The headline read:

BLACK SWAN – WORLD PREMIERE

He scanned the article beneath, translating as he went.

"Have you heard anything about this new ballet, *Black Swan*?" he asked.

"No," the courtesan replied. "Why? Should I?"

"I don't know. It's just that it's been written by the late Roussel."

"Oh?" Josephine replied.

But Ulysses was already done with the newspaper article and was now patting his pockets, as if looking for something. And then he remembered.

"Can you pass me my jacket?" he said, motioning towards the scruffy article hanging from the end of the bed with his sling-draped arm.

Josephine did as she was bid. "There you go," she said as she passed it to him.

The bloodied and folded manuscript paper was still where he had hidden it before fleeing the garret room. But it was only as he was unfolded the sheet of parchment that he noticed what had been scrawled on the reverse for the first time.

Ulysses peered more closely at the mark. At first he had taken it to be a blot of ink or a smear of blood but now, as he brought it closer to his face and studied it more carefully, he could see the loops and whorls were too many and too well-intentioned – it was clearly handwriting. The trouble was deciphering what it was supposed to say.

He turned the folded sheet over for a moment and regarded at the words that had been crossed out at the top of the page again:

Black Swan

"What do you make of this?" he said, pushing the paper in Josephine's direction, showing her the reverse with its strange word-smear.

"Hmm," the girl hummed as she studied it herself. "I think it's a name. This here" – she pointed at the end of the smear – "it looks like it was meant to be 'Montmartre.' In fact I'm sure it is, only whoever started writing this didn't finish it…" Her words stumbled into silence as she saw the blood and realised why the message had been left incomplete.

"What about the rest of it?" Ulysses pressed, watching as the colour drained from the girl's cheeks. "We are attempting to solve a double murder here, after all, so things are bound to get a bit squeamish."

Josephine swallowed hard, her gaze lingering on the mysterious dark smudges on the back of the parchment.

"See here? That's 'M.' for 'Monsieur,' then this bit is 'Lum...'
'Lumière,' I think, or something very much like it."

"Monsieur Lumière," Ulysses repeated, trying the name out
on his tongue, "resident of Montmartre. So how far away do
you think he lives?"

"Thank you," Ulysses said, as Josephine helped him into
his scuffed jacket. "For all that you've done. And Madame
Marguerite. And her son, whatever his name is. You will pass
on my thanks to them, won't you? And I promise I'll wire them
the money I owe them just as soon as I get back to England
and get things straightened out there."

"If you really want to thank me," the girl said as she
smoothed down his lapels, "you won't go."

Ulysses smiled. "I have to."

"But you need to rest," Josephine persisted.

"What I *need* to do is hunt down a homicidal eight-foot tall
gorilla!"

He folded up the sling he had already removed from around
his neck and placed it in a jacket pocket, moving towards the
bedroom door.

The girl suddenly skipped past him, bracing herself in the
doorway, blocking the dandy's way out.

"Josephine," he began.

"You can't go!" she cut him off.

"I have to," he said calmly, yet firmly.

"Why? Give me one good reason."

"There's just something I have to do. Now, if you'll let me
past..."

"But you can't go alone." Josephine was struggling to find a
decent excuse now.

"I won't be alone, will I?" Ulysses said softly.

The courtesan's face fell and her chin dropped onto her
chest. A single tear traced a path across her cheek. Catching
her chin with his right hand, wincing slightly as he did so, he
raised her head and met her gaze again.

"Because you'll be here," he said, placing his left hand on his
breast, "won't you?"

*   *   *

JOSEPHINE WATCHED FROM a third storey window as the man who had called himself "Ulysses" crossed the street below, continually scanning the road to both left and right as he did so, his eye-patch almost hidden by the hat now pulled down over his head. With his stubble gone as well he looked like a very different man to the one who had arrived two days ago.

"Good luck, my dashing hero," she said, the tears running freely down her face, "and may God go with you."

She watched until he turned the corner at the end of the street and was gone swallowed by the labyrinthine streets of Montmartre.

And she continued to stare at the empty space long after he was gone.

CHAPTER EIGHT

Call Me Ishmael

"Is it ready?" Le Papillon asked as he regarded the caged beast.

The primate was asleep. It lay on the tilted gurney, secured by the clamps about its wrists and neck, the huge gorilla-shaped cage shut fast around it. The air was redolent with the musky animal smell of the thing.

"Oh, it's ready, alright," Moreau said, grinning inanely. There was a manic gleam in his eye.

Eight feet tall, eight hundred pounds in weight, its already intimidating strength enhanced by the cybernetics implanted into almost every part of its body, it was an awe-inspiring sight.

"And he has a name now," the doctor added.

"*He?*"

"After all, I couldn't keep on referring to him as 'that thing' or 'it' now, could I?"

"Couldn't you?" Le Papillon looked askance at the doctor. "So what's *he* called?"

"Ishmael."

"Any particular reason?" the anarchist asked, his gaze

wandering over the massive musculature and metallic enhancements of the savage beast.

"I don't know, it just seemed... appropriate. Noble."

"Next you'll be telling me that this thing –"

"Ishmael."

"Ishmael – if you must – is some manner of noble savage. The Caliban to your Prospero, as it were."

"Who?"

Le Papillion scowled. "Never mind. It's not important." For someone so obviously intelligent, Montague Moreau's education was sorely lacking in places. "So, are we ready?"

Moreau took a seat in front of the Babbage engine control unit built into his desk. He flicked a switch and the mish-mash of machinery the device was connected to began to crackle and hum. Le Papillon wrinkled his nose as the tinny smell of ozone filled the chamber, mixing unpleasantly with the odour exuding from the ape.

"Ready when you are," Moreau said, evidently thrilled by the anticipation of what they were about to do.

"Time is, as they say, of the essence," Le Papillon said. Following the doctor's example, he lowered a pair of tinted goggles over his eyes. "Fire away."

His gaze flitting between the screen in front of him – an emerald rotating wire-frame image of the enhanced ape displayed upon it – and the cybernetically-enhanced creation itself, Moreau took a lever in his left hand and activated the mechanism.

The crackling hum rose in pitch and sporadic bursts of electric blue began to bathe the cage. As the anarchist watched, the sparking serpents snaked their way towards the crown of electrodes embedded in the great ape's skull.

The gorilla's eyes flicked open.

Le Papillon took a surprised step backwards.

"You're sure you have it under control?" he asked the doctor. "You're sure it's safe?"

"For you and I? Of course," Moreau said, far too casually for Le Papillon's liking. "For whichever target I implant inside its brain, not so much," the scientist-surgeon smirked.

The cyberneticist depressed a button on the control panel;

the clasps holding the electrified cage closed released, and the cage sprang open.

Moreau's fingers danced over the rattling keys of the console as he typed a string of commands into the ordinateur.

The massive animal sat up and yawned. It slowly turned its head from left to right and back again, its obsidian eyes scanning every inch of the room as it did so.

Le Papillon took another step back.

Moreau typed something else into his Babbage engine and the ape stepped down from the cage and gurney, great slabs of muscle moving beneath its rippling, black-furred hide. Biceps as thick as tree trunks tensed as the beast hefted the heavy steel vambraces that sheathed its forearms.

Sparks popped from the cage as the last of the electrical energy dissipated. Inconsequential wisps of smoke rose from the silver fur of the giant gorilla's back as a last few desultory arcs discharged themselves within the ape's muscular body.

Still keeping one eye on the hulking brute, Le Papillon lent over towards Moreau. "You have inputted the target's designation?"

"As we speak," Moreau replied, his hands flying over the console keyboard.

"Then Monsieur Lumière's time has come."

With one final, bold keystroke, Doctor Moreau's hands came to a standstill, the middle finger of his right hand hovering over the enamelled *enter* key.

"Wait!" Le Papillon suddenly snapped, with uncharacteristic irascibility.

Doctor Moreau looked at him, eyebrows arching in surprise.

"I want you to enter a second target."

"A second target? But I thought there was only one left that needed eliminating..." He broke off as realisation dawned. "Oh, I see."

"Can you do it?"

"Easy," the cyberneticist laughed. "I don't think Ishmael is likely to forget the one that got away, do you?"

"Then do it."

"Do you want him to hunt the bastard down, then?"

"After it has eliminated Mousier Lumière," Le Papillon

replied, peering the length of the cellar at the newest addition to his collection – a black and orange butterfly of the species *Danaus plexippus*, mounted in a stark white frame all by itself, as if frozen in a moment of time.

"But of course," Moreau chuckled, his twitching fingers darting over the keyboard again, lines of algorithmic code appearing on the screen in glowing green characters in synchronicity with his deft keystrokes.

"Precisely," Le Papillon said, a scowl knotting his face. He didn't like being second-guessed by anyone.

Moreau stopped typing and turned, giving Le Papillon an expectant look.

"Activate," the anarchist said.

The doctor struck the *enter* key.

With a grunt, the giant gorilla lurched forward, making for the arched doorway leading from the cellar into an adjoining passageway, which in turn ultimately connected with the labyrinthine tunnels of the Paris sewer system, and a multitude of ways out of Le Papillon's subterranean lair.

Le Papillon followed, keeping a wary distance between himself and the beast, as the hulking primate squeezed through the archway and into the corridor beyond. Doctor Moreau stayed where he was, observing the creature's progress via the monitor built into his control desk.

He saw what the ape saw. Bio-electrical impulses travelling along its optic nerves were relayed via the electrodes in the ape's skull to the transmitter positioned between the animal's shoulder blades. The transmitter – which was now protected by a shielding collar that surrounded the creature's neck – then converted those signals into radio waves which were beamed to a receiver in Moreau's control console. From there they became grainy images on the screen in front of him.

The huge ape moved almost silently along the corridor as it squeezed itself between the narrow walls. The only sounds it made were the padding of its leathery feet on the rough floor, and the scrape of its shoulders against the ancient brickwork. There was a single-minded purpose to its movements. It had been given its target and now it had murder on its mind.

A moment later it was swallowed by the shadows that

awaited it in the tunnel beyond. And then it was gone.

Le Papillon allowed himself a brief smile of satisfaction. Everything was back on course.

The butterfly had flapped its wings, and on the horizon, beyond the monolithic landmarks of the Parisian skyline, the storm clouds were massing.

PART TWO

Black Swan

~ May 1998 ~

Things fall apart; the centre cannot hold;
Mere anarchy is loosed upon the world...

– William Butler Yeats, 'The Second Coming,' 1920

I am not fond of expecting catastrophes, but there are
cracks in the universe.

– Sydney Smith, 1771-1845

CHAPTER NINE

Monkey Business

FORTUNE, AS IT is so often said, favours the bold, and for someone whose very DNA oozed charm, it wasn't hard for Ulysses Quicksilver to acquire an address for the mysterious M. Lumière.

Despite his photo-fit being proudly displayed on newsstands throughout Paris, nobody recognised him, even when he walked straight up to them and addressed them directly, asking if they had heard of a certain M. Lumière and, if they had, whether they would be so kind as to tell him where he might be found – all in flawless French, of course.

It helped that he had temporarily flipped the eye-patch up out of the way, hiding it under the brim of the hat he had borrowed from Madame Marguerite's dressing-up box. Pulling his fringe down as best he could, he hid the knot of scar tissue that filled his left eye-socket.

And so it was that he came to M. Lumière's apartment building later that evening, as the setting sun painted the domes of Sacré-Coeur a mixture of peach and burnished gold.

It was as unremarkable as any other building in the district: seven storeys tall, its façade all French windows and narrow wrought iron balconies. The mysterious M. Lumière kept the penthouse apartment.

Ulysses walked on by without once breaking his stride. He had developed a mistrust of front doors of late. As recent events had demonstrated so clearly, front doors were for salesmen and the police. Coming in by the front door warned people you were on your way and left the caller at a disadvantage. Ulysses felt he needed every advantage he could get at the moment, considering his current situation.

It didn't take the resourceful dandy long to find a way round the back, where the caged ladder fire escapes were hidden away along with all manner of exposed pipework.

Exercising his shoulders, he tested Doctor Cossard's surgical skills and caught his breath as he felt the stitches holding the ragged edges of the bullet wound pull taut.

The sensible thing to do would be to take things easy. But then sensible had never really been Ulysses Quicksilver's style.

And yet, in the greater scheme of things, the sensible thing ultimately was to solve the mystery of the Rue Morgue murders, clearing his name in the eyes of the French police in the process, thereby enabling him to leave the French capital and return to England, to prevent the love of his life from ever setting out on a particularly ill-advised voyage to the Moon. And for any of that to happen, right now that meant paying M. Lumière a call.

Two storeys from the roof, Ulysses paused to catch his breath. He hadn't realised how much such simple physical exertion – such as climbing a ladder – would take its toll. And that was after two days of rest and recuperation at Madame Marguerite's, being nursed by the lovelorn Josephine.

A shadow, big and black, darted past above him, instantly catching Ulysses' attention.

"*Merde!*" he hissed.

There was only one possible explanation as far as he could see and it meant that he had been on the right track all along. Only, Ulysses thought disconsolately, sometimes he hated being proved right.

Reaching the top of the fire escape, ignoring the sharp pain in his shoulder, he swung himself over the raised parapet and onto the roof.

Naturally there was no sign of the brute now, but it had been here, he was sure of it, and that meant that, unfortunately, he knew where it was now.

Ulysses scampered across the roof. Reaching the parapet on the other side, he leaned out and looked down.

Any doubts he might have had about having located the Lumière apartment were dispelled the moment he saw the curtain flapping through the open French doors on the balcony directly beneath him. Sounds rose from the apartment below, sounds that only confirmed his worst fears and set his heart racing: a man's helpless cries, the crash of furniture, and the snorting barks of something large, bestial and angry.

He grabbed the parapet with both hands, judging the distance to the balcony at a glance. "Here goes nothing," he muttered and swung himself over the edge of the roof.

He landed in a crouch, wincing at the pain in his shoulder. Rising, he peered through the open French doors into the room beyond.

It looked like a sitting room that doubled as a study. Photographic portraits lined the walls in regimented fashion and there was a tall, glass-fronted cabinet to his left filled with clockwork toys. What was left of the rest of the furniture was now just so much splintered wood and torn upholstery; a chaise longue leaned peculiarly against one wall.

To Ulysses' right the sitting room door was open, revealing a hallway beyond where he glimpsed the closed front door. On the far side of the room stood a writing desk, a gleaming golden parrot perched on a stand on top of it, next to a device fashioned from a gramophone and a profusion of copper wire.

The parrot was jerking and twitching on its perch, grating electronic squawks emanating from its beak.

Pressed up against the desk was a clearly terrified middle-aged man. He was wearing a tweed three piece suit, his greying hair was swept back from a high forehead and he wore a goatee upon his pronounced chin.

But the presence dominating the scene, that made the otherwise spacious sitting room seem small by comparison, was the eight hundred pound gorilla in the room.

Ulysses entered as the ape picked up a chair and hurled it at the wall above the man's head. The parrot and the gramophone crashed to the floor where the broken chair joined them a moment later.

As if half a ton of gorilla wasn't unsettling enough, the great ape's massive form was enhanced with all manner of cybernetic attachments. There were the heavy iron vambraces sheathing its forearms, the snaking cables that were wound around its limbs, and the metal-reinforced joints of its hips, its knees and its riveted knuckles. The primate's body was criss-crossed with lines of stitching and the scars of old sutures which appeared almost white against the charcoal grey flesh, leaving hairless trails through its thick black fur.

And there were the electrodes projecting from the top of its head, but Ulysses didn't remember the thick steel collar from his last encounter with the beast. It completely covered the box of blinking lights that had been bolted between the animal's shoulder blades.

There was an unpleasant, acrid smell in the room that seemed to penetrate its every corner; a combination of lubricant grease, animal musk and ammonia.

Ulysses went for the gun he kept holstered under his left arm, only neither the holster nor the gun were there, of course. And not for the first time since arriving in Paris, he wished his sword-stick wasn't still lost somewhere in the past.

There was no doubt in the dandy's mind that the ape was wholly fixated on accomplishing only one goal – that of killing the middle-aged man cowering before the desk.

Thanks to all the noise the ape was making and the desperate howls of its victim, the brute was wholly unaware of Ulysses' presence. If he was to find out what was going on, and why the composer and the ordinateur engineer had been murdered by the gorilla, he needed to keep M. Lumière – for he was sure that's who the man was – alive. And the ape's obsession with its assigned target might actually enable him to do just that.

But to get the animal's attention without also possessing the means to defend himself from it was surely tantamount to madness.

He quickly scanned the room. There were broken pieces of furniture that he could improvise as cudgels, but he doubted the delicate mahogany posts would stand up to giving the ape a good thrashing.

He looked again at the ape. He supposed he might be able to pull out a few cables, touch them together and create a short circuit; that was bound to have an effect on the beast, although he wasn't entirely sure what that effect would be. And to test out his theory he would need to get so close to the beast that he would put himself in immediate danger.

The ape roared and lunged.

Lumière screamed.

Beyond the sitting room-cum-study, the front door opened.

All eyes turned towards the young woman who had let herself into the apartment.

Lumière gave a whimper. The young woman gave a strangled cry of fear. The ape gave a snarl.

The time for ingenious plans and clever tricks was over. It was either now, or never.

"Hey!" Ulysses shouted.

The wide eyes of the pretty girl framed in the doorway met his. Lumière was making a strange snivelling sound and didn't seem capable of stopping.

The gorilla froze in its advance on the sobbing wretch and slowly turned its head, fixing its cruel gaze on Ulysses.

"Er, hello," Ulysses said. The ape let out a low growl, its lips peeling back to expose large chisel-like teeth and yellowing, tusk-like fangs. "My, what big teeth you have. Now why don't you pick on someone your own size? But no, that would be silly, wouldn't it? I suppose there can't be many your size around; at least not in Paris. At least I hope not."

Confusion creased the great ape's features, and for a moment the monster appeared to be wracked by indecision.

"Come on then!" Ulysses shouted, some of his old bravado returning as he glanced about the room whilst keeping himself between the open French doors.

Night was settling across the city, the street below a deeply shadowed canyon now that the sun had set beyond the Montmartre Cemetery. But the terrible tableau inside the penthouse apartment was bathed in the warm yellow glow from the corner behind Ulysses.

He spun round, grabbing the standing lamp in both hands and holding it out before him like a quarterstaff. With one sharp swipe he knocked the lampshade off against the jamb of the open French doors. A second strike shattered the light bulb, the bared metal points at its cap sparking as electricity arced between the exposed wires.

"Come on then," he growled, advancing towards the savage brute, thrusting the crackling tip towards the ape's face.

The monster rose to its full height, raising its massive arms above its head. Its knuckles scraped grooves in the plastered ceiling, sending a shower of white dust down on their heads. The return sweep of the ape's long limbs set a chandelier swinging, the jangling of its suspended teardrop crystals creating its own discordant protest.

"Come on!"

The gorilla grunted loudly and beat its chest. As the beast dropped onto all fours, Ulysses braced himself, sure that this was it.

The beast snorted, batting at the lampstand as Ulysses kept up his goading.

Any moment now, it would launch itself at him. Surely, any moment now.

Only it didn't.

"Come on!" Ulysses shouted, in French and then English, just to make sure he covered all the bases. "What's wrong with you? I'm right here. Come and get me!"

The ape seemed frozen into inaction, an expression

somewhere between utter confusion and unbridled rage knotting its leathery features. Bolts of blue-white lightning arced among the humming electrodes plugged into the ape's skull, mirroring the snapping bursts of electricity popping from the broken light bulb.

Behind the beast, the whimpering man shuffled tremulously towards the door, the young woman beckoning him towards her.

"Come on, you evolutionary loser!" Ulysses screamed.

The monster put its huge hands to its head, letting go again just as quickly as electricity sparked through its fingers from the crown of thick electrodes. With a snarl of frustrated fury, the gigantic primate turned its back on Ulysses.

Lumière was halfway to the door. The beast grabbed the man with one huge hand. He let out a wail of terror as the ape pulled him within reach of its other sledgehammer fist.

"No!" Ulysses screamed, leaping at the ape, still holding the lampstand.

It was the futile action of a desperate man. With one sharp twist the deed was done. M. Lumière was dead.

The cry of alarm died in Ulysses' throat.

The great ape cast the body carelessly aside. It bounced off the desk, a slack arm pulling a drift of technical drawings onto the floor after it.

Its primary target eliminated, the gorilla was free to turn its angry attention to the daring dandy. There was murder in its beady black eyes.

Slowly, Ulysses backed towards the open windows and the balcony beyond, holding the lampstand out before him.

M. Lumière was dead, which meant there was only one lead left for Ulysses to follow, if he was to solve the mystery of the Rue Morgue murders – the murder weapon; the beast itself.

If he could only follow it as it fled the murder scene, the ape might very well lead him to its masters. Only judging by the way it was clawing its way towards him now, the carpet rucking beneath its huge fingers, the gorilla wasn't going anywhere in the foreseeable future, at least not until Ulysses was dead.

Ulysses could feel the curtain flapping at his back. He was going to have to decide which was more important to him – having a lead to follow or still having his life. All he had to do was stop the ape, save the girl and get out of there alive.

Ulysses glimpsed movement away to his right, beyond the hulking heavily-muscled mass of bestial biology and crude cybernetics that was currently obscuring much of his view of the room.

"*Non!*" came the woman's voice. "No!" she cried again and a moment later a vase full of dried blooms smashed against one armoured vambrace.

The ape snarled, half turning in the direction of this new annoyance.

A crystal decanter hit it square in the face, shattering against its scarred snout. The ape shook its head in surprise and gave a bark of irritation.

The obsidian pearls of its eyes narrowed as they focused on the young woman and a rumbling growl rose from within its broad barrel chest. The woman gave a startled gasp of terror.

Still snarling, the ape turned back to the dandy, which was when Ulysses struck.

He landed a blow with the lampstand across the cyber-ape's snout, the jagged metal and glass remnants of the broken bulb scoring bloody gouges across its nose and lips.

"Run! Get out of here!" Ulysses shouted.

The girl didn't need to be told twice, dashing from the room and slamming the door shut behind her.

Barking with pain, putting one immense paw to its face, the primate lashed out with its other arm, furious primitive instinct overriding whatever instructions it was receiving from its mysterious master.

The swipe sent Ulysses flying across the room as if he were nothing more than a ragdoll.

He collided with a display case, glass and wooden staves shattering around him. Clockwork devices tumbled to the floor in a cascade of broken cogs and springs as Ulysses covered his head with his hands in a vain attempt to protect himself.

*   *   *

THE APE WAS on him in seconds. Picking him up in one huge hairy hand, the raging beast hurled him violently across the room.

Ulysses slammed into the flimsy sitting room door, the force of the impact splintering the panels before the hinges gave and it came away from its frame altogether. He landed in the hall at the young woman's feet. Hearing her subsequent shriek of alarm, Ulysses woozily opened his one remaining eye.

"Get... out..." he said, barely managing to maintain his grip on consciousness.

He was dimly aware of a dull throbbing sensation from his shoulder. Part of him was surprised that he wasn't in abject agony. Instead, a warm glow was spreading throughout his body. Nonetheless, somehow he knew that if he tried to sit up, even if he just tried to lift a finger he would suffer the consequences and know pain again. All he wanted to do was sleep.

But there was another part of him – his stubborn, intractable core – that would never give up, that would fight the oncoming oblivion to the end.

In his barely conscious state, he was still vaguely aware of what was going on around him. He heard the shuffling leathery footfalls of the silverback as it followed him from the devastated sitting room. He was aware of the clacking of the young woman's footsteps as she continued to back away from the beast.

He felt the ape's eyes on him then, those pitiless black beads of concentrated hatred and evil intent. Its rank breath gusted into his face and ruffled his hair. He was forced to fight the desire to gag. There was only one way out of this now; all he could do was play dead and hope for the best.

A rough finger prodded him in the side, sending stabbing pains through his ribs.

Ulysses let his body go limp as the ape rolled him onto his back.

He thought he heard the woman say something, but her voice was muffled, as if his ears were full of cotton wool.

And then Ulysses felt the change in the air currents as the gorilla shifted its great bulk and moved away from him. He heard it knuckle its way back across the devastated sitting room and the banging of the French doors as it exited the apartment the same way it had entered.

And then it was gone, and with a groan Ulysses lost his battle with oblivion.

CHAPTER TEN

Unanswered Questions

ULYSSES CAME TO with a start, the ape's snarling face and bloodied snout fading along with the rest of the disturbing dream. He tried to sit up and felt ropes bite at his wrists. Blinking his eye into focus, he slowly took in his new surroundings.

He was tied to a bed in what was clearly a young lady's bedroom.

"Oh boy," he groaned, "not again."

"Again?" exclaimed the woman seated at the end of the bed. It was the girl from the apartment, the one who, like him, had happened to interrupt the ape's assault on M. Lumière. "This happens to you a lot, does it?" she demanded in Parisian-accented French.

"Well, not as often as you might think," Ulysses admitted and winced.

He went to put a hand to the stabbing pain at the back of his head, in that moment forgetting that he was still tied to the bed.

"It's just that this is the second time in as many days that I've come to on some strange young lady's bed," he explained.

He looked again at the knotted rope restraining him. Then he looked at the room, taking in its tasteful, feminine décor.

"So you just happened to have a hank of rope lying around, did you?" he muttered to himself.

"Appearances can be deceptive," the young woman said.

He looked at her properly for the first time, taking in her auburn hair, piled haphazardly on top of her head, making her appear all the more appealing as a result; the intense look in her flint-hard stare; the sculptural definition of her cheekbones, streaked with grime; her long, slender limbs; her well-endowed bosom, emphasised by the low cut dress and the string of pearls she was wearing; the leather apron worn over the top of said dress; the heavy ironworker's gloves.

"But sometimes what you see is what you get," Ulysses countered, trying his most rakish grin on her.

"Why don't you just tell me who you are and what you were doing in my... In *that* apartment?"

"No. Why don't I tell you all about you first?"

A smile curled the corner of the woman's otherwise stern mouth. "Go on then. Why not?"

"Very well."

Ulysses took a deep breath and began.

"You look like you've just stepped out of a workshop and from that, coupled with the fact that we met at M. Lumière's, someone clearly possessed of some ability when it comes to clockwork, and possibly audio manipulation as well," he added, recalling the gramophone-like device that had been damaged during the ape's rampage, "I would have to say that you are also of a technical bent. And yet you still believe that to find a place in society you have to conform to accepted gender stereotypes, hence the dress and the pearls.

"And you haven't bothered to change, that or you haven't had time to change yet, so I would say that either we haven't been here long or there is some pressing matter that you must attend to, possibly resulting from your... Yes, from the way you let yourself into the apartment unannounced by the front door – the similarity in facial features, although not that great a similarity... As a consequence of your uncle's death."

The young woman bristled. So he was right, Lumière had been her uncle.

Ulysses was in full flow now and there was no stopping him. "It's not the first time you've done something like this, judging by the wear and tear on the apron, which clearly fits you so well, and the same could be said of the gloves. You're clearly stronger than you look too, having somehow managed to manhandle me here – wherever here is – so I would have to say, at a guess, that you are an engineer, possibly an inventor of some kind, and you were visiting your uncle because... because... Ah yes, because either he needed your help with something, or you needed his."

The woman met his gaze for several long, uncomfortable seconds without saying anything. Ulysses could see the tracks of dried tears in the smudges of grime on her face, and from the way she was staring, hardly daring to blink, she was clearly on the verge of crying.

"So that's what you think, is it?" she said sharply.

"Yes."

"Whereas, if I were to hazard a guess, judging by your appearance alone, I'd have to say that you were a wanted murderer on the run from the gendarmes."

"Come on. I really look like a criminal to you?"

She tossed the folded newspaper in her hands onto his lap.

"Yes."

Ulysses looked down, only to be met by a hauntingly familiar, yet still slightly sinister, simulacrum of himself that had been circulated throughout the Parisian press.

"It's the eye-patch, isn't it?" he harrumphed. "It's always the eye-patch."

"It does give you a certain... I don't know what," the girl agreed.

"But as you yourself said, appearances can be deceiving."

"And as you said, sometimes what you see is what you get."

"Ah. Fair comment."

"It said in *Le Journal* that you're wanted for murder."

"It did? And who am I supposed to have done away with to make myself so popular that the press can't stop printing column inches about me?"

"A composer."

"I was framed, maybe not intentionally, but it doesn't make any difference in the end."

"So you're taking the rap for someone else?"

"Not through choice, I assure you."

This woman was hard work. Oh to be back in Josephine's bedroom right now, with someone who he felt would be on his side no matter what happened.

He suddenly felt exhausted, overwhelmed by it all. Everything was a battle. Just staying alive was a battle, or so it seemed to him, and right then it felt like a battle he was losing. But that was all he needed to tap into that well of inner strength and pep himself up again. For he might be many things, but he was not a loser; he would never be a loser.

He tested his bonds again. It wasn't only his wrists that had been restrained; it was his ankles as well.

"There's no point even trying," the woman said. "I know what I'm doing when it comes to knots."

He glanced down at himself then, realising that he was missing his shirt. His chest had been bound with a wide bandage. He took a deep breath and winced. It was his ribs. The other bandage and dressing were still in place around his shoulder.

"Looks like you know what you're doing when it comes to first aid," he said.

The woman nodded.

"So you must believe I'm innocent," Ulysses decided, with relief.

"How do you work that out?"

"Well why would you go to the trouble of making sure I was fit and healthy otherwise?"

"How about to make sure you're in a fit state to answer to your crimes in a court of law and so that you're in the peak of physical fitness so you endure the full term of your sentence?"

Ulysses wilted, then brightened again. "So you noticed."

"Noticed what?" the young woman said, making a point of looking at something on the other side of the room.

"The peak of physical fitness thing."

"It was merely an observation." She blushed.

"And I'm the President of France," Ulysses laughed.

"You broke into my uncle's apartment," the woman pointed out, returning to the matter in hand.

"If you're going to be pernickety about it, I didn't break in. The ape had already done that for me!"

The girl said nothing.

"Much as it pains me to point this out, you saw the brute kill your uncle with its bare hands. I was trying to stop it!"

"And you failed," she said bluntly. There was no screaming, no tears, no recriminations, just the weight of undeniable failure weighing down Ulysses' shoulders. "How did you know the beast was going to be there?"

"I didn't, okay? It was just dumb luck."

The young woman's eyes seemed to blaze red with the fires of accusation. "Luck?"

"Bad luck. The only kind I ever seem to get."

The woman looked like she was about to speak.

There came a loud knock from somewhere nearby. The sound made Ulysses start and his heartbeat quicken.

The girl rose from the end of the bed and left the room. "Who is it?" she called.

"It's the police, miss," came a gruff, and slightly muffled, voice.

"Bloody hell!" Ulysses cursed. "Not again!"

Ulysses tugged at the ropes binding his wrists, kicking his legs against the knots constricting his ankles; the metal bedstead banged against the bare floorboards.

He heard a tut from the other side of the bedroom door.

The gruff voice came again. "Are you alright in there, miss?"

Ulysses tensed.

"Yes, I'm fine," the young woman called back. Ulysses heard the rattle of a safety chain and then the click of a catch being released. "I just knocked over my umbrella stand.

"Sorry about that. Now, what can I do for you, officer..."

"Sergeant Lecoq, miss." Ulysses could hear the gendarme's gruff tones much more clearly now that the door was open. The bedroom was clearly off the main hallway of the property, wherever that was, although he didn't think it could be too far from Lumière's place in Montmartre for the girl to have got him here all by herself.

On most other occasions Ulysses wouldn't have particularly minded being tied to a young lady's bed, any time other than right now to be precise.

He listened intently to the exchange taking place on the other side of the bedroom door.

"What can I do for you, Sergeant Lecoq?"

Had she called the police or not? And if she hadn't, what were they doing here?

Ulysses could come up with only one reasonable assumption.

"May we come in?" the sergeant's voice came again.

"No. As you can see I'm in the middle of something. Whatever you have to tell me, you can tell me here."

"Are you sure, miss? I mean–"

"I'm sure, thank you, sergeant."

"Well, I'm very sorry to tell you that I am the bearer of bad news."

"What bad news?"

"It's your uncle, M. Gustav Lumière."

"My uncle?"

"He's dead, miss. I'm ever so sorry."

The tears were coming again now. "Dead?"

"Murdered."

"Murdered?"

"Yes, miss. I can only offer you our utmost condolences."

For a moment it went quiet out in the hallway. Then, "Who did it? Who killed him?"

"We're still searching for the villain, miss."

"But you have a suspect. I saw his face in the paper."

"Yes, miss. And don't you worry, we'll get him. I am very sorry for your loss." A moment's hesitation. "Do you want someone to stay with you?"

Ulysses heard her breathe in, as if to answer, but no words came.

"You wanted to say something, miss?"

"Er... No. No, there's nothing more to say, is there?"

"No, miss. Once again, I am sorry for your loss. You have our sympathy."

Ulysses heard the door close. He strained to listen to the retreating footsteps of the police.

A moment later, the bedroom door was flung open.

The girl stood there, hands on hips, her eyes blazing like the coals of a forge, her merciless gaze upon him.

"Then you believe me," Ulysses said, a tentative smile shaping his features. "You're prepared to give me the benefit of the doubt?"

"I'm prepared to give you the benefit of the doubt. For now."

"Ah. Okay." It wasn't quite the response he'd been hoping for. "I see."

"So why don't you do something about removing that doubt," she went on. "Tell me everything, and you can start with your name."

HE DIDN'T TELL her everything, of course; only the bits he thought she'd believe.

He told her about how he stumbled upon the body of the dead composer Roussel, although he failed to mention the locked door or precisely how he had ended up in the composer's garret in the first place. He told her about being chased by the gendarmes and his initial encounter with the ape.

She assumed that he had been shot by the police. He didn't contradict her.

He told her he'd laid low for a while, scanning the papers for clues, and how he had made the connection between the composer's death and that of the ordinateur auteur. He skipped the bit about Madame Marguerite's boarding house and went straight on to the blood-stained clue scrawled on the back of the rejected piece of manuscript paper, and his enquiries around Montmartre, which brought him neatly to his arrival at her uncle's apartment.

He kept the whole agent of the English throne thing out of it, just to keep things simple.

When he had finished, she remained ambiguously silent.

"Look, I take it you searched my pockets while I was out for the count." She nodded. "So you know I'm not armed. I didn't even have a knife on me when I ran into Monsieur Killer Gorilla."

Still she said nothing, her wide eyes locked on his increasingly desperate gaze.

"And I took on that beast to save you. So come on, untie me, and let's see if we can't find out who wanted your uncle dead and why, together."

"Would you do that?" she suddenly blurted out, setting to loosening the rope around his ankles. "Only I'm worried Uncle Gustav might have got himself mixed up in something…"

"Dodgy? Illegal? Revolutionary?"

Her eyes said it all. "Something like that, yes."

As the girl untied him, the dandy felt waves of relief wash through him. At last things looked like they might be getting back on track. Now that he had a willing accomplice, someone else who had witnessed the ape commit murder, he had a better chance than ever of getting to the bottom of this mystery and clearing his name.

And once that was done, he would at last be able to return to England and get back to the important business of saving those most important to him.

"So, seeing as how we're going to be partners," he said, sitting on the edge of the bed, rubbing at his wrists, the girl beside him, smelling of engine oil and lavender, "how about you tell me your name?"

"Cadence," she said, and offered him her hand. "Cadence Bettencourt."

"I take it M. Lumière was your maternal uncle then?"

"That's right. And my only living relative."

"Well, it is a pleasure to meet you, Mademoiselle Bettencourt."

She smiled, her cheeks flushing.

"So, time and tide, as they say."

"I beg your pardon?"

Ulysses rose stiffly to his feet, wincing at the twinge this invoked in his bruised ribs.

"We should get going. There's no time to lose. We don't want the trail to go completely cold. I would suggest we start back at your uncle's place."

The girl began to remove her gloves and apron.

"What were you working on?" Ulysses asked, his curiosity piqued.

"Oh, just a pet project of mine. Something for getting round town in the rush hour."

She placed the folded gloves and apron carefully on her bedspread.

"You know," she said, "I had been suspicious of my uncle for some time, truth be told, but as he was my only living relation I didn't want to pry, or do anything that might upset him or end up driving him away.

"Uncle Gustav once said to me that if I ever found myself in trouble I should contact Valerius Leroux. I had no idea at the time what he was talking about but he clearly must have known that he had got mixed up with the wrong crowd."

"And who is this Valerius Leroux?" Ulysses asked. "And what does he do that makes him the man to turn to in a crisis?"

"He... He arranges things."

"What sort of things?"

"Things that need arranging, I suppose. I don't know any more than that, but he has money and influence."

Ulysses could think of one or two things that he could do with having arranged. Perhaps employing this Leroux was the most effective way for it to be achieved. Suddenly Magna Britannia didn't seem as far away as it once had.

"Then it's a deal."

"I'm sorry?"

"I'll help you track down your uncle's killer if you'll arrange a meeting between myself and Valerius Leroux."

"But of course," she said and then caught herself. "But why?"

"I find myself in need of a travel agent."

"Right then, like you say, sounds like a plan," the girl said, making for the front door. When Ulysses didn't move to follow her, she spun about on her heel.

"What is it? What's the matter? Why are you still standing there?"

"Um..." Ulysses glanced down at his bandaged torso. "I think it might draw undue attention to our activities if I were to go out and about without my shirt, don't you? So would you mind telling me what you've done with it?"

CHAPTER ELEVEN

Mona Lisa Smile

Cautiously, Cadence opened the door. Pushing it open, she flinched at the protesting squeak of its hinges.

"Here, let me," said Ulysses, stepping past her into the penthouse apartment.

The place was just as he remembered it. After the gorilla had thrown Ulysses through the sitting room door, clearly believing him to be dead, in the next instant it had pricked up its ears and fled the flat.

Not knowing what else to do, and considering that the unconscious Ulysses might be the only person who could help her make sense of her uncle's death, she had managed to hoist him onto her shoulders and proceeded to carry him out of the apartment. She had left the apartment under the cover of darkness and, amazingly, got him all the way back to her place without attracting any unwanted attention.

"But how did you get me from your uncle's apartment building to your workshop?" he had asked, intrigued. It might have only been half a mile, but just the same. "You didn't carry me all the way, did you?"

"*I* didn't," was all she would say, and refused to be drawn on the matter.

The broken door was still lying in the hallway, a couple of spots of Ulysses' blood upon it. Stepping past it he peered into the devastated sitting room-cum-study.

"Is he...?" Cadence whispered from behind him.

"No, he's gone."

Ulysses stepped carefully into the room, taking care where he trod.

Lumière's body was gone, but the piles of papers that had cascaded to the floor remained where they had fallen beside the desk. They looked like schematics for circuit designs. The room was cold, the windows having been open all night.

Ulysses recovered a half-folded schematic from the floor. The design looked like that for a device intended to be inserted into the auditory canal, judging by the careful drawing of an over-sized human ear beside it. Its curious shape made it look like a sucker-mouthed fish.

"What was your uncle working on?" Ulysses asked.

"His field was acoustics," she said. "You know; the recording, transmission, modulation and projection of sound waves."

"Indeed. Interesting."

He bent down and retrieved something that had rolled under the desk.

It was the golden parrot. It was still attached to its perch but it was badly dented, having been partially crushed.

Ulysses peered into the automaton bird's glittering crystal eyes.

"Could this be repaired, do you think?" he asked. "I mean, I don't know how much you know about electronics and audiology–"

"Enough," she said, taking the broken object from him.

"What was it?" Ulysses asked. "His pet or something?"

Cadence shot him a scolding glance. "Archimedes is a state-of-the-art automaton."

"Called Archimedes."

"Yes, what of it? Uncle Gustav liked the company."

"Well, when you start naming the state-of-the-art automaton that you keep around your apartment for company, it's what we call a pet."

Cadence gave a very Gallic shrug as she set about turning the dented device over in her hands. She depressed a switch secreted under one wing and when that didn't do anything, popped open a panel in its breast and tested a connection.

"I can fix him," she said.

"Hmm?" Ulysses asked, pieces of the gramophone in his hands.

"Archimedes. I can repair him, only not here. Back at my place."

"Good. I mean, we might be able to learn something from it."

"How do you mean?"

"It's a parrot, isn't it? And an automaton at that."

"So?"

"Well, parrots repeat things." He showed her the pieces of gramophone. "Do you know what this was before everything went... apeshit?"

"No. Some sort of recording device no doubt, or something to do with sound modulation."

Ulysses placed the pieces carefully on the desk. Leaving the clutter surrounding Lumière's workspace, he crossed the room, his eyebrows knitted in thought. He took in the pile of matchwood and crystal splinters that was all that was left of Lumière's cabinet of clockwork curiosities. The tiny treasures were now just so much twisted brass and unwound spring mockeries of the wonders they had once been. Looking at the broken toys he remembered the pain his collision with the cabinet had caused.

"I think we're done here," he said, striding across the room and through the empty door frame.

The robo-parrot under one arm, Cadence hastened after him, clearly more than happy not to have to spend another minute in the room where her uncle had died.

Out on the landing, they waited as the lift ground its way up from the ground floor.

"Right. Get yourself back to the workshop," he said. The lift arrived, Ulysses pulled open the safety gate, and the two of them got in.

"What are you going to do?" the young woman asked.

"You made that call to Leroux, didn't you?"

"I did."

The elevator began to descend.

"Can I borrow your personal communicator?" Anticipating her answer would be in the affirmative, Ulysses held the palm of his hand out flat before her.

"What do you want it for?"

"He said to meet him at the Louvre, didn't he?"

"That's right. Look, tell me; who are you going to call?"

"I think it's time the gendarmes received an anonymous tip-off, don't you?" he said, smiling slyly.

The lift arrived at the ground floor with a jolt.

"And while they're tidying things up here" – pulling open the gate, Ulysses stood aside as Cadence stepped out – "I'll be meeting with your friend Leroux at the Louvre."

"Quite magnificent, isn't it?"

Startled at hearing someone address him in English – even if it was English spoken with a strong Gallic accent – Ulysses turned from studying the painting to study the man standing beside him.

The man was wearing a navy suit cut in the latest style, a white shirt and an ostentatious silk bow-tie. His fine blond hair was swept back from a high forehead forming a pale widow's peak, while his skin appeared as smooth as alabaster. He looked like he would have given Ulysses a run for his money as the Best Dressed Bachelor that season, if due to circumstances beyond his control, Ulysses hadn't been out of the running.

"It certainly has a certain *je ne sais quoi*," Ulysses said with a smile.

"Her smile is," the man said with a flourish of the handkerchief grasped tightly in his left hand, "how do you say?"

"Enigmatic?"

"Just so. Enigmatic. And, of course, *magnifique*!"

The man turned to meet Ulysses' enquiring gaze.

"Monsieur Quicksilver, I presume," he said, offering his right hand.

Every movement he made was balletic and precise.

"Valerius Leroux." Ulysses accepted the hand and shook it firmly. The returned grip wasn't in any way so firm. It made Ulysses feel uncomfortable. Fortunately in the next moment Leroux let go of Ulysses' hand.

"It is a pleasure, Monsieur," Leroux said, bowing as if they were in the Palace of Versailles at the Court of the Sun King, rather than in an art gallery, although they were in front of arguably the most famous portrait in the world. "I have heard so much about you."

"Really? From Mademoiselle Bettencourt?"

"Quite so. But enough of this. I understand that you are planning on leaving our fair City of Lovers."

"You understand right."

"I am sorry to hear that, truly I am." He sounded almost hurt.

"Believe me, if circumstances were different, I would quite happily stay. But maybe some other time, eh? The question is, would I be correct in thinking that you're the man to speak to regarding my travel arrangements?"

"Just so." Leroux shot darting glances to left and right as he ran the fingers of one hand through his fine, pale blond hair. "Walk with me," he said, grabbing Ulysses by the arm. Ulysses winced. "Oh, I'm sorry. Did I hurt you?"

"No, it's alright. I'm fine," Ulysses lied through gritted teeth. "It's nothing."

"Hmm. Something tells me you lead a rather – how shall we say? – interesting life, Monsieur."

"That's one way of putting it."

The two men headed out of the Italian gallery.

"So, Ulysses – may I call you Ulysses?"

"What? I mean, yes. Yes, of course."

"So, Ulysses, what line of work are you in?"

"I'm… Well you could say that I'm in exports."

Leroux gave him a look as if to say, *and my mother's the Queen of Magna Britannia,* but what he actually said was, "Exports?"

"And imports."

"Very well."

"So you'll help me?" Ulysses said, sounding more anxious than he had intended.

They passed from Spain into France, not stopping to enjoy any of the paintings in those galleries as Leroux led Ulysses inexorably downstairs, heading for the exit.

There was an ever-present hubbub of hushed voices and ringing footsteps, the weird acoustics of the galleries turning every sound into strange echoes. Brilliant light came in through the high windows and the atmosphere was redolent with the smell of floor polish. The other visitors to the museum moved in clusters, obediently trailing their guides through the galleried halls, or as couples, not looking at the art at all, only having eyes for each other.

No one was looking at Ulysses. If the wandering and wondering eyes of the tourists were lingering on anyone, it was his new best friend, the effete Valerius Leroux. Most, however, were too busy enjoying all the wonders the Louvre had to offer.

Leroux pulled open his jacket to reveal a bundle of documents and tickets protruding from an inside pocket.

"False papers, a passport, and one ticket for the Paris-London Express that will carry you straight through your Mr Brunel's Trans-Channel tunnel and get you out of France and back to the bosom of your beloved Magna Britannia."

"You are even more accomplished than I was led to believe."

"You don't know the half of it," the Frenchman said with a sly wink.

"How…" For a moment Ulysses was lost for words. "That is simply remarkable. Now, what do I owe you?"

"Ah, yes," Leroux said, smiling broadly. "Now we come to the matter of recompense; the francs and cents, if you like. If you will forgive me, Ulysses, you may speak like a gentlemen, but you dress like one who has fallen on hard times. What could you possibly give me in return for my help?"

"I have money. And plenty of it. Just not on me right now. I promise you, Valerius, as soon as I am back in England I will have the money wired to you before I do anything else. With interest."

"Hm. So you say, but how do I know this? I do not know you from – what is the expression? Ah yes – from Adam! No. We need to think of an alternative; how you might pay me in... how do you say? In kind? You scratch my back – is that the expression?"

Ulysses didn't like the way this conversation was going.

"So, as you can see, I can help you," the Frenchman said, smiling enigmatically. Ulysses knew that look; it was one he had employed enough himself in the past. He swallowed hard, feeling his stomach knot. "So now the issue is not what I can do for you, but what can you do for me?"

CLEARING A SPACE before her – carefully pushing aside the tins of enamel paint, the oily rags, the jam jars filled with washers and a variety of tools – Cadence Bettencourt set the robo-parrot down on her workbench.

Uncle Gustav had always kept Archimedes in excellent working order, but the bird hadn't come off so well in its encounter with the mechanised ape. His gleaming brass outer shell – that had been so lovingly polished by her uncle that it shone like gold – was scuffed and horribly dented in places. Archimedes' left wing was virtually hanging off, the articulation screw bent horribly out of shape, the poor thing. The eyes were refusing to light as well, even though she had already checked the battery.

The damage Archimedes had suffered was clearly more than simply superficial. She was going to need to take a proper look inside.

Taking the parrot's head in her hands, she gave it a twist and gently loosened the screw-thread holding it in place. Five more twists and the head was off. Delicately she lifted the head free, twisted wires unspooling after it. Making sure that none of the wires became disconnected, she laid the head on the workbench.

Everything was done with the utmost care.

As far as she could see the head itself was intact; all of the connections were secure. That was a good start at least.

Taking a screwdriver, she applied it to the inspection hatch and removed the panel completely, allowing her to access the parrot's internal workings. It didn't take her long to find the disrupted connection.

Unsurprisingly, it was on the same side that the parrot was most badly dented. With the front off, she did what she could to re-shape the automaton's body-shell, pushing out the dent from the inside. If Archimedes was ever to look as fine as he had done before his run-in with the gorilla, he was going to need the attentions of a jeweller or an expert panel beater, or, failing that, to have his outer shell re-cast. But it would do for now, allowing her to reconnect the offending wires more easily.

Taking up a soldering iron and donning a pair of tinted goggles, she set the heated tip and a length of fine solder to the ornate teak-framed Bakelite circuit boards inside.

She could have carried on in this way all day. She found electrical engineering so therapeutic.

Setting the soldering iron down, she inspected her work through an arrangement of armature-mounted magnifying lenses. Happy that she had done the best she could, she set to repairing the wing – a relatively easy task by comparison.

All that remained then was to put Archimedes back together and see if she had succeeded in returning him to working order.

Re-attaching the front panel, and having tightened the screws at each corner, she set the parrot upright on the workbench. Taking the moulded metal head in her left hand, with the right she fed the loops of cable back inside the bird's body cavity, finally locating the head on the neck thread and locking it back in place again with a few gentle twists.

Her heart thumping in excitement and anxiety, she pressed the button hidden beneath the bird's tail.

Nothing happened.

She gave the automaton a tentative shake and tried the switch again.

Accompanied by a soft background hum that she could feel vibrating through her hand, the bird's eyes glowed green, the illumination slowly increasing in intensity until they shone like a couple of torch-beams.

"Hello, Archimedes," Cadence said with a sigh of relief.

Accompanied by a succession of stilted clicks, the robot bird ruffled its feathers and flexed its wings. Its head clicked first left, then right.

In a sudden flurry of automated movement the bird leaned back on its perch and looked at Cadence.

"*Raawk!* Who's a pretty girl then?" the bird squawked, its synthesised voice edged with a coarse static burr. "*Raawk!*"

Clearly there was still some fine-tuning to be done.

And then suddenly the parrot's electronic squawk cut out as some pre-programmed subroutine was triggered within its Babbage brain. The automaton started again, but now it sounded like Archimedes was doing a poor impression of her Uncle Gustav, parroting a message it had recorded on a previous occasion.

"Beware Leroux!" the parrot squawked. "You cannot trust Leroux!"

"So we're agreed then, we have a deal," Valerius Leroux said as the two of them exited the museum together.

"You drive a hard bargain, M. Leroux, but yes. We have a deal," Ulysses said with a sigh.

"You promise to acquire a specimen for me upon your return."

"I promise."

"Then let us shake on it, like Englishmen."

"Like Englishmen," Ulysses said, accepting Leroux's hand

with little relish, fully aware of the unpleasant feebleness of the handshake to come.

"Thank you, Monsieur Quicksilver. Then here are your papers, your passport and your train ticket for the Trans-Channel Express," Leroux said, handing Ulysses the selection of documents. "It has been a pleasure doing, er, business with you."

"Pleasure was all mine," Ulysses muttered sardonically.

He looked at the glass and brass structure behind them once more. It had been commissioned from some designer back in the 1980s, it was said, in response to the rise of the Industrial Revival movement back in Magna Britannia. The modernity of the pyramid was in stark contrast to the seventeenth century façade of the original twelfth century castle. Then, turning on his heel, Ulysses set off across the Cour Napoleon.

"I bid you farewell, Monsieur," the fixer called after him, "and *bon voyage*!"

Picking up the pace, Ulysses headed north-west across the concourse. He needed to get back to Montmartre as quickly as possible, and despite what he had told Cadence prior to leaving for his meeting, he didn't want to stay out on the streets any longer than he had to.

The screaming started out on the Rue de Rivoli that marked the northern perimeter of the Palais du Louvre. Hearing it, Ulysses kept walking, trying to deny his subconscious, pretending that the threat wasn't focused on him this time. But it was no good, he knew such foolish notions were nothing but a lie. He was Time's Arrow. Those who would threaten the balance of the Universe would always be coming for him.

And then it was there, the screech of car tyres and the trumpeting of omnibus horns heralding its passing.

Eight feet tall, and almost as broad, every joint and muscle enhanced with augmetic artifice or energising cables, its hide a mixture of thick black fur and surgical scars, it knuckled its way towards him, bounding along on all fours.

And there would be no escaping it this time.

CHAPTER TWELVE

Fight or Flight

KNOWING THAT HE didn't have a hope against the beast one-on-one, Ulysses did the only thing he could. He turned tail and ran.

Twice he had run into the ape and now the ape had run into him. It couldn't be a coincidence. Ulysses sprinted back across the Cour Napoleon, past the glass and brass pyramid, momentarily catching sight of the retreating Valerius Leroux again, and the stony expression on his face. When everyone else was staring in horror at the advancing beast, Leroux was calmly striding away towards the north side of the plaza.

Ulysses wondered at the anger of the ape, as he sprinted across the paved square, dodging panicking bystanders and sending the pitches belonging to purveyors of tourist tat tumbling in his wake. Had it been enhanced, along with the rest of the ape, or was it just the animal's natural aggression, exacerbated by the situation it now found itself in? After all, Ulysses could well believe that having a dozen electrodes rammed into your brain could put a crick in anyone's day.

Screams and the clatter of postcard stands crashing to the ground chased him across the courtyard. Unable to resist a moment longer, Ulysses dared a glance over his shoulder as he raced on.

Finding the pyramid between it and its designated target, rather than taking a detour around the structure, the gorilla bounded up one angled side, several diamond panes crazing under its weight.

Reaching up with one long arm, it grasped the top of the pyramid and hurled itself over the pinnacle. It landed with a thud only twenty yards behind Ulysses; paving slabs cracked under it.

Panting for breath, his pulse pounding like the drumming hoof-beats of a Grand National winner, Ulysses returned to the business of running away.

At the back of his mind there was an awareness that he needed to lure the cyber-ape as far from the crowds as possible, but then he was in danger of getting himself cornered within the Cour Napoleon with no way of getting out alive. Besides, in the middle of Paris on a sunny day in May, keeping the killer ape away from innocent bystanders seemed like a nigh impossible task.

And that told him something about the person who had had first Carmine Roussel, then Pierre Courriel Pascal, and lastly Gustav Lumière killed; the same person who must have set the beast to hunt Ulysses down. That person, the true killer, was desperate. They were desperate to eliminate Ulysses and desperate enough to have the assassination carried out in broad daylight, with hundreds of eye-witnesses present, and in doing so expose their secret weapon to the world, thereby exonerating Ulysses of any wrong-doing.

But that information was only going to be of any use to Ulysses if he could get away from the beast bearing down on him now.

The arched colonnade of the Pavilion Sully was only a matter of half a dozen bounding strides away. Ulysses legged it under a shaded archway and straight through the doors in front of him, barely registering the colourful banner hanging at the entrance, bearing the words:

Peau
La Mode des Animaux

and adorned with images of lithe woman dressed as zebras and tigers.

Ulysses skidded across the polished floor of the hallway beyond, sending a tottering young man into a fluster as he pulled open another door and barged his way into–

–the sudden burst of noise and the dazzling glare of a dozen camera flashes going off in his face, that took him by surprise as much as had the re-appearance of the ape. He pushed on regardless.

Despite the retina-searing bulb flashes and some very bright lights above his head, much of the room was in darkness, or rather was actually decorated in black, the shadows exacerbated by the brilliance of the lights focused on the stage on the far side of the room. The stage and its décor were a minimalistic white where near-naked models paraded up and down the catwalk to the polite applause of the surprisingly severe audience.

"Bugger!" he exclaimed.

In his efforts to escape the maniac gorilla and, at the same time, lead it away from members of the public, he had led the monster right into the middle of a crowded fashion show.

He glanced back at the door as he excused his way between the fashionistas of Paris, pursued by cries of "Monsieur!" and "*Sacre bleu!*" His heart was racing even faster now; he knew what was coming.

With a crash the door flew off its hinges, flattening the two security men standing closest to it as the ape burst into the room.

Inevitably there were more screams, which were reciprocated by the savage beast with a bellowing primate roar.

The animal wasted no time in clearing a way across the room in its pursuit of the fleeing dandy. Chairs, and those seated upon them, went flying as the great ape pushed its way further into the room.

Ulysses made it to the stage, pulling himself up onto the catwalk and into the path of the tottering models. The chaos consuming the other side of the room was only just beginning to register in the models' minds.

For a moment, Ulysses found himself faced with joggling breasts and what felt like acres of smooth, supple flesh painted with all manner of wonderful animal print patterns.

"Sorry, Mademoiselle," he gasped as he brushed past one of the hysterical girls. He glanced down at his arm, sure that he must have just smudged the marvellous make-up that had been applied to every part of her supple body. But there was nothing.

And then he found himself looking into the face of a woman whose skin had been tattooed or textured to look like snake skin. In fact it must have been a very cunning prosthesis, because he could see every individual raised scale.

As the catwalk parade began to dissolve around him, he made it through to the back of the stage – with its huge photographic reproduction of a tiger-striped woman snarling at him – and bumped into another elfin woman, this one dusted pink with exotic plumes curving up from the base of her spine. The feathers must have been attached to the waistband of the tiny thong she was wearing, although there didn't seem to be enough material to secure them to. Perhaps they had been glued on, but if that was the case, it had been done by someone with the skill of an expert special effects artist.

And there was another model, her skin mottled like that of a cheetah, the paint job so convincing that it looked like her naked body was covered with a pelt of downy fur. Orange-gold eyes flashed in his direction and for a moment he felt he could hear the growl of the big cat they belonged to echoing across continents from the baking jungles of its savannah home.

Unaware of what was happening at the front of stage, the piped music and the general hubbub masking the screams and animal roars, the models backstage were carrying on as if everything was running normally.

That was, until the great ape tore through the image of the

tiger-woman and burst through into the space behind, trailing shreds of chipboard, splintered wooden battens and torn cardboard-mounted photographs.

Ulysses picked up the pace again, throwing everything he could in the way of the charging ape as it continued its relentless pursuit – costume racks, make-up tables and lighting rigs – anything he could lay his hands on as he dashed past.

Only he couldn't help noticing that there weren't many clothes on the clothing racks.

Now the roars of the massive silverback were drowning out the music backstage. A screaming model – with skin mottled like a giraffe's hide – suddenly found herself face to face with the ape. Hands pressed to the sides of her head in abject horror she howled at the brute, eyes wide and staring, rouged lips open even wider.

A growl of aggravation rumbled up from within the beast's enormous ribcage. With a swipe of one huge hand, the ape picked the girl up and threw her across the room. She landed with a crash amidst a stack of folded chairs, her screams silenced in an instant.

Ulysses stumbled over a trailing cable and instinctively grabbed at the nearest thing to him to stop himself falling. One hand grabbed hold of something soft and feathery. There was a scream – more like a cry of pain this time rather than a wail of fear – and whatever he was clutching onto came free.

Staggering forwards he regained his footing, and as the ape crashed through the improvised barricades he had thrown down behind him, he glanced at what he was now holding in his left hand. It was an exquisite peacock's feather. There was blood at the tip of the quill.

And then he was leaving the pavilion that had been especially erected to house the 'Skin' fashion show, within the Cour Carrée of the Louvre Palace. Barrelling through another door, he skidded across a polished floor past dusty, glass-cased Egyptian antiquities, before stumbling out of the building and into brilliant sunlight.

Blinking at the sudden sunshine, his eye having to adjust

after the backstage gloom, Ulysses looked left and right. Automobiles and omnibuses sped past on the Rue de l'Amiral de Coligny and in that split second he assessed the best way to go to continue his flight from the enraged puppet animal.

The cough of a steam engine had him looking into the sun, shielding his eye with a hand.

It was coming out of the sun, and it was heading right for him.

And then it swung about overhead and Ulysses was able to discern the shape of it quite clearly.

It looked like a velocipede, but one that had sprouted a complex steam-powered propulsion system, not to mention a pair of glider wings and two stabilising tail fins.

The aerial steam-powered velocipede had begun its descent and was coming in at a steep angle – too steep, surely. And just when Ulysses thought the bike and its pilot were going to have a rather unpleasant, not to say painful, encounter with the pavement, its steam engine revved, the front wheel jerked upwards and the flying machine landed.

Bracing her legs to balance the velocipede, flicking the machine into neutral and setting the engine into a purring idle, Cadence Bettencourt sat back on the padded leather saddle, as the articulated wings retracted behind her. Lifting her flying goggles from her face she turned her eyes on Ulysses.

"So this is the little run-around you didn't want to tell me about," he said.

"Well," she said, "what are you waiting for?"

The dandy didn't need telling twice and jumped onto the padded leather seat behind Cadence. As he did so he saw the parrot's head protruding from a pannier behind him.

"You brought the automaton with you?"

"His name is Archimedes," she said, gunning the throttle. "Now hold on."

Ulysses barely had time to put his arms round the girl's waist and pick his feet up off the ground before the steam velocipede was haring off along the pavement.

Behind them a gaggle of leopard-spotted and zebra-striped

models spilled out of the Musée Louvre and onto the pavement, screaming in abject terror.

"What's all that about?" Ulysses said, hoiking a thumb at the feline and zebrine models pouring out through the gallery doors behind them.

The parrot whistled. "Who's a pretty girl then?"

Cadence glanced in a rear-view mirror.

"Oh, that. It's all the rage. Animal body modification."

"Incredible," Ulysses muttered. It was unbelievable what people were willing to do to themselves in the name of fashion and some warped concept of beauty.

Cadence gunned the throttle again, and swung the purring velocipede off the pavement and into the horn-honking traffic.

Accompanied by the crash of breaking glass and a bellow of animal rage, the ape hurtled out of the museum after the models, sending a number of confused passers-by flying too.

It only took the beast a moment to relocate its target and then it was bounding after them.

"I take it you discovered the truth about Leroux at the eleventh hour," she called back over the roar of the wind.

"Leroux?" he shouted back.

"Beware Leroux!" the automaton squawked.

"You mean it wasn't Leroux you were running from?"

"Why would I be running from him? I was running from *that*."

Cadence glanced in the mirror again and saw the ape.

"This thing flies, right?" Ulysses said. "So why aren't we flying now?"

His arms tight around the girl's waist, he dared another glance backwards. As he had feared, the ape was gaining on them.

"It needs a long enough runway to get up to speed."

"How fast do you need to be travelling?" Ulysses screeched, sounding more desperate than he had intended.

"Forty-four miles an hour."

"Forty-four miles an hour?"

"Forty-four miles an hour!" the bird parroted.

"Then what are you waiting for?"

Cadence laughed at him then. "At midday, in the middle of Paris? Might as well be eighty-eight miles an hour!"

Ulysses' eye was still on the beast.

"Then what do you suggest? You do know there's half a ton of cybernetic gorilla pursuing us, don't you? Do you know any good shortcuts?"

A car horn parped behind them and the Doppler scream of an omnibus horn wailed past.

"Don't worry," Cadence said, "I've got a few tricks up my sleeve, as you English would say," and promptly swung the contraption left onto the Quai du Louvre.

There was the screech of brakes behind them, and the sound of something big and heavy colliding with a truck.

Something that had been niggling at Ulysses' subconscious since the girl had picked him up finally worked its way through to his surface thoughts.

"Why did you think I'd be running from Leroux..." And then realisation dawned.

"Beware Leroux!" the parrot squawked again.

"Oh, so it was him!" he exclaimed in excitement. "He was the one who had your uncle killed, along with the other two men."

"Exactly!"

"Well, that puts a whole new colour on things. Now we know who's responsible all we have to do is–"

A symphony of hooting drowned out what Ulysses said next, as Cadence dodged and weaved, throwing the velocipede left and right between chugging steam-trucks, horse-drawn carriages, charabancs, and fresh-out-of-the-factory automobiles.

Ulysses could hardly take his one eye off the street behind. The gorilla had vanished amidst the hurly-burly of the traffic for a moment, but the dandy knew it could only be a matter of time before it made a reappearance.

And then he saw it, swinging through the trees that lined the road, as if they were in the cloud forests of the Congo rather than one of the busiest metropolitan centres in Europe.

"It's above us!" Ulysses shouted over the roar of the traffic and the velocipede's chugging steam-engine.

"Let's see how it copes when there aren't any trees then," Cadence threw back and took a sharp right.

Bouncing over the pavement, missing several rigid cast iron bollards, they turned onto the Pont Neuf, heading for the Île de la Cité.

Ulysses tried to get a good look over Cadence's shoulder at the speedometer, praying that it was somewhere close to the magical forty-four miles an hour. It wasn't that he particularly fancied taking to the skies on what was little more than a souped-up bicycle with wings, but that option was far preferable to being beaten to a pulp by eight hundred pounds of crazed cyborg gorilla.

"You know you were wondering how the ape would cope without trees?" Ulysses said. "Turns out it's doing pretty well, actually."

The velocipede hurtled over the bridge, the lane they were in clear ahead of them, its velocity increasing all the while, the needle creeping past the thirty mark now.

Thirty.

Thirty-five.

Forty.

A battered old truck suddenly pulled out in front of them, into their lane of traffic.

Cadence pulled hard on the brakes, almost losing control of the velocipede as the back wheel locked and slewed round behind them.

The truck was piled high with pumpkins, its backboard clattering, the worn bolts holding it in place rattling noisily as the vehicle bumped and jolted around the road.

"Overtake that truck!" he shouted at Cadence.

"*Raawk!* Overtake the truck!" shrieked the automaton.

"Look, will you just shut up!" Ulysses snarled at the bird.

"What do you think I was going to do?" she asked grumpily, gunning the bike's throttle again, and pulling in between the truck and the pavement.

"Shut up! Shut up!" repeated the parrot.

A gentleman was walking the other way across the bridge, clearly enjoying the sunshine, cane in hand, and completely oblivious to their presence. That was until Ulysses leant over and snatched the cane from him. Leaning the other way across the bike now, deftly spinning the cane from one hand to the other, he hooked the looped end around one of the rattling bolts on the backboard of the truck and tugged hard as the velocipede powered past.

The back of the truck flipped open, dispensing the vehicle's cargo of pumpkins across the road in a smear of orange, slippery flesh.

"Merci, Monsieur!" Ulysses called, swinging the cane backwards and into the surprised clutches of its owner.

He heard the angry roar of the gorilla and the clatter of mechanical components as it came a cropper amidst the smashed squashes. He knew his little obstacle didn't have a hope of stopping the beast but it might slow it down a tad.

And then they were passing over the Île de la Cité itself and skidding across the second span of the Pont Neuf.

"Where are you going?" Ulysses demanded. He didn't like being so reliant on anyone other than his redoubtable manservant Nimrod, and he hadn't seen the old chap in months. It was even worse when he was somewhere he wasn't as familiar with as he was his precious London.

"Look, don't start asking me where I'm going," Cadence threw back. "I know what I'm doing!"

Ahead of them, on the landward side of the bridge, where the Pont Neuf met the crosswise Quai des Grandes Augustins, a large removals lorry blocked the way ahead.

Cadence slammed on the brakes even harder than before, leaning into the skid as the contraption swung left, its back wheel locking for a moment again. And then, the engine snarling like a caged beast, they were rocketing away, heading east along the south bank of the Seine, the river itself only a few yards away to their left.

Cars, buses and lorries came at them head-on, with more

horns blaring and headlights flashing, their drivers raging in impotent fury at the girl on the bike, as she turned the velocipede onto the pavement. Besides, they soon forgot about the girl when the ape came into view.

Cadence sent tourists and Parisians running for cover, tumbling to left and right as she steered the speeding bike along the sidewalk.

The partially retracted left wing hit a stall selling tourist tat and Ulysses thought he heard something vital snap.

He was trying to see what damage the wing had suffered when the gorilla landed on top of an artist's riverside gallery, demolishing the flimsy wooden structure beneath its heavy, iron-braced forearms, sending oil-painted canvases of famous Parisian landmarks flying in all directions, like garishly-plumed birds of paradise taking to the skies.

"Look out! Look out!" the parrot screeched, its synthesised voice possessed of a rather convincing degree of fear and alarm.

The gorilla turned another sales pitch to matchwood as it smashed its way through in its pursuit of the accelerating velocipede, this time sending a cascade of miniature gargoyles and grotesques crashing into the road.

Cadence cried out. Ulysses snapped his head back round, facing forwards again in an instant.

"You have got to be kidding me," he gasped, seeing the gaggle of frantic nuns scattering before them.

A lorry hurtled past to their immediate right, clipped the tip of the other wing, and then there was nowhere else for them to go.

Giving the throttle all she had, Cadence pulled the velocipede hard left. It climbed the makeshift ramp provided by a stack of second-hand books and took off over the parapet of the river wall as the speedometer needle registered forty-four miles an hour.

CHAPTER THIRTEEN

The Silverback of Notre Dame

AND THEN THEY were flying.

The pitch of the velocipede's engine rose as the contraption soared through the air with startling grace, the formidable façade of Notre Dame appearing over the tops of the trees that lined the Quai de Montebello further on. The Seine was a colourless mirror below them, its surface presenting a rippling inverted impression of the buildings lining its sculpted banks. Ahead of them, only a few tantalising yards away, rose the stone wall of yet another of the many bridges that connected the Île de la Cité to the rest of Paris.

Ulysses held his breath and clung on, his arms tight around the Cadence's waist.

Forty-four miles an hour, she had said, that was the magic number. With Cadence's fingers still tight on the throttle that was what the speedometer was reading now, only they weren't flying – they were falling.

The damage sustained by the extendable wings had resulted in them becoming twisted at the wrong angle. Ulysses realised the tail had been knocked out of kilter too and was no longer helping to stabilise the vehicle's arcing flight over the Seine. If anything, it was causing it to wobble so that Ulysses feared the girl might lose her battle to control the bike altogether.

In that moment of heightened stress he held his breath, taking in everything around him in minute detail. He saw the parapet of the bridge looming before them, the reflection of the bike upon the waters below, the enraged face of the bellowing beast as it extricated itself from the splintered remains of an artist's stall behind them.

"Come on! Come on!" Cadence hissed at the velocipede.

"Come on! Come on!" the automaton cried from the pannier.

And then the velocipede touched down. The back wheel clipped the parapet, throwing the contraption forward, both engine and tyres screeching as traction was achieved, and in the next instant the bike hared off again.

Cadence swore fruitily as she tried to retain control of the wildly weaving bike at the same time as trying to dodge the slow-witted gawping members of the public who hadn't yet had the good sense to get out of the way.

It wasn't that she was particularly trying to preserve anyone's life, other than her own and that of her passenger. It was just that if they collided with someone, chances were they would be thrown off the velocipede and left at the mercy of the pursuing primate.

Within seconds – having avoided a smoky haulage wagon, charabancs painted in the colour of the French flag, and a bicycle-riding onion salesmen – they were careening across a pedestrian crossing, to a chorus of screams from nurses pushing perambulators and the abusive shouts of cantankerous old men armed with gnarled walking sticks, and onto the cobblestoned square that lay in the shadow of the Western Façade of Notre Dame cathedral.

The bestial roar had Ulysses looking back over his shoulder and Cadence revving the throttle again, steering the velocipede between the crowds of tourists and the unlicensed salesmen trying to flog replicas of the cathedral in myriad forms to the susceptible – everything from clumsy watercolours, through mass-produced ceramic casts of the Western Façade, to machine-stamped key-fobs.

The gorilla exploded from the stand of stalls at the edge of the square, sending easels and prints spinning through the air like a flight of startled pigeons to the screams of the terrified tourists.

"Shit!" Cadence gasped, catching sight of the beast out of the corner of her eye.

"Look out! *Raawk!*"

With a swipe of one massive arm, the monster caught the tail fin of the velocipede, pulling the assembly away from the bike. Momentum kept the contraption hurtling forwards but it was wildly out of control now.

Panicking people fled before them, scattering left and right as the bike ploughed onwards, the façade of the cathedral looming large now ahead of them.

Cadence applied the brakes and nothing happened.

She swore again, and yanked hard left on the handlebars.

The velocipede went into a skidding slide, engine parts kicking up fat sparks from the cobbles as they made contact with the ground.

"Off!" Ulysses shouted, as the velocipede piled into the railings erected in front of the cathedral.

The fence had probably never been intended to stop hurtling steam velocipedes from damaging the eight hundred year-old stonework, but right now it had that fortuitous effect nonetheless.

"And don't even think about saving the parrot!"

Pulling the gasping girl after him, Ulysses barged through the sluggish, startled crowds at the entrance and into the gloom of the cathedral's interior.

Usually he would have done anything he could to keep innocent bystanders safe from harm but desperate times, as the saying went, called for desperate measures. He didn't have the means to hurt the ape, he knew that, so his best bet was to try and trap it or trick it into injuring itself, somehow. He hadn't worked out the details yet. As ever, he was making it up as he went along.

The life of his true love was what was really at stake here. Everything else – hunting down the Rue Morgue murderer, escaping the ape, proving himself innocent of the crime of which he had been accused by the gendarmes and popular public opinion – was all simply the means to one end. Saving Emilia Oddfellow from the fate that awaited her on the Moon.

After the bright May sunshine outside, the medieval church seemed possessed of an almost preternatural gloom. It was as if they had stepped back in time.

The tiny, high windows and subtle chandelier lighting dotted throughout the building kept things very much as Ulysses imagined the church must have looked when it was first finished some time in the 1200s. Of course the semi-darkness only served to make the stained glass all the more striking.

Ulysses had visited Notre Dame once before, before making his world record-breaking attempt on the Paris-Dakar rally. Unfortunately now wasn't the time for sight-seeing, but that previous visit had left him with a useful working knowledge of the layout of the cathedral, including the location of the chapels and shrines and tombs to various saints, churchmen and knights, along with the best place where you might be able to escape from a rampaging cyber-gorilla.

"This way!" he said, pulling Cadence towards a narrow doorway half hidden behind wax-dripping candelabra and information signs.

Yet more screams chased them all the way to the aged tower door. It was unlocked and turning the heavy iron handle, Ulysses pushed it open, setting off up the stone spiral staircase beyond.

His legs burning, sweat pouring from his brow, he didn't slow his pace one jot, taking the stairs two at a time, and hauling Cadence after him all the way.

Their footsteps echoed throughout the spiralling passageway. Through the open door at the bottom of the staircase they caught distorted cries of alarm and gruff primate barks.

But soon all Ulysses could hear was the pounding of their footsteps on the stone stairs, their breathless panting, and the *dub-dub dub-dub* tattoo of his own heartbeat in his ears.

At last the staircase gave out onto a landing and from there, through another creaking door, the two gasping fugitives found themselves in the attic-like belfry of the cathedral's South Tower. Curtains of dusty spider webs fluttered in the breeze while dried leaf litter had collected in the corners of the chamber, along with the debris of deconstructed pigeons' nests.

Apart from the contented cooing of a number of still resident pigeons, the fluttering of the spider webs and the ever-present breeze, the atmosphere within the belfry was still.

The great bourdon bell, Emmanuel, hung before them in the gloom, verdigrised with age. It was an ancient thing that had marked the passing hours for more than three hundred years.

"Hang on," Ulysses said, his voice sounding loud within the stillness of the loft space, holding up a hand for quiet even though Cadence hadn't said a word.

"What?" she half-whispered.

"Listen. Do you hear that?"

"Hear what? I don't hear anything."

"Indeed. That's what I'm worried about."

"The ape," Cadence said slowly.

With a splintering crash that hurt their ears, half a ton of metal, meat and bad attitude burst through the belfry floor and landed with a crash in front of Ulysses, trailing broken floorboards. With the tower loft now open to the cathedral below, a cacophonous chorus of screams and panicked shouts rose to meet them.

The gorilla locked its beady gaze on Ulysses and growled, nostrils flaring, its massive chest and shoulders heaving as it recovered its breath for a minute.

Behind him, Ulysses sensed Cadence backing away towards the door.

Ulysses flexed his hands.

The ape took a purposeful step towards him, resting the great hairy knuckles of its ham-sized hands on the rough boards before it.

Once again the dandy adventurer found himself wishing he had a gun or his trusty sword-stick to hand. But surely there was something here in the belfry that he could use to at least slow, if not actually stop, the beast?

The first time he had run into the beast, it was the damage he had done to one of the ape's mechanical components that ultimately saved him. The second time, he had had to play dead. If he couldn't harm the brute physically, perhaps he would do best to try his original approach again and take out some vital component or other.

The beast snorted and took another knuckling step forward. No matter what its controllers had set it to do, it was going to enjoy settling its grudge with the dandy, Ulysses was sure of it.

Ulysses shot another desperate glance around the attic, at the peg-pinned joists, the exposed boards, the stone walls. Surely there was something here he could use?

The gorilla shuffled its massive bulk forward another step.

Ulysses took a wary step backwards, his one eye glancing from the killer gorilla to the beams and back again. If he could somehow work his way up onto one of those joists he might then be able to drop down onto the ape's back and from there disconnect something vital from the primate's cybernetic rig.

All he needed was a distraction.

But the ape had had enough. Rising to its full height, it beat its heavy fists on its broad, muscular chest, making a bellowing declaration of its murderous intent that left Ulysses in no doubt as to what it was planning to do to him.

Once again Ulysses did the only thing common sense and instinct told him he could do, given the circumstances. He turned and ran.

He heard the grunt of anger and effort as the ape kicked off behind him. The dandy barely managed to keep ahead of its bounding advance.

The ape leapt again.

One heavy steel vambrace clipped the Emmanuel, the thirteen tons of bell metal chiming in response.

Ulysses threw his hands over his ears, his face a rictus of pain as the bell's reverberations passed right through him, setting every bone in his body vibrating in response, or so it seemed.

But he kept running for the door.

Cadence was there, at the threshold to the belfry, doubled up, crippled by the pain of the great bell's peal.

Unable to stop himself, at the door Ulysses turned and looked back to see what had become of the ape.

Whatever agony he was having to endure, it was nothing compared to the ape's suffering.

He could hear the great beast's yowling over the reverberations of the bell as the animal staggered back across the belfry, its huge hands clutching its head.

That was all Ulysses needed to know.

Re-entering the loft space, gritting his teeth against the dolorous clanging, he picked up a broken end of floorboard and struck the bell again.

His assault did little to raise another note from the bell, but did cause him to cry out in pain as his shoulder jarred at the impact. He tried again, in spite of the aching bullet wound, only this time his swing connected with the clapper.

The first shock of the clapper the brazen wall made the framework upon which it was mounted quiver, and a clear booming note rang from its vibrating surface.

The ape screamed again, its agonised hollering all but drowned out by the tolling of the bell.

Barely-tamed lightning crackled around its electrode-implanted skull in a halo of electrical fire, the thick steel rods humming like tuning forks inside the ape's brain.

Ulysses dealt the clapper another resounding blow, feeling his teeth shaking in response to the thrumming *bong* the Emmanuel bell returned.

The whole tower trembled; woodwork, leads, cut stones, all groaned at once.

The altered primate could barely walk now. It stumbled backwards, eyes shut tight against the pain, its chisel-filled mouth open in one unending howl, sparks flying from its skull-rods.

The animal's eyes suddenly snapped open, the beady black pupils back-lit by the intense red glow of overheating metal components. But to Ulysses' mind the crimson light was the unforgiving blaze of interminable hatred.

The ape took one more step back –

–and disappeared through the hole it had made in the belfry floor. It dropped like it was half a ton of solid granite.

With the great bell still thrumming behind him, Ulysses sprinted to the splintered gap and, apparently heedless of the risk to himself, hauled himself half over the edge to peer down into the vaulted void of the church below.

But there was no sign of the ape. The stone-flagged floor far below was devoid of any cybernetically-enhanced primate carcass.

He was so used to the continuing screams that he barely noticed their presence.

Risking life and limb, pulling himself further through the hole, he peered down into the inverted cathedral, twisting his head this way and that.

The clear high sound of breaking glass had him shifting his position again in time to see the gorilla swing from a supporting buttress and through the ornate rose window in the western end of the building. Broken glass rained down into the church, the work of medieval craftsmen that had survived the centuries up until that moment sparkling like cut diamonds in the sudden sunlight as the screaming ape fled the cathedral.

And then the monster was gone.

Pulling himself back up through the hole into the belfry, Ulysses rolled onto his back before scrambling to his feet and catching the look in Cadence's eyes.

"The chase is back on," he said, an excited sparkle in his eye. "Only now the hunter has become the hunted."

CHAPTER FOURTEEN

The Game is Afoot

"YOU HAVE TO trust me on this," Ulysses insisted as he and Cadence Bettencourt ran back down the worn stone staircase of the South Tower. "The ape won't be interested in chasing us anymore."

"How can you be sure of that?"

"Because I've seen something like this happen before."

Cadence grunted. She didn't sound particularly impressed but she was still keeping up regardless. It seemed that she had decided that it was a better bet to keep Ulysses close than to lose him in the midst of this debacle.

"It's clear to me now that whenever the ape suffers any sort of technological malfunction, some pre-programmed behaviour has it break off from the fight and – I'm hypothesising here, of course – return to base so that it can be repaired. You know the type of thing, I'm sure. Lovelace behaviour-algorithm: If injured, return to Base. Execute."

"So basically, you think it's running away?"

"Yes. We'll be perfectly safe."

"And I take it your definition of 'safe' might be somewhat different to everybody else's?"

Ulysses didn't even deign to answer that last quip.

DETECTIVE INSPECTOR AUGUSTE Dupin was just climbing out of the police-cab outside the cathedral of Notre Dame when the rose window exploded outwards in a starburst of whickering crystal shards as something burst through it.

It was something appalling; something that should not have existed. It was big and black and covered with thick hair, as well as myriad scars. Its muscular body was bound with all manner of electrical cables, its forearms were sheathed inside heavy iron cuffs and every joint in its body appeared to have been reinforced with thick metal screws.

All eyes were on the devastated window and the creature now dropping towards the cobbled plaza. It only took a moment for instinct to kick in and then the gendarmes hurried to get out of the way.

The great ape landed on the bonnet of Dupin's cab. The engine block, axle and chassis buckled under the impact of half a ton of cybernetic gorilla, the back end bouncing into the air.

The axle snapped and one wheel was sent flying off into the stunned crowd. The other wheel folded in half, the tyre bursting with a loud *pop*.

Dupin fell to the floor as he tried to launch himself out of the way. Ignoring the pain of grazed knees and elbows, his attention was fully on the ape. At a blink he took in every minute detail of the beast.

He saw the blazing red-hot glare in its beady black eyes. He saw the sparking electrodes in its misshapen head. He saw the terribly muscled arms bound with cables and the wires plugged into its massive torso. He saw the forbidding yellow tusks cramming its mouth, and the hands capable of snapping a man's neck as if it were no more than a twig. The beast was truly terrifying.

For a moment the primate's furious glare fell on the Detective Inspector and he felt a knot of primal fear constrict his stomach.

And then the great ape took off again, the windshield of the cab shattering as the cyborg leapt clear again and landed in the middle of the cobbled square, sending more screaming tourists scattering. Before the shocked gendarmes could train their guns on the monster it was gone, swallowed by the narrow streets and crowding tenements of the Île de la Cité.

"Jesus Christ," spluttered the youthful detective sergeant, "what was that?"

"That, I suspect," Dupin replied with a chilling calm that surprised himself, "was our killer."

"What?" The detective sergeant was flabbergasted.

"That was the Rue Morgue murderer."

"COME ON!" ULYSSES panted, sprinting for the door. "We can't let it get away. Do you think that velocipede of yours will still fly?"

Ulysses burst back into daylight to be met by angry gasps of surprise, the clatter of pistols being primed and trained on him, and shouts of, "Stop, police!"

The dandy skidded to an abrupt halt, automatically raising his hands in surrender.

"It's him!" one of the gendarmes at the periphery of the crowd called out. "It's the Rue Morgue murderer!"

"It's the murderer," came a cry from the crowd.

"It's the Rue Morgue killer."

"It's him, did you see? It's the murderer."

Ulysses didn't dare move a muscle. He shot Cadence a glance and saw that she had her hands up and was staring unblinkingly at the semi-circle of armed officers before them.

Ulysses couldn't help wondering what the gendarmes made of the two of them, him looking like a pirate on shore leave and Cadence in her velocipede leathers.

There was a commotion at the back of the crowd and a police-cab trundled away across the square after the ape. He didn't fancy the gendarmes' chances of catching up with the beast.

As he and Cadence stood there, waiting and watching, a man in a long beige coat with smartly coiffured black hair emerged from the police line and confidently approached them.

Everything about his manner suggested that he did not fear for his safety. So, Ulysses thought, either he was confident he could take a man wanted for murder in a fist fight, or he suspected what Ulysses already knew – that the dandy wasn't guilty.

"You know we've been looking all over the city for you?" the man said.

"I did have an inkling," Ulysses replied, "but you should have been looking for that ape."

Slowly lowering his hands, he offered one to the policeman. This had the gendarmes anxiously re-adjusting their aim on the scruffy-looking individual.

"Ulysses Quicksilver, at your service."

Slowly, not once taking his eyes off the fugitive's face, the other man took Ulysses' hand and shook it. The man opened his mouth to speak, but before he could the dandy interrupted him.

"Let me guess. You must be Detective Inspector Dupin."

"That's right."

"How did he know that?" spluttered a younger man standing a few paces behind the Detective Inspector.

"Calm down, sergeant. I would think he read my name in the papers, wouldn't you?"

"Any relation?" Ulysses asked.

"I'm sorry?"

"To the famed Auguste Dupin, I mean."

"Yes, as it happens."

"Well, I suppose I should thank you, Inspector."

"For what?"

"For not having your men shoot me on sight. I take it we have an understanding?"

"An understanding?"

"You understand that I wasn't responsible for the Rue Morgue murders."

Behind the Detective Inspector the gendarmes began shooting each other confused glances.

Dupin fixed Ulysses with a hard, appraising stare.

"I don't know what you are, but you're not the murderer. But I can't quite shake the feeling that you might yet be able to help us with our enquiries just the same."

"So what brings you to Notre Dame on a lovely day like today?"

"That thing."

"The over-grown monkey," the detective sergeant piped up.

"I think you'll find it's a gorilla," Ulysses corrected, "or at least it *was*."

"Same difference."

"No, not really."

"As soon as I heard the reports coming in from the Louvre and elsewhere about a giant gorilla on the rampage I had a feeling I had found what I'd been looking for all along. And you?"

"Being chased by the aforementioned cyber-ape," Ulysses said. "An unfortunate side effect of trying to solve the Rue Morgue murders for you, Inspector."

"And who might you be, Mademoiselle?" Dupin said, turning his attention to Cadence.

"Cadence Bettencourt," she said, lowering her hands, but making no move to get better acquainted with the inspector.

"Bet-ten-court," the detective sergeant repeated as he wrote the name down in his notebook.

"That's right. Niece to Gustav Lumière," she added, "the monster's third victim."

"Ah," Dupin said, his face suddenly lighting up. "So it was you who called in about the ape." His expression darkened once more just as quickly. "You could have given us your name."

"That was my fault, Inspector," Ulysses stepped in gallantly. "Mademoiselle Bettencourt did that as a favour to me, to give me a chance to try to clear my name."

"You could have come straight to us as well," Dupin pointed out, his face severe.

"I could, but I was the most wanted man in the city at the time. Do you really think I would have been able to progress my investigation so quickly if I had?"

"Perhaps."

"Well, there were other complications to take account of as well," Ulysses went on.

"And you might yet face charges. Both of you," Dupin added.

"For what?" Cadence cut in, indignantly.

"Endangering innocent lives. Withholding evidence from the police. Obstructing a police investigation," Dupin said. He turned back to Ulysses then. "You could have killed one of my men up on that roof!"

"They could have killed me! But thankfully nobody died and now we're all friends so let's say no more about it, shall we?" He looked pointedly at the guns still pointing in his direction.

Dupin turned to the gendarmes, as if only just remembering that they were still there. "Put those away. Now!"

Reluctantly the officers did as instructed.

"So, you believe me," Ulysses said, the relief plain in his voice.

"I believe you know more than you've told me so far," the Inspector replied, "which actually isn't very much. I also believe you might also be able to help with the matter of another unexplained death."

Ulysses raised an eyebrow at this last comment.

"Indeed I might, but I would suggest our more pressing problem right now regards the killer gorilla that's fleeing through the streets of Paris as we speak."

"You might have a point there. But what's the connection?"

"I'm sorry?"

"Between the victims. A penniless composer and this young lady's uncle."

"An acoustician," Cadence interjected.

"And you, Monsieur Quicksilver."

"And don't forget the ordinateur auteur," Ulysses added.

"There's another?"

"Indeed, but one that's been passed off as a suicide. A certain Pierre Courriel Pascal. But as to the connection... I don't know. At least, not yet. But the villain of this piece–"

"Leroux," Cadence interrupted again.

"Beware Leroux!" came a croaking electronic voice from within the wreckage of the velocipede. A couple of the gendarmes looked round in surprise.

"Or so we believe," Ulysses added. "Anyway, he clearly feared I was close to uncovering the connection otherwise he wouldn't have risked sending his killer after me in broad daylight.

"Whatever he has planned, it's going to happen soon else he wouldn't have risked exposing himself like that. But he must also believe that we won't be able to stop him in time and thereby thwart his plan – whatever that might be."

"You can deduce all this but you can't come up with a connection?" Dupin said, sounding like a disappointed school teacher.

"Actually, I do have one idea."

"And what's that?"

"I think his unstoppable scheme has something to do with the late Roussel's latest composition, *Black Swan*."

Dupin's face went dark. "That premiere is today, at the Paris Opera."

"But if we can track the ape back to wherever it's heading, I believe we might be able to stop Leroux before he has a chance to put his plan into operation."

"So this Leroux could be anywhere," the Inspector said.

"No, not anywhere. He will be wherever that ape is going. And if not him, then his accomplice at least."

"You don't think this Leroux is working alone?" Cadence asked.

"Hang on, are we talking about Valerius Leroux here, the philanthropist and renowned butterfly collector?"

"That's the bastard," Cadence growled, her eyes glistening with tears.

"Bastard! Bastard!" came the crowing voice again.

"But if we don't catch up with that ape, I fear that when we run into him again – *if* we run into him again – by then it will all be too late. The damage will have been done."

"I have officers in pursuit as we speak," Dupin said.

"Begging your pardon, Inspector, but they haven't got a hope of catching that brute before it goes to ground," Ulysses said.

"And I suppose you have?"

"Do you think that thing will still fly?" he asked Cadence whilst eyeing the velocipede.

The engineer joined him in his appraisal of the crumpled contraption.

"If it's the only chance I've got of paying Leroux back for the murder of my uncle, I'll damn well make sure it does."

Up in the air, feeling the wind rushing through his hair was utterly exhilarating. Ulysses had enjoyed many an aerial flight before, but nothing quite like this one.

"Down there!" he shouted over the roar of the wind.

Below them, Paris was laid out like a street map, their bird's-eye view allowing Ulysses and Cadence to see things that were denied to the police pursuing the ape on the ground.

They saw the flashing light of the police pursuit vehicle and heard the wail of its siren as the velocipede purred through the sky above the city, its canvas wings snapping in the wind.

The police-cab was rattling along a canyon-like street between tall, crowding tenements. It was clear from Ulysses' vantage point that the gendarmes in pursuit were proceeding through a combination of sheer guesswork and the desperate knowledge that they couldn't let the beast get away. The truth of the matter was that the cyber-gorilla was now bounding across the rooftops of the city again, having already left the police several streets behind.

As Cadence swung the velocipede around after the ape, closing with it all the time, the beast suddenly disappeared from view.

Cadence cursed. "Where did it go?"

"Down."

"Down where?"

"Down there!" the parrot-simulacrum squawked.

With the careful application of rudder and aileron, the velocipede commenced its descent.

Ulysses thought he caught sight of the gorilla once more as it swung itself from a balcony to an alleyway below but then it was gone again.

Mere moment later, the velocipede was on the ground, at the end of the same cul-de-sac, its tyres finding traction once more on the cobbles.

Ulysses' heart was hammering like the pistons of the velocipede's steam-engine. They couldn't have lost it; they had been so close!

Cadence took the velocipede to the end of the alleyway and killed the engine.

"What do we do now?" she said with a frustrated sigh.

"What now? What now?" echoed the bird.

There was nothing there.

Nothing but the heavy iron disc of a manhole cover set into a steel ring within the cobbles, not quite fully back in place, the muck and grime at its rim smeared with great fat fingerprints.

"We keep after it, Mademoiselle Bettencourt," Ulysses said, dismounting from the back of bike and cautiously approaching the manhole. "After all, the game is now, most definitely, afoot!"

CHAPTER FIFTEEN

Old Ghosts

"Opera, I will admit, is not to everyone's taste," the man known variously as Le Papillon and Valerius Leroux said, stopping at the entrance to Dr Montague Moreau's makeshift laboratory, "but one cannot help but wonder at the melodrama it provokes within its audience."

"Far as I'm concerned, going to the opera's like getting drunk," Moreau grunted.

"Really?" Le Papillon sighed. "Do enlighten me, please."

"In that it's a sin that carries its own punishment with it."

The anarchist's house guest had his eyes locked on the monitor attached to the control console in front of him. The grainy image displayed upon it was being relayed directly via the optical feed from the nerves behind the gorilla's eyeballs.

"That aside, even the sublime *Madame Butterfly* will be as nothing compared to the melodrama my own commission will wring from the hearts of every one of this great city's inhabitants when *Black Swan* opens on the stage above us in only a matter of" – he glanced at his wristwatch – "less than a quarter of an hour."

Le Papillon thought that such a dramatic revelation deserved more than the disinterested grunt the doctor gave it, so absorbed was he with his pet's progress through the city's sewer systems. This vexed the butterfly collector. An artist needed an audience, or at least an appreciative comment every now and again.

"I must admit, I will miss this place," he said, as he looked around his lair for the last time. His gaze lingered first on his butterfly collection – so proudly, and immaculately, displayed on his study wall – and then the dramatically-altered pipe organ.

The former had taken him years to collect, catalogue and ultimately display to best effect. If it hadn't been for the latter he probably wouldn't have been here now, standing on the edge of eternity, on the verge of creating his greatest artistic masterpiece yet.

If it hadn't been for the haunting echoes of his great-grandfather's private organ recital, here in the bowels of the Palais Garnier, his great-grandmother might never have discovered his lair and found her Angel of Music, hiding his deformity in the subterranean depths.

The destruction of it all was a high price to pay, but it had all been a means to the end, and only he – with his vision of eternity – could see the bigger picture, could understand how the world would be changed afterwards.

But what did it matter if his home and all his possessions were lost in the process? Great art always demanded sacrifice, and what he had planned would be the greatest ever created, putting to shame the works of such men as Da Vinci, Monet and Rodin.

It mattered not. He was an artist, a creator. He would start again, rebuild. After all, where was the challenge, the joy, in maintaining the status quo? Things changed, no matter how hard people struggled to deny it. Things aged, they decayed; it was impossible to halt the spread of entropy. Change was the only constant, chaos the only logical choice in an illogical world.

Besides, when he was done and his work completed, he would have enough money to build his own Opera House. His butterfly collection was a rare thing but it was also complete, the specimens locked within their timeless bubbles, frozen in a moment of eternity. He needed a new challenge, a new subject to collect. Stamps, perhaps, or maybe capital cities.

Once he was done with Paris, he could move on to Berlin, or Rome, or Madrid – see what wonders he could work abroad upon the face of the Earth. And when the Earth held no more challenges for him, he was sure there was work for him to do on the Moon. Then again, a man of his very particular talents was sure to find gainful employment on Mars.

No, on this day Valerius Leroux would die in the disaster that would envelop Paris. But Le Papillon, like the butterfly emerging from its chrysalis, would rise again in the aftermath of the catastrophe and begin his work anew, continuing in a never-ending cycle of death and rebirth.

That was one thing the disgraced former Prime Minister of Magna Britannia had been right about. The great nations of the world, humankind itself, needed to evolve or it would die like every planet-dominating species before it. Only a year before, Uriah Wormwood had offered the stagnating behemoth of an empire a unique opportunity, and the agents of order – misguided idiots hide-bound by their prehistoric concepts of order and stability – had resisted the change.

But the world had changed nonetheless, maybe not as much as Wormwood might have hoped, but it had most definitely changed. And besides, change could only ever be diverted, slowed temporarily. It could not be stopped.

Those who couldn't handle that truth branded Le Papillon a villain, a terrorist, an anarchist, insane. He was a bastard, and he was happy to admit that, but then it was in his blood. He was from a long line of bastards, his grandfather the illegitimate result of the deformed genius Erik's obsessive love for the ingénue Christine Daaé.

Le Papillon returned his attention to Doctor Moreau. "Something is troubling you," he stated bluntly. "Did the ape... *Ishmael*" – he spat the name, rather than spoke it – "complete *his* mission?"

"Well..." Moreau began.

Le Papillon bristled. "Well? Is that all you have for me? *Well*? A simple yes or no is all I require."

"No is never a simple answer, is it?"

"When I am forced to risk exposing this whole operation prematurely, I do not expect 'Well' as an answer." The man's face was suddenly as pale as the marble from which it appeared to have been carved. He stood perfectly still, centring his anger, fists bunched, his knuckles as white as his alabaster visage.

"Well, look at it this way," Moreau said, still not making eye contact with the lepidopterist. "That little risk you're talking about has led the police to the very man they were hunting for the Rue Morgue murders. So I'd say that rather gets them off our back, wouldn't you? Besides, Ishmael will have lost those bloody gendarmes as soon as he took to the rooftops again. They'll never catch him and they'll never connect him to us."

"But what of Quicksilver? What of him?"

"He'll be under arrest and in police custody by now."

"But he met me, in person."

"He'll never believe that the man who was helping him flee the country, whilst on the run from the police, was the same man who sent a cybernetic gorilla to kill him."

"You say that..." No plan ever survived contact with the enemy. "Where's the ape now?"

"Ishmael's in the sewers, heading home."

"Home?"

"You know what I mean."

"Yes, I know exactly what you mean." Le Papillon scowled. "How long until it reaches us?"

"Ten minutes, tops."

"Then I want us ready to leave in five."

Moreau turned to face him at long last. "Five?"

"Is the portable unit ready?"

Moreau jerked his head towards the object on the table behind him, his eyes back on the monitoring systems. The device was the same size as a handheld kine-camera and looked like a small cathode ray screen attached to a large magnifying lens handle. It was covered in all manner of lights, switches, dials and buttons. It was also currently connected to the doctor's control desk via a coiled cable and was humming gently to itself.

"Yes, I can see that it's there, but is it ready?" Le Papillon pressed.

"It will be when it's finished charging."

"And how long will that take?"

Quitting the console with an annoyed huff, Moreau got to his feet and turned his attention to the humming device. "Couple of minutes," he said gruffly. "How about your little box of tricks over there?" The doctor nodded towards the corrupted and cannibalised pipe organ.

"I merely need to flick the switch to activate it," Le Papillon said, a smirk of pride suddenly manifesting itself upon his face. "And I believe I can hear the orchestra tuning up even as we speak."

A monitor hidden amongst the additions Pascal had made to the grand instrument displayed the feed from a camera hidden within the orchestra pit several storeys above. On it, the anarchist could see the conductor flexing his arms as the musicians under his command warmed up.

The strident ringing of the telephone cut through the background electrical hum taking over the cellar lair. He had built this place back up from the derelict ruin it had become following his great-grandfather's death to the bijou abode it was now, having rediscovered it when his mother brought him to the Palais Garnier as a child.

The telephone continued to ring.

"Aren't you going to get that?" Moreau asked, disconnecting the handheld unit from the main console and bundling a pile of papers into a doctor's bag open on the workbench behind him, along with all manner of other odds and sods.

Breathing in deeply through his nose, to demonstrate his irritation, Le Papillon strode the length of the cellar past the humming pipe organ, to his immaculate study space.

Such rudeness! The man was an oaf, little more than an uncouth lout, despite all his obvious talent with cybernetics and its associated Babbage and Lovelace disciplines. If he hadn't needed to keep him around in order to keep the ape in check, the anarchist would have stove his skull in there and then using his cunning box of tricks, and left him to suffer the same fate as those who were even now taking their seats ready to experience the world premiere of the late Carmine Roussel's posthumous masterpiece.

Soon, of course, he would need neither the ape nor the organ grinder. He would savour that moment, when it came.

Reaching for the phone trembling on his desk he lifted the handset. "Yes?"

"What's going on, Le Papillon?" came the familiar, yet still unnervingly distorted English-accented voice.

The lepidopterist hesitated, composing himself before answering.

"Everything is still on schedule."

"Is it? Is it really? My intelligence would suggest otherwise," the voice came again, its cadences a crackling snarl.

"Your... intelligence?"

"I have been monitoring police channels–"

"Checking up on me, are you?"

"And something seems to be – how shall I put this? – awry."

"Nothing is awry. There is nothing to worry about. Everything is going according to plan."

"And that includes a silverback going on the rampage through central Paris, does it? I take it that was you."

"Very well, there was a slight hitch – one of yours actually – nothing more than a fly in the ointment, shall we say? We sent the ape to deal with it."

Le Papillon could sense the tension at the other end of the line.

"What do you mean, one of ours?"

"An Englishman." The tension was making him feel uncomfortable, and he didn't like to be made to feel uncomfortable. "Name of Quicksilver."

"Ulysses Quicksilver? What's Quicksilver doing in Paris?"

the voice shrieked, forcing Le Papillon to move the handset away from his ear.

"At this moment? Being locked away in a nice police cell, I should think." He hoped he sounded more convinced than he felt.

"Do not underestimate Quicksilver."

"Soon it won't matter where he is or what he's doing at the time," Le Papillon said, his arrogant confidence returning.

"Spare me the details, I don't need to know. Just make sure you've looked his corpse in the eye before you start boasting that he's dead. He's been dead before."

"Talking of mortality," Le Papillon interjected, "as the old saying has it, time and tide wait for no man, and so I must bid you farewell. You know how it is: things to do, an apocalypse to arrange, a populace to massacre. But before I go, can you confirm that payment will be made to the designated Swiss bank account as arranged when we first made our Devil's bargain? After all, an apocalypse doesn't come cheap."

"When Paris falls, the minute it hits the news here, the money will be transferred to your account."

Le Papillon heard a click and the line went dead.

The echoing chords and opening phrases of an overture wafted through the cellar walls to the anarchist's ears.

"Doctor Moreau?" Le Papillon called, suddenly transfixed by one particular specimen mounted on the wall in front of him. "The swan is flying and the storm is about to break. It is time we were gone."

Placing the handset carefully back on its cradle, Le Papillon made his way back through the cellar, a framed specimen case in one hand.

He stopped before the pipe organ, with its spilling cable guts and flowering trumpet horns, listening to the sounds being produced by the musicians of the orchestra and their maestro united to produce a performance of the utmost beauty and harmonious delight.

Caught up in the rapture of the moment, he wondered if this was how his great-grandfather had felt when, lost within his music, Le Papillon's great-grandmother had found him there and learned his terrible secret.

His hand hovered over the activation button for a moment as a lilting refrain lifted him from the mundane into an ethereal realm of light and beauty, taking him out of the world for a moment to join the ghosts of his forebears in the eternal.

Roussel really had been a genius. His death was such a loss to the world, and yet the world did not know it. But after today the man and his music would be remembered forever, Le Papillon had made sure of that–

A finger descended and the deed was done. Change had won out in the end and the world would never be the same again.

CHAPTER SIXTEEN

The Final Curtain

ULYSSES BOLDLY LED the way through the stinking darkness of the Paris sewers, impressed by Cadence's own indefatigable resolve, his face set in a permanent grimace.

What was it about villains and their underground lairs? Why could they only ever be reached by traversing the channels that transported society's effluence through the dark? There was probably a moral in there somewhere, and Ulysses might have searched for it himself if it wasn't for the vile, gag-inducing miasma that had a grip of his lungs now.

They advanced by the light cast by one of the velocipede's lamps. Cadence had removed it with a handy screwdriver taken from the utility belt at her waist. Its battery-powered yellow glow pushed back the gloom.

The clopping sound their booted feet made on the railed path along which they advanced was accompanied by the gurgle of brackish water and an echoing drip.

Progress might have been bold, but it was also slow, Ulysses half expecting the ape to jump out at them from a dismal alcove or adjoining tunnel at any moment. It wasn't hard to follow the monster's passage through the hidden sumps and culverts. It had clearly been forced to crouch to proceed along the mouldering brick tunnels. There were scuff marks in the sludge on the walls and scratch marks had been gouged in the brickwork by the beast's hulking augmetics.

And it was these scratch marks that eventually led Ulysses Quicksilver and Cadence Bettencourt to the deserted cellar.

A wheel-locked steel door, corroded by the accumulated foetid faecal fumes of ages, opened onto a dank brick-lined passageway.

The first thing that struck Ulysses was the music. It carried through the vaulted cellars in a polyphonic tide, one melody surging to rise above another before that too was subsumed by an alternative counterpoint phrase.

The tunnel led into a network of vaulted cellars and sunken chambers.

The first chamber they came to was a makeshift laboratory, complete with a metal caged gurney and Babbage-unit control desk. The darkness was permeated by a blue glow of electrical discharge that made Ulysses' hair stand on end. He had spent more than enough time in such places to last him a lifetime – the lab under Umbridge House on Ghestdale, not to mention Doktor Folter's torture chamber-cum-surgery at the heart of Castle Frankenstein – and so hurried on.

From the laboratory, the cellars opened out into a wide vaulted space, lit by wall-mounted lights. The grand space looked less like a cellar and more like some kind of auditorium. It was dominated by an immense organ, a masterful creation of the organ-maker's artifice.

But the marvellous mechanical pipe organ had clearly been the victim of some terrible musical desecration. Its internal workings had been exposed to the world and all manner of electrical components – yard after yard of spooled wires, something that looked like a recording cylinder, not to mention several large trumpet-like protuberances – had been inserted into it. The marriage didn't appear to have been a particularly happy one; the end result certainly wasn't pretty, although it did possess a certain spectacular quality all of its own.

Buried at the heart of the construction was the core of a Babbage unit, or at least some form of ordinateur processor. A mass of cabling led from the machine to great holes in the ceiling above.

Ulysses moved on again, the waves of vibrating energy pulsing from the organ-thing giving him earache and making him feel light-headed.

The smell of the place was a strange melange of ozone, hot metal, an acrid animal scent, camphor and furniture polish.

Beyond the auditorium, the cellar shrank back into a passageway with arched openings leading off it, one of these leading in turn to an immaculately laid-out study. It all appeared very homely, in a clinically measured way, from the precisely mounted insect specimen cases – the majority of which were butterflies and moths – to the way the titles were aligned in the bookcase beside the spotless desk and the wingback armchair set at a precise forty-five degree angle in one corner.

But there was something wrong, one thing out of place amidst the order that drew Ulysses' eye in an instant. A space, a gap in the otherwise near total coverage of specimen cases.

He resumed his wary exploration of the cellar lair, lamp in hand. There were other rooms; bedrooms – one immaculately presented as if no one had ever slept there, the other a total mess – a kitchen, a larder, a dining room, even a bathroom. But there was not another human soul present, beyond him and his companion, and there certainly wasn't any sign of the ape.

The place was deserted, like the *Marie Celeste* had been, as if whoever had been living there had just stepped out for a minute.

"Where are we?" Cadence asked.

"It's hard to be sure," Ulysses said, joining her before the peculiar organ, despite the discomfort he felt stood before it.

He paused, concentrating on ignoring the pain and listening instead to the hum of the machine and the lilting music wafting from great sound amplification horns.

"But given the length of time it took us to cross the city by sewer and that we suspect Leroux is behind the Rue Morgue murders, one of the victims being Carmine Roussel whose last work *Black Swan* is premiering this very day – right now, probably – at the Paris Opera, and considering the music that's being piped through this pipe organ right now, if I were to hazard a guess, I'd have to say that we were somewhere beneath the Opera House itself."

The device was humming loudly, the vibration a strange counterpoint to the orchestral overture, the instrument's open stops lending the music its own unnerving acoustic qualities. Ulysses could feel the vibration rising through the soles of his feet and making his legs feel like jelly. And was it his imagination or was the sensation intensifying?

He looked again at the machine. And that was when he saw it.

Resting on the upper register of the keyboard was a small, polished walnut frame, and pinned to the back board within was a single butterfly.

It was coloured orange and black, like a leaded stained glass window at sunset on a summer's day, with white speckles around the edge of each wing.

"He knew we were coming," Ulysses whispered.

"Leroux?"

"Or me, at least. He knew I was coming and he didn't try to stop me. Which must mean that either he knew I'd be too late or..."

"Or what?"

"Oh shit!"

"What?"

"We've just walked into a trap."

The dandy took in the cables, the winking lights of the ordinateur, the thrumming trumpets, shifting from foot to foot at the uncomfortable vibrations passing through him now. The humming sound *was* rising in intensity.

"And this must have something to do with this, must be some integral part of the snare. That's the only explanation."

"Shit!" Now it was the girl's turn to swear.

"What? What is it?"

"I know what this is," she said, her wide eyes scrutinizing the design of the organ. "Uncle Gustav hypothesised that such a thing could be created but I never thought…"

"What? Tell me!" Ulysses pressed. He could feel the fillings in his teeth vibrating in sympathy with the emanations coming from the curious device.

"It's a sonic bomb."

"A what?" Ulysses had to yell to be heard over the thrumming noise of the throbbing organ.

"It manipulates sound waves, modulating and concentrating them until the collected acoustic force is released in an explosion that acts not unlike a massive seismic event."

"Like an earthquake, you mean?" His nose was running. He wiped the back of his hand across his upper lip and it came back red.

Cadence nodded.

"So what happens if this thing goes off?"

She looked at him, her face pale. "Everyone dies."

"How long have we got until detonation?"

"I don't know," Cadence said, suddenly flustered. "I mean everything about this suggests that the music the orchestra is playing has clearly been composed in order to create the greatest acoustic tension possible as it builds."

"How long?" he shouted.

"Ten minutes?"

"What happens if we can stop the orchestra before then?"

"The damage has been done, the feedback loop has already been created. Stopping the orchestra will only lessen the force of the blast, not dissipate the sound energy already collected and focused by the machine."

It was getter harder and harder for the two of them to communicate.

"Then we haven't a moment to lose," Ulysses said, taking off his jacket and starting to roll up his sleeves. "Call Dupin and tell him what's going on. Tell him he's got to stop the performance and get everyone out as quickly as possible."

"I can't," Cadence said, her personal communication device in her hand. "There's no signal down here."

Typical, Ulysses thought. "Then get to topside as quickly as you can and tell him in person. Now run!"

"And what are you going to do?"

"Try to defuse this bomb. What else?"

Blood was dripping from his nose and onto his shirt, spotting the floor in front of the organ-bomb.

"No!" Cadence shouted over the painful pulsing hum of the organ.

Ulysses shot her a furious glance.

"No," she went on, "because we're going to do this the other way round."

Ulysses opened his mouth to argue.

"Because I'm the one with the engineering expertise. I'll stay behind and dismantle the bomb while you warn Dupin."

A strict middle-class Neo-Victorian upbringing taught him that he should protest, that good manners dictated that he should ensure the young lady was safe and take the more risky course of action himself, but Ulysses couldn't fault her logic.

"Very well," he said, "but I want you to know that I'm only going under protestation. And promise me, if it can't be done, you'll get out of here yourself. Don't take any risks."

"I think by far the greater risk," she shouted over the relentless thrumming, "would be to..."

The rest of what she said was drowned out by the noise emanating from the weaponised pipe organ.

Turning on his heels, Ulysses set off at a run.

ANOTHER STEEL, WHEEL-locked door led him to a flight of brick-laid steps that in turn brought him to a caged elevator. This he rode to a basement tunnel, and from there, via more doors – including one disguised to look like the back wall of a broom cupboard – and a service passageway, he found himself at last backstage at the Paris Opera.

The fact that he had been right about their location didn't

give him any sense of pride. A madman was prepared to unleash hell on the centre of Paris and hundreds if not thousands of people would die in this terrible terrorist atrocity if Ulysses and Cadence between them failed to avert the disaster. If Cadence failed to deactivate the bomb, Ulysses had to at least ensure that the Opera House had been evacuated.

It was a mercy to be free of the painful, nosebleed-inducing sonic vibrations.

Following the appropriate painted signs, picking up a number of disapproving looks along the way, he came at last to the foyer of the Palais Garnier to find Detective Inspector Dupin and his men already there.

"Quicksilver!" the policeman spluttered in surprise. "Where did you spring from?"

"There's a bomb under the Opera House!" Ulysses gasped. "We have to get everyone out now!"

Dupin didn't need to be told twice. The look in Ulysses' remaining eye, coupled with the fact that he was there at all and hadn't flown the coop when he so easily could have done, was a good enough guarantee for the Inspector that the dandy was telling the truth.

They set off together towards the auditorium, taking the steps of the grand staircase two at a time. Bypassing the flustered front of house staff they met at the doors to the main auditorium. Through the combination of a flash of Dupin's badge and the fierce expression on Ulysses' face, they burst into the gold-ornamented grandeur of the Paris Opera's theatre.

The orchestra was in full swing, the ballet itself almost under way, the music swelling to fill the performance void, enhanced by the acoustics of the place. Dancing string melodies merged with parping brass, the tinkling of a piano and the crash of percussion, while the intruders' unprompted entrance was met by a chorus of tuts, mutterings of disapproval and a fair amount of annoyed head-turning.

"You have to leave," Ulysses said, turning to the man at the end of the row nearest to him. "Now!"

"Hey, get your own seat, buddy!"

"This is the police!" Dupin announced loudly to all around him. "You must leave immediately."

The commotion they were making and the confusion that followed it was spreading throughout the auditorium now, the clamour causing heads to peer from balconies and boxes above.

The orchestra, however, played on.

"You have to go now!" Ulysses screamed, grabbing another man by the arm and physically hauling him out of his seat, much to the other's obvious chagrin. "Get out while you still can!"

The conductor turned at that, fixing Ulysses with a fierce glare from his pedestal, but kept on conducting regardless. It was clear that nothing was going to halt the premiere of *Black Swan*.

The music swelled to a marvellous crescendo. Despite the desperate nature of his current situation, a part of Ulysses' mind could still appreciate that Roussel's final magnum opus had been a triumph.

A tremor passed through the floor of the auditorium, making Ulysses and the policemen start, and members of the audience jump in their seats.

Ulysses looked about him in panic, suddenly fearing for Cadence's safety.

Then came another.

Even the orchestra felt it this time, the conductor faltering. There was a cracking sound from above him and a piece of ornamented plaster thudded onto the carpeted floor beside Ulysses.

Someone was screaming. He suddenly realised it was him. "Get out! *Get out! GET OUT!*"

A third tremor and the massive chandelier suspended high above the prized seats of the stalls began to jangle and shake.

"*GET OUT!*"

There were screams all around him now. And panic, and terror, and people running for the doors.

Ulysses joined the mass exodus of the Opera, the tide of

humanity carrying him towards the exit as plaster shards rained down upon their heads.

He was barely through the auditorium doors himself when he felt the seismic shockwave that heralded the city's demise.

And then the world turned upside down.

PART THREE

White Noise

~ May 1998 ~

*Lives of great men all remind us, we can make
our lives sublime, and, departing, leave behind us,
footprints on the sands of time.*

– Henry Wadsworth Longfellow

CHAPTER SEVENTEEN

Aftershocks

WHITE NOISE.
  Red pain.
  Darkness...

HE'S AWARE OF the ringing in his ears before he's aware of anything else. It's like it's never left him, like it's always been there; a background buzzing, as if there's a furious fly trapped in his auditory canal.

He tries to move but his body resists in painful protest. He's lying on his back, of that much he's certain, his arms and legs splayed out either side of him. His legs are trapped, his left arm too. He tentatively tries his right arm again, feeling grit rub against the palm of his hand.

He opens his one remaining eye but is met by nothing but darkness. He blinks, and waits, hoping that his vision will somehow become accustomed to the gloom of this lightless pit in which he now finds himself.

If only he could hear anything other than the constant

buzzing in his ears, he might be able to find out more about his surroundings.

There's blood in his mouth, the hot battery tang of it coating his tongue. There's something sticking into his back. He tries to adjust his position, but his legs are still trapped.

He blinks against the impenetrable darkness, the utter blackness making his eye sore with straining. It's more comfortable to keep it closed.

He strains to listen, his whole body tensing in frustration, until he is forced to give up in annoyance.

Panic waits for him, there in the darkness, but if he panics now he's lost. Panic is the cringing beast that waits at the edge of the conscious mind, in the shadows at the edge of the impenetrable forest of the subconscious. Waiting, ready to pounce, and seize control when all reason has fled.

At least he can breathe. He can feel something on his chest, but it's not heavy and moves with him as he takes a long, slow breath through his nose.

The air smells of plaster and charcoal. Dust particles tickle his nose, causing him to take a sharp involuntary breath. He coughs as more of the disturbed dust fills his mouth, spitting in an attempt to clear his mouth of saliva and blood.

His heart is pounding. He can feel the throb of the pulse in his wrist where something is pressing again it.

He can't even move a hand to wipe the mess of spittle from his lips.

He takes another careful breath. And another.

And another.

He focuses on nothing but his breathing, and as he does so he calms his thumping heart.

Beginning to relax at last, he now focuses on the pressure of the pulse in his wrist and the throb of the pulse in his ears, visualising the blood being pushed around his body with every surge. And as he does so, his mind makes a connection between the dull thud of his heart and the pulsing of the sonic bomb buried in the basement in the phantom's lair beneath the Paris Opera House.

And he remembers...

The immaculate study. The makeshift laboratory. The smell of animal musk and camphor and hot batteries. The brutalised pipe organ. The Monarch butterfly in its walnut frame, resting on the upper register of the pipe organ's keyboard. The swelling sound of the orchestra filling the cellar. The pulses emanating from the weaponised instrument increasing in intensity with every arcing musical phrase, making his head throb and seeming to synchronise with the desperate beating of his heart.

Saying goodbye to Cadence Bettencourt, leaving her to disarm the sonic bomb. Blood streaming from his nose. The flight through the subterranean labyrinth of secret tunnels and maintenance passageways beneath the Paris Opera. Meeting Inspector Dupin again in the foyer. The soaring triumph that was Carmine Roussel's posthumous greatest work, and his last thanks to Le Papillon's murderous actions. Their desperate attempt to evacuate the auditorium, Ulysses himself being carried along by the wave of panicked humanity.

That was when the world had turned upside down. Then nothing, for he knew not how long, and now this; white noise, red pain, and impenetrable darkness.

He tries moving his trapped legs once more, slowly this time, gritting his teeth against the pain, and feels something shift. He cries out as the pressure against his shins increases, the crushing weight on his legs intensifying.

His voice sounds muffled in the claustrophobic darkness, but in the silence that follows his pained exhalation, as he is forced to draw breath again, he hears a voice. Muffled. Urgent.

"Hello!" he shouts, and coughs as he inhales another cloud of dust. "Hello! Over here!"

Voices again; more than one now.

It takes him a moment to realise that they are speaking French.

"Over here!" he calls again.

Footsteps. A sound like feet on mountain scree. The crack and tinkle of breaking glass.

He cries out again as something presses down on him from above. More urgent chatter and the pain eases.

And there's light now; only a chink, but it's better than nothing. Blinking urgently, he sees the swirling dust, coloured silver now, the pieces of broken plaster resting on his chest, and the curving arch of a once ornate candelabra, the weight of it crushing his legs.

The voices are clearer now and closer. Hands pull at the rubble and suddenly the light is more than he can stand and he squeezes his remaining eye shut against its glare.

"Monsieur Quicksilver?"

The intolerable pressure on his legs eases. The release from pain causes him to gasp in relief.

He can move his arms now too.

He feels a hand grab his and someone pulls him from the rubble.

"YOU'RE SURE YOU'RE okay?" Inspector Auguste Dupin asked as a look of anxious concern writ large upon his face.

"How's the saying go? That which doesn't kill you..."

"Only you look like shit. Like..."

"Like the Paris Opera House just fell on me?" Ulysses Quicksilver said.

"That wasn't what I was going to say, but the analogy works just as well." The rumour of a wry smile curled the corner of Dupin's mouth.

Ulysses hadn't made it further than the entrance foyer of the Palais Garnier when the sonic bomb detonated. He was still there now, after a fashion, sitting on the marble steps of the grand staircase. Only now the foyer benefited from what a desperate property developer might have described as an *al fresco* aesthetic.

Dawn was just breaking over the rooftops of Montreuil and early morning sunlight poured into the ruin of the now not-so-grand lobby. Dupin had told him he'd been trapped under the debris for hours. He had told him he was lucky to be alive.

There were certainly plenty of others who hadn't been so lucky.

The roof of the Opera Garnier lay about Ulysses' feet. Much of it was now blocking the Place de la Bastille and the Rue Halévy beyond. The police were still helping ballet-goers from the rubble, but a number of shrouded bodies were already lying in the lee of what had once been the ticket office.

All things considered, Ulysses thought, it could have been a lot worse. They could have all died along with the Opera House.

There was no way of knowing yet how many had lost their lives in the disaster, how many had been injured, or how many might yet succumb to their injuries, but – he kept telling himself, like it was some kind a mantra – it could still have been a lot worse.

Dancers, musicians, backstage staff, passers-by, drivers of vehicles crushed by the collapsing structure as the edifice slid into the road like a calving glacier – it could number hundreds, if not thousands, but not everyone was dead, and Ulysses was still very much alive.

No matter how selfish such a thought might be, to Ulysses, at that moment, that was all that mattered. It wasn't that he valued his life more highly than anybody else's, but that he valued the life of Emilia Oddfellow more than anybody else's, including his own. As long as he was still alive, then he might yet save her, her father and his younger self, from the apocalyptic fate that awaited them on the Moon.

God alone knew where Leroux, the phantom of the opera, and the ape had got to – and there had been that other bedroom in Le Papillon's basement-lair too, the question of the identity of its owner still niggling at Ulysses' subconscious – but the worst had already happened.

And besides, this was Paris. This wasn't his jurisdiction. It wasn't his turf – although his role as agent of the throne of Magna Britannia could take him anywhere in the world to protect British interests – and the destruction of the Paris Opera wasn't his problem. It was tragic, admittedly, but that still didn't make it his problem.

The French police knew now that Ulysses hadn't been behind the Rue Morgue murders. Thanks to him they also knew the identity of the enigmatic terrorist known as Le Papillon, and where to start looking for him. The British dandy had done enough to get the ball rolling for the Parisian authorities. Having cleared his name, now all he needed to do was head back over the Channel to good old Blighty.

He smiled, patting his jacket pocket. He even had the falsified documentation, passport and train ticket Valerius Leroux had passed him at the Louvre.

"What happened to your friend?" Dupin asked.

"My friend?"

"The girl. The one you were with at Notre Dame. The one with the velocipede. Mademoiselle Bettencourt?"

Ulysses blanched, feeling the blood draining from his cheeks.

In all the commotion, he had forgotten that she had been working to disarm the bomb when it went off.

How could he have been so selfish? How could he have been so preoccupied as to forget Cadence when she had sacrificed her life in an effort to save the Parisian elite visiting the Opera House for the premiere of Roussel's *Black Swan*?

He looked at the gaping hole in the ground behind him. In places, the rubble lay a good six feet lower than ground level.

The detonation had been deep down beneath the Opera House, so deep that it would have brought down the cellars and labyrinth of tunnels that riddled the ground beneath the city streets, like the subsidence of a vast sinkhole. Nothing could have survived under all that.

Even if Cadence had given up on disarming the bomb before it went off, and not been caught at the epicentre of the blast – pulverised to a paste by the lethal sound waves – she would surely have been crushed by the tons of earth, brick and Opera House that had collapsed into the huge hole afterwards.

His gaze drifted across the piles of rubble and broken walls, and splintered columns. Smoke was rising from somewhere nearby, while the clouds of dust raised by the rescuers and shambling survivors as they stumbled from the rubble were turned gold by the early morning sunlight. The police were still pulling people from the rubble alive, but Cadence Bettencourt wasn't ever going to be one of them and that saddened Ulysses.

He had liked her. She had been resourceful, clever, charming. Attractive. He would have considered her a prize worth trying to win over, if his heart hadn't already been spoken for by another. That aside, her death was just another pointless waste, one of hundreds, no doubt, following Leroux's abominable attack on the Paris Opera.

And it had all been so convoluted. What had been the point of that? Why a sonic bomb? Why not just plant half a ton of dynamite in the sewers and be done with it? What had been the point of all that tomfoolery involving the pipe organ?

"Are you sure you'll be alright?" Dupin pressed. "It's just that there's still much to be done and... I'm needed elsewhere."

"Come on," Ulysses said with a weary sigh, "I'll give you a hand."

"Are you sure?"

"Look, will you stop asking me that?"

It was the morning of Sunday 17th May, 1998. There was still a month or more before the doomed Apollo 13 made its fateful journey to the Moon. He could help out here for an hour or two.

"Yes. I've got plenty of time."

"I mean, don't want to get yourself checked over by a professional?" Dupin said, looking at him now like he was concerned for his mental state as much as anything else.

"Why, is there a doctor in the house?"

"Probably, somewhere under all that rubble. But you could have concussion. Or worse."

"I'll be fine," Ulysses said, punctuating his declaration with a wheeze of pain as he got to his feet. His shins ached from where the candelabra had lain across them, and his shoulder was aching too. In fact, there wasn't a lot of him that didn't hurt, one way or another.

His one-eyed gaze alighted on the shrouded bodies again for a moment. And besides, he was a lot better off than those who had fallen victim to Le Papillon's attack on the Paris Opera. Like those poor wretches now lying under the blood-stained sheets, who had gone out the night before expecting an evening of delightful music and diverting conversation, not death and destruction at the Opera.

Like Cadence Bettencourt.

CHAPTER EIGHTEEN

Fait Accompli

"YOU'LL NEVER GET away with this, you know?"

The butterfly collector suppressed a snigger. "But my dear, I already have."

Leaning against the parapet, Valerius Leroux looked out across the city. Once more in the guise of Le Papillon, the agent of chaos – wearing what could once have been a French Foreign Legionnaire's uniform with the addition of a utility belt and other accoutrements, his aristocratic features hidden behind a goggled mask – he stared at the site of the Opera Garnier.

Dust hung in the air over the site of the demolished landmark – once referred to as "the most famous opera house in the world" – even now, hours after the sonic bomb had brought it crashing to the ground. His heart leapt at the memory.

His sonic bomb. He had done this. Hundreds, if not thousands dead, and it was only just the beginning; a prelude to the main act.

The echo of emergency sirens had faded long ago, although he could still see the red and blue lights blinking between the crowded tenements of the Gaillon district. From his vantage point he could also make out the traffic jams and congestion chaos his opening salvo had caused. One little building razed to the ground and practically the entire city had been brought to a standstill.

He smiled, imagining the shock the populace of Paris were going to receive when he put the final stage of his plan into action. And it wouldn't be long now.

He turned back to where his colleague was finishing off connecting the other device to the tower's superstructure. "Is it ready?"

The rope tether creaked and groaned in the wind, the balloon anchored above them straining to be free.

"Won't be long now," Dr Montague Moreau replied not looking up from his work, his speech impaired by the screwdriver clamped between his teeth. "Just need to double-check these last connections, then you can turn it on, sit back and enjoy the show as the shit really hits the fan."

Le Papillon's jaw tensed at the scientist's earthy tone, but he made no comment. Instead he said, "Good. I've been waiting months to see my plan come to fruition. As have other... interested parties."

"So that's why you're doing this, is it?"

He spun on his heel, fixing the girl with a needling stare. She was straining against the bonds securing her to the ironwork beside the elevator doors, but it was a futile effort, one that only allowed her to believe in the illusion of hope. The auburn tresses hanging down about her head shook as she raged, giving her the appearance of some wild, red-haired Celt – a Boudicca for the new steam age.

Le Papillon admired the Queen of the Iceni. She would have appreciated what he was attempting to do here, he was sure of it. She had been an agent of chaos too. All she had wanted to do was watch the world burn, just like him.

"I thought your actions might at least have been driven by some political or philosophical ideology," the prisoner went on. "A bold, if misguided belief in something. At least then the hundreds of deaths you've caused might have meant something."

"Hundreds? Try thousands."

The girl blinked back tears of rage. "But it all boils down to money in the end, doesn't it? You're just a common thief. A petty crook."

The terrorist froze. "There is nothing common or petty about me, I can assure you."

"Alright then, try amoral, psychotic, or simply downright evil."

"Labels, that's all they are. Words. They mean nothing!" Le Papillon spat, surprising himself with the vehemence of his response.

The girl had touched a nerve. But he was better than that; he was beyond such primitive animal responses. He would not give her the satisfaction of seeing him rise to her goading. And he would not let her stop him from enjoying his moment of satisfaction as his ultimate plan came to fruition.

"I can't believe my uncle trusted you!" his prisoner cried.

"Yes, but he did. And now he's dead and soon you will be too."

When Le Papillon had interrupted her, she had been on the verge of stopping the countdown and disarming the bomb altogether. The ape could easily have killed her with nothing more than a flick of the wrist, but at the last moment Le Papillon had stayed its hand.

The girl – what was the word? – intrigued him. Yes, that was it. Besides, a spectacle like the one he was about to put on needed an audience. Montague Moreau didn't count – he had been involved in the scheme for months and knew what to expect. And God alone knew what was going through the mind of the ape – other than Moreau's remote-control-triggered electrical impulses.

The lepidopterist was planning on enjoying the spectacle himself, of course, but a show was nothing without an audience. The general populace of the city would be too caught up in becoming bit-part players in the experience to appreciate the full extent of his accomplishment. But from her prime position atop Monsieur Eiffel's tower, Cadence Bettencourt would have a grandstand seat at the fall of the second Gomorrah.

There would be time to have her killed once the show was over, the start of which was only a matter of minutes away.

As Paris was gripped by panic the night before, the emergency services rushing to deal with the aftermath of the destruction of the Opera House, Le Papillon, Dr Moreau, Cadence Bettencourt and the Moreau's pet cyber-ape had made their way to the top of the Eiffel tower, travelling by balloon – the same balloon that was now tethered to the mast that protruded from the top of the tower. The rope ladder that hung from it would be their only escape route when the time came to depart the city once and for all.

The drums containing the different parts of the device had been transported to the tower in the basket of the balloon as well, but days before. Emptied of their contents, they stood stacked neatly in front of the decommissioned lift. Le Papillon didn't want anybody turning up unannounced just as they were putting the final part of the plan into action.

The device wasn't particularly large, especially when you took into account what it had been designed to do. But of course the device itself was little more than a receiver-cum-transmitter.

It was humming quietly to itself, generating a fluctuating rising and falling cadence of disharmonics. It had been operational since the night before, receiving the signal being broadcast from the Opera Garnier and the premiere performance of Roussel's *Black Swan*, via the adapted pipe organ in the basement and the radio mast at the top of the Eiffel Tower.

"What are you planning to do with that?" Cadence Bettencourt asked, twisting her head in an attempt to see what Moreau was up to.

The scientist gave her a lascivious look. "Wouldn't you like to know?"

"To be honest, I think I already do."

Her bluntness and confident tone caught the cyberneticist by surprise.

"Of course I'm only theorising here, but that box of tricks bears more than a passing resemblance to the kind of recording devices my uncle was working on up until his death. So what I'm thinking is that thing's been active since last night, that before the organ-bomb in the basement of the Opera House blew up it relayed the performance of Roussel's *Black Swan* to this device, which it received via the radio mast up there." She glanced skyward. "I'm guessing that a recording of that very performance is now stored in that ordinateur memory core ready for you to employ the destructive waves again as you see fit."

Moreau looked from the girl to his employer.

Le Papillon scowled.

"I'm right, aren't I?"

"Is it ready?" the terrorist grunted.

"Ready when you are," Moreau replied, getting to his feet.

"And the balloon's ready to go?"

"We just have to untie the tether, pull up the anchor and away we go."

"And the ape?"

Unhurriedly, Moreau put down his toolkit on top of one of the empty barrels and picked up the portable control unit that looked so like a handheld kine-camera. Holding the remote loosely in one hand, the doctor casually flicked a switch.

A large hand grabbed hold of the parapet, making Le Papillon start – although he did his best to mask his surprise – and the massive cyber-altered silverback swung itself up onto the top tier of the tower.

CADENCE GASPED.

The gorilla squatted on the balcony, fixing her with a beady, black-eyed stare.

Unable to help herself, she flinched, even though she couldn't hope to escape it, tied to the structure of the tower as she was.

Or couldn't she? Her hands out of sight, tied behind her back, she began to move them up and down, rubbing the knots of rope against the rough corner of the pillar.

The huge ape sniffed the air, great nostrils flaring. The lines in its furrowed brow deepened.

The beast seemed to remember the last time they had met as well as she did. The chase. The cathedral. The pursuit. Everything about the disgruntled expression on its simian features told her that there were still old scores to be settled, that it would yet have its revenge.

But for the time being, another directed its actions, if not its thoughts. She was safe for as long as the anarchist dictated that was how he wanted the situation to remain.

"Well, now that everyone's here" – Le Papillon looked from the ape to Cadence, and finally to the doctor – "let us begin. Activate the device."

"Your wish is my command," Moreau chuckled, and flicked a switch.

Lights flashed on the cogitator unit as the ordinateur engine began burbling to itself.

Positioned only a few feet from the device, Cadence heard the ordinateur recording rewinding, followed by a click and a moment's eerie silence. Then the crackling overture to the ballet began as it was played back through the device, the overlapping melodies and polyphonic rhythms redoubling and redoubling again, creating jarring disharmonics within the acoustics that set her teeth on edge.

She could see that it was having a similar effect on the doctor and the terrorist, although they obviously weren't suffering as much as she was, not being so close to the machine or actually tied to the vibrating superstructure of the tower themselves.

The ape moaned, its face suddenly beset by myriad tics as arcing sparks danced between the electrodes piercing its skull, the metal rods humming in tormented sympathy with the rising acoustic charge.

She could feel the metal at her back throbbing under the stress of the altered acoustics, feel it thrumming through her bones, making her head ache as the sounds grew louder and louder. It seemed to her that the sound was being transmitted through the girders and pylons of the edifice itself, as if the Eiffel Tower was a colossal tuning fork.

Cadence gritted her teeth, biting back a moan of pain. She wasn't sure how much longer she could take this. Her eyeballs felt like they were throbbing with every pulse emanating from the strange device. She felt dizzy and wondered how long she would be able to remain conscious if this torture kept up for much longer.

Hot spots of blood began to drip from her nose. Unable to wipe them away, she felt the dribble over her lip and onto the rope binding her, or down the front of her leather jacket.

And then, just when she feared she was going to pass out, there was a burst of energy, like the sonic boom of the sound barrier being broken, as a wave of acoustic force was released from the resonating superstructure of the tower.

"Don't pass out now, Mademoiselle Bettencourt," Cadence heard Leroux chuckle through the audio haze of white noise ringing in her ears. "You should watch this. After all, it was your uncle who helped make all this possible, who helped turn my dream into reality."

"More like a living nightmare," Cadence spat, blood flying from her lips. Then she screwed her eyes shut so as not to witness the end of the world, and in doing so deny the man responsible for her uncle's death the satisfaction of having an audience to share the spectacle to his hellish show.

THE PULSE RIPPLED outwards from the superstructure, much of the force channelled into the ground through its splayed feet. It was as if a gigantic pile driver had been slammed down into the earth beneath the tower.

Trees surrounding the Parc de Champs de Mars were shaken by the blast, the blast stripping them of their leaves, as surely as if they had been caught in the teeth of a sudden tornado. At the same time, the ground beneath the concrete foundations of the tower fractured and a curtain of earth and water erupted from the expanding cracks, falling back to earth as muddy rain.

Le Papillon heard the distressed cries of early morning dog-walkers and those who took their morning constitutionals in the park at that time, and laughed through his mask as he saw them scurrying like ants in a futile attempt to escape the inescapable.

And that was all they were to him, scurrying ants before the might of his intellect, his ruthless ambition, and the magnitude of the scheme he had put into operation.

The fractures rippled outwards from the tower, sending more fountains of mud into the air, while in the streets beyond the park buildings began to fall.

The whole tower shuddered. Le Papillon tightened his hold on the ironwork of the parapet, as did the adapted gorilla perched on the handrail.

As the feedback loop doubled and redoubled in force, the tower became merely the epicentre of the blast. It stood at the eye of the earth-storm now assaulting the city, spreading out across Paris in rippling, destructive, seismic waves.

Le Papillon peered over the edge, at the ground almost a thousand feet below. Boats bobbed on the Seine as rippling waves spread from the southern bank of the river. The Pont d'Iéna shook, sending a chugging steam-carriage halfway across it slewing sideways, mounting the pavement and colliding with the carved stone balustrade.

A moment later the bridge cracked clean across its middle. In the Jardin du Trocadéro, a six-foot-high tidal wave of rippling earth spread outwards, away from the Eiffel Tower, carrying a crest of turf, broken paving slabs and plants with it.

"Look at that!" Moreau whooped, peering through one of the pivoting tourist telescopes mounted at the corner of the platform.

Le Papillon followed his gaze. In the distance, the façade of the Palais de Chaillot cracked and crumbled as if it was constructed of nothing stronger than royal icing.

The tolling of bells rang out across the city, erratic and out of sync, clearly audible above the lower pitched seismic rumble that could be felt more than heard. The anarchist's eyes had picked out the shaking steeple of Saint Pierre de Chaillot less than a mile away to the north.

A moment later, under the relentless shaking of the city's foundations beneath it, the church spire collapsed, toppling into the street below like a felled tree. Tiles and stones came crashing down on to the heads of terrified passersby, whose screams were drowned out by the noise of the death-rattle.

A sound like an eroded cliff face crashing down onto a shingle beach sent Le Papillon hurrying to the other side of the platform.

The grand dome of the Eglise du Dome, at the heart of Les Invalides, had given way and caved in.

Le Papillon's heart leapt. Everywhere he looked, tenements were toppling, landmarks fractured and fell, monuments crumbled to dust. He had done this. He had achieved this. The death of a city; a metropolis murdered by his hand.

From behind him came the girl's heavy, heartfelt sobs.

"I told you you shouldn't miss this, my dear," he jeered. Far away, the slow-turning sails of a red windmill, visible above the tumbling rooftops, broke off and went spinning into the street below. "After all, the Moulin Rouge never put on a show like this!"

CHAPTER NINETEEN

Earthquake

ANOTHER SHUDDER PASSED through the ground at Ulysses' feet and the rear wall of the auditorium of the Paris Opera House tumbled into the great depression in the ground.

Arms outstretched for balance, legs braced, the disorientated dandy steadied himself.

Ulysses and Inspector Dupin exchanged glances.

"What was that?" the Inspector hissed. "An aftershock?"

"So long after the initial seismic event? I don't think so."

Another tremor passed through the ground like a ripple across a pool, this one stronger than the last.

"A pre-shock then?"

"Is there such a thing?"

"How would I know?" Dupin retorted. "I'm a police officer, not a seismologist. Besides, I thought you said the bomb had already detonated."

"I did. I mean it did. You know it did," Ulysses protested, looking to the rooftops around him as another shudder sent tiles and window boxes cascading into the roads demarcating the Place de la Bastille.

The sound of church bells ringing – with no sense of rhythm or timing – reverberated across the city.

How long was an earthquake supposed to last? Ulysses wondered.

Somewhere nearby, a church steeple came crashing down into another street with the roar of a landslide.

Could there have been a second device? But if so, where had it been located?

The beleaguered buildings surrounding the square finally gave up the ghost, their foundations buckling, the tenements toppling like dominoes.

Considerations such as what was causing the earthquake and where were forgotten as primal instinct kicked in. Ulysses and Dupin ran for safety as dust clouds swept across the square, obscuring everything in a dense grey veil.

As the ground bucked and rocked beneath them, like an ice floe on an Alaskan river in the spring thaw, they instinctively ran to the only place they felt was safe, given the circumstances: into the crater in which the ruins of the Opera Garnier lay.

The two of them staggered to a halt as the dust came down around them, unable to see for more than a few feet in any direction, barely able to see each other, let alone the startled gendarmes, medics and rescue workers or their charges now stumbling about in the cloud of debris. It reminded Ulysses of the sandstorm he had run into in the desert during the Paris-Dakar rally years before.

Putting a scuffed sleeve across his nose and mouth, he closed his remaining eye and breathed in through the rough fabric of his battered jacket.

The thunder of toppling buildings continued, as did the quaking beneath his feet. Underground pipes burst, sending torrents of pressurised water jetting into the air that then fell back to the ground as rainbow-shot showers, suppressing the dust. Gas mains fractured, the igniting hydrocarbons blasting manhole covers from the crazed tarmac streets.

"This isn't natural," Dupin coughed through the dust and smoke.

"I thought you weren't a seismologist. But you're right. There's no geological fault line under Paris, is there?"

"None that I know of. I mean, we would have heard about it before now, wouldn't we?"

"Indeed." The clouds of dust were starting to clear now, revealing scenes of even greater devastation and more lost souls, made phantoms by the earthquake and the pall of grey that covered them.

Dupin took in the scene, his mouth agape in horror. "Well, I would hazard that Le Papillon is not done with Paris yet."

"I would agree. A butterfly flaps its wings…"

"But where is he?" The look on Dupin's face was one of bewildered anger. Anger he felt at the wanton destruction of the city he loved, but directionless; he needed someone to blame, someone to unleash his anger upon.

"I'll find him. You stay here. Help these people get through this."

"But where will you look?"

"I'm guessing that if I find the epicentre of this on-going earthquake, our anarchist won't be far away."

"How do you know he's not miles away already?"

"I don't. But I have a feeling he will have wanted to watch this. He's been planning this for months. And he likes an audience, too."

"You think your friend might still be alive?"

"I can only hope," Ulysses said, feeling his cheeks flush with colour, "but I won't know till I find the bastard himself."

It seemed to Ulysses that the anarchist got a kick out of watching others suffer, particularly savouring the anguish of those forced to observe the destruction he wrought. It was as if he fed off their guilt and sorrow. That was his *raison d'être*, what gave him his thrill.

"I should come with you," the Inspector said, picking his way across the dust-covered rubble of the Opera House.

"No," Ulysses answered firmly. He could hear the rage in the inspector's voice. He had a suspicion he knew what Dupin would do if he caught up with Le Papillon. It was what Ulysses would probably do, but Ulysses was a free agent with the ultimate alibi – he was in London while this debacle was going on, or at least a younger version of him was – whereas Auguste Dupin was a respected member of the Parisian police force who needed to keep his nose clean, a representative of the law who needed to be seen to uphold justice rather than indulge in vengeance.

Dupin was the kind of hero Paris deserved at the moment, a white knight who, in the aftermath of this unfolding disaster, would help put things right again. But Ulysses Quicksilver was the kind of hero it needed right now, one who was prepared to do whatever it took to stop the madman who had unleashed hell on the City of Lovers, transforming it into a City of Nightmares. While Dupin needed to keep his hands clean, whether he knew it yet or not, Ulysses could get his as dirty as he liked.

"Stay here!" he shouted back over his shoulder. "Do what you're best at."

"And what's that?"

"Helping people."

"And what are you going to do?" the inspector asked Ulysses' back as he scrambled clear of the sinkhole into the devastated Rue Auber.

"What needs to be done."

"Wait!"

Ulysses stopped and turned at that.

"Take this," he said, tossing the dandy a pistol.

Ulysses snatched it out of the air.

"And I supposed you'd better take these as well, in case." A pair of handcuffs followed.

"Thank you, inspector," Ulysses said, giving a slight bow. "I didn't know you cared."

"Never mind that now. Isn't there somewhere else you need to be?"

ULYSSES SET OFF at a run, senses alert to everything going on around him, reasoning that the best way to avoid the apocalyptic effects of the earthquake was to keep on the move. But which way should he to go?

Even as he ran – ears straining for the tell-tale sounds of a building's foundations giving way or window panes cracking as a house's façade crumbled, his one eye scanning the street ahead of him, on the lookout for toppling telegraph poles, streetlamps and out-of-control steam-wagons – a part of his mind considered where the epicentre of the earthquake might be and thereby how best he might reach that particular location.

They had been warned of the impending round of secondary tremors, or aftershocks – or whatever they had been – by the wholesale destruction of entire streets to the south. Ulysses reasoned that, considering his current location, the focus of the seismic assault was on the other side of the river, the Musée d'Orsay side.

It hadn't taken long, from the first warning signs that something was wrong to the secondary quake hitting the Place de la Bastille. So it couldn't be too far away either. He was no expert, but it couldn't have been more than a couple of miles at most.

A lamppost toppled to the ground, throwing sparks and broken glass into the street in front of Ulysses as he fought to stay on his feet.

Somewhere, someone screamed.

The trouble was, Paris was a big place. To cover it on foot and find the source of the seismic pulses was a nigh on impossible task, but then what other option did he have?

Ulysses did a double-take, looking more closely at the toppling buildings around him as he ran on. It took him a moment to realise that these streets were looking more and more familiar – although it took him a moment longer to recognise where he was.

He had always had a strong sense of direction. Even though he had travelled to the Opera underground (via the labyrinth of sewer tunnels that wound beneath the city) and that conversely he had taken in much of the layout of this part of the city from above (whilst riding on the back of a flying steam-velocipede), he had nonetheless worked out where he was. He was approaching the spot where he and Cadence had chased the gorilla to a dead-end, and where they had come to ground in their pursuit of the cyber-ape, after turning the tables on the beast inside the belfry of Notre Dame cathedral.

Glancing down an alleyway, reliving the memory of their aerial pursuit of the brute above the rooftops of the city, cold shock suddenly gripped him and he skidded to a halt, as a loosened casement window crashed onto the fractured pavement behind him.

It was the cul-de-sac where Cadence had parked the steam-velocipede. Ulysses peered through the drifting clouds of dust and trailing smoke. And then he saw it.

Incredibly, the bike was still there: surrounded by broken bricks and shattered roof tiles, admittedly, but it was still in one piece. And that bike was the solution to the challenge now facing him.

He was all too aware of the shaking gutters and shingle-clatter of roof tiles shaking loose above him as he sprinted along the alleyway. He leapt broken beams, piles of bricks, his eye always on Cadence Bettencourt's run-around, knowing full well that one collapsing tenement could rob him of his means of escape and pursuit, not to mention his life!

"Who's a pretty boy then?" came a synthesised squawk. Still sitting in its pannier at the back of the bike, its head rotating in apparent simulated agitation, was Lumière's parrot.

"Nice to see you too," Ulysses said.

Grabbing hold of the handlebars, he swung himself into the driver's seat, taking a moment to study the controls. He had only ever ridden the velocipede as a passenger but everything seemed quite straightforward. After all, there weren't many things he hadn't driven or piloted at one point or another in his life, either in his role as an agent of the crown of Magna Britannia or simply for pleasure, having the role of dandy and hedonistic thrill-seeking playboy off to a tee.

Activating the ignition, Ulysses was relieved to hear the

engine fire first time. Revving the throttle, he kicked the stand-rest up and, muscles tensing against the weight of the machine, turned it in a tight circle to face the open end of the alleyway. He revved the throttle again and released the clutch.

Engine roaring, tyres screeching, the steam-velocipede took off.

"*Rawk!* Here we go again!" Archimedes squawked behind him.

Feet safely off the ground and on the bike's footrests, Ulysses jinked the machine between the piles of rubble and over piles of fallen debris, regularly glancing at the speedometer. The bike wobbled and shook beneath him and it took all Ulysses' concentration not to lose control of the steam-powered contraption.

Slowly the needle crept tantalizingly ever closer to the desired forty-four miles an hour. Ahead of him loomed the end of the alleyway and the crumbling façade of the buildings beyond. There wasn't much of a runway left before he'd run out of room and time altogether.

Ulysses glanced from the speedo to the red button at the end of the throttle under his right hand. He hadn't noticed it when he had been on the bike before, since Cadence's gloved hand had kept it hidden from view. What did it do? It had to have a purpose, and Ulysses guessed, since it was attached to the throttle, it would have something to do with maintaining the bike's acceleration. But he was no engineer; there was only one way to find out.

With crashing roar, like an avalanche of glass and brick, the architecture at the entrance to the alleyway finally gave in to the endless seismic shocks. The walls buckled, and the upper storeys of the crumbling tenements toppled slowly into the street.

Pulling back on the throttle again, Ulysses depressed the button.

With a throaty scream, the velocipede rocketed forwards, a jet of flame erupting from its twin exhausts, Ulysses bracing himself as the bike leapt into the air.

The toppling tenements loomed large above him as he pulled back on the controls, the engine roaring, booster jets screaming, and Ulysses wondering if perhaps it wasn't just too little, too late.

"Take cover!" the parrot screamed.

And then – like the Argo evading the Clashing Rocks of Cyanea – they were through, the two buildings coming down together in a deafening crash of bricks and crumbling mortar.

"Lucky bastard!"

Ulysses looked back over his shoulder at the robo-bird and gave a look which started as a scowl but turned into a grin as he regarded the flapping droid.

"Indeed," he said, smiling from ear to ear.

Bringing the bike around over what was left of the Gallion district, Ulysses cast his gaze over the destruction that was still being wrought by the earthquake right across the city. Buildings lay toppled everywhere he looked, spreading out from a central point, in every direction throughout central Paris.

He climbed higher.

Reading the pattern created by the fallen buildings, Ulysses steered Cadence's contraption south-west.

There ahead of him, the tallest and most instantly recognisable landmark in the whole of Paris rose above the devastation.

"Of course," Ulysses hissed under his breath, and turned the bike towards the looming iron spire of the Eiffel Tower.

CHAPTER TWENTY

Tower of Destruction

ULYSSES FELT AS though he could see the waves of sonic energy emanating from the interlaced girders of the Eiffel Tower, the resonating harmonics being created within the superstructure of the landmark distorting the air around it. Or was it just the heat-haze from the late spring sun?

Whatever the cause, there was no doubt now in Ulysses' mind that the tower was the epicentre of the earthquake. Le Papillon had clearly done something to turn the edifice into a sonic pulse transmitter – just as he had turned the pipe organ beneath the Opera Garnier into a sonic bomb. And doubtless his gullible, and already dead, accomplices had had a part to play.

How had such a thing been achieved? And could it be undone?

Actually, Ulysses reflected, it probably could. He had conquered giant robots and time-warping devices that punched holes in the very fabric of the space-time continuum, so surely he could find a way to de-weaponise the Eiffel Tower – even if it meant blowing it sky high.

The velocipede passed over the Jardin des Tuileries – the once glorious public gardens now looking like they were in the initial earth-moving phase of an ambitious landscaping project. From there he crossed the Seine, every bridge spanning the river as far as the eye could see reduced to broken spans and fractured pilings.

His target was only a mile away now. Where precisely on the tower was Le Papillon's diabolical device? And was his nemesis, Valerius Leroux, really there too?

Above the tower Ulysses saw a tethered hot air balloon. From this distance, it looked like a child's party balloon.

That confirmed it. A hard smile spread across Ulysses' lips. He was going to get the chance to get his hands dirty after all. Le Papillon was there, Ulysses was sure of it, waiting and watching as a city died. Enjoying the results of his handiwork.

He thought of Cadence. He thought of Josephine and Madame Marguerite, and wondered whether they had somehow miraculously survived the earthquake. If there was any justice in the world, then fate would have spared them. But then Ulysses knew from bitter personal experience that life was horribly unfair.

The velocipede soared ever closer to the tower. It was only half a mile away now.

He could see movement up on the top platform; people. One of them stood at a telescope. It was a man, someone he hadn't encountered before. Another he did recognise, the tumble of auburn hair giving her away.

His heart leapt, but in the very next moment apprehension dug its claws in. If he could see them, they would most definitely already know of his approach, the noise of the purring steam engine giving him away if nothing else, even over the sounds of mass municipal destruction occurring at the foot of their ivory tower.

"WE'VE GOT COMPANY," Moreau said, turning from the telescope he had had his eye to a moment before.

"Ah," Le Papillon said, eyes narrowing behind the goggles of his mask as the whirring optics within zoomed in on the approaching aerial velocipede. "Now that I was not expecting."

His jaw tensed. For one who sought to create chaos within the world, Le Papillon didn't like it when his own plans went awry. It was Quicksilver, he was sure of it. It had to be.

"You know what they say," came the girl's voice from behind him. "No plan survives contact with the enemy."

"Hmm... The enemy? Rather an unfortunate fly in the ointment."

Le Papillon unholstered his pistol and heard the girl gasp. Had she really been so naïve as to believe that he would allow the British agent to approach unhindered? He was in no doubt as to what Quicksilver would do to him. The dandy was here to kill him, so the lepidopterist would just have to kill him first.

Without uttering another word, Le Papillon took aim and fired.

Cadence Bettencourt screamed.

Ulysses heard the dull crack of the pistol shot and before he could do anything to avoid it, the bullet spanged off the engine housing, ricocheting through one of the velocipede's tail-fins.

"*Merde!*" Ulysses hissed under his breath. That had been too close. Clearly the direct approach wasn't going to work.

Adjusting the angle of the wings with the bike's foot-operated aileron controls, Ulysses steered the contraption into a downward glide.

There was another pistol crack and the sharp sound of another ricochet.

"*Merde! Merde!*" the parrot squawked. "Beware Leroux! You cannot trust Leroux!"

"You're not wrong there," Ulysses agreed, his body alive now with the adrenalin flooding his system.

He had to get out of the range of the gun.

He heard the metallic echo of one more shot as the velocipede passed into the shadows under the tower's secondary platform. The splayed structure of the edifice itself was now shielding him from any more pot-shots the terrorist might try to take against him.

The engine began to splutter. Ulysses glanced over the side of the velocipede as he banked around a girder. The turbo boost had automatically cut out.

He was going to have to land. The second platform was now out of reach, but only a matter of twenty feet below him were the much broader promenades of the first tier. And thank God they were wider: flying Cadence's steam-powered velocipede was one thing, landing it something else entirely.

What did they say about a good landing? Something about it being one you could walk away from?

To give himself enough runway to land on, he was going to have to bring the bike around outside the tower again, and no doubt back within range of Valerius Leroux's pistol.

Bracing himself for the worst, Ulysses swung the spluttering bike around the south-west leg of the thrumming tower. But no shots came. He could only guess that Le Papillon had already given up hope of catching him that way, or that the butterfly-collector had something else planned, perhaps even making his getaway by balloon at that very moment.

And then the promenade of the first tier was before him again, the balustrade surrounding it only inches away from the bike.

His heart pounding, Ulysses held his breath and made a final adjustment. And then the back wheel of the bike made contact with the surface of the walkway.

There was a squeal of rubber, and moment later the front wheel made contact too. Ulysses slammed on the brakes.

He could feel the thrumming vibrations besetting the tower, and if there had ever been any doubt in his mind that the tower was the earthquake machine, they were gone now; the fillings rattled in the teeth.

The bike skidded, jerking from side to side, threatening to throw Ulysses off. The opposite edge of the platform was before him, an ominous one-hundred-and-eighty-six-foot drop to the traumatised ground on the other side.

Fighting both the controls and the hurtling momentum of the bike, he steadily regained control. He killed the engine, keeping the pressure on the brakes. The screech of protesting tyres continued right up until the bike juddered to a halt, its front wheel touching the decorative ironwork of the balustrade.

"Lucky bastard!" Archimedes squawked again.

"Yeah, whatever," Ulysses retorted, as he gladly dismounted from the bike.

He took the gun Inspector Dupin had given him from his pocket and checked its load. Every chamber contained a bullet. Smiling to himself, he ran for the lift.

Reaching the lift, Ulysses punched the call button.

Nothing happened.

He tried again.

Still nothing. No grinding of gears; nothing.

Ulysses shook his head in despair. Of course the lift wasn't working. Le Papillon and his accomplice would have made sure of that, just as they had made sure there hadn't been anybody around to bother them when they set about the business of turning the Eiffel Tower into an earthquake machine.

Craning his head back, he looked up to where the pylons converged hundreds of feet above him. There was no way round the problem; he was going to have to take the stairs, all eight hundred odd feet to the top.

Grabbing hold of the railing at the foot of the first flight, he hesitated, looking longingly at the abandoned velocipede. If only he had been able to approach the tower with greater stealth, perhaps even now he would be atop battling to rescue Cadence from the villainous Le Papillon, saving a damsel in distress from a dastardly villain once again, just the way he liked it.

But this was the real world and the steam-velocipede was too much of a liability. Cadence was alive, but now that Le Papillon knew Ulysses was on his way the dandy didn't know how long that would remain the case.

Much as it galled him to admit it, her safety was secondary to that of the city. The needs of the many outweighed the needs of the few. The butterfly had flapped its wings and a city was falling even now as a result. Leroux had to be stopped, regardless of the fate that might befall Cadence Bettencourt.

Ulysses took the first of more than a thousand steps that would take him to the top of the Eiffel Tower.

"Well, here goes nothing," he said with a sigh.

"Here goes nothing!" the clockwork bird parroted.

And with that, Ulysses Quicksilver set off.

"Are we done here?" Le Papillon asked his partner-in-crime.

"Well, the machine will keep running until it drains its power source or somebody switches it off. Just depends if you want to stay and watch to the end of the show."

He was tempted, but he had seen enough. The Arc de Triomphe, the Musée D'Orsay and the Louvre all turned to rubble. This was a disaster from which the French capital would never recover.

"No. All good things, as the English say." The terrorist turned to his accomplice. "Turn it off. We're taking it with us."

"We're going?" Moreau sounded disappointed. "You're worried about Quicksilver? No one can get us up here, you know?"

"Quicksilver can."

Moreau gave a snort of laughter. "You're joking, right?"

"He's on his way as we speak."

"What? But we deactivated the lifts."

"It doesn't matter," the other snarled, his voice suddenly shrill with anger and frustration. "

"Like Napoleon said," – the girl was laughing through her fearful tears now – "no plan survives contact with the enemy."

"Shut up!" Le Papillon snapped, silencing the girl in an instant.

He turned back to Moreau.

"Deactivate the machine," he said, his voice icily calm again.

"Are you ser – ?"

"Deactivate the machine, dismantle it and load it into the balloon."

The anarchist glanced at the hulking ape, squatting on the parapet of the tower, staring dispassionately at the destruction befalling the city below. "Get the ape to help you if you need to, but don't take too long about it."

Montague Moreau stared at him open-mouthed with shock.

"What about...?" He nodded towards their prisoner.

"Forget about her. She's not important."

"And what are you going to be doing?"

"I'm going to deal with... our little problem."

"You're really going to go up against him – the man who's survived not one, but two run-ins with Ishmael and survived the detonation of the sonic bomb, not to mention the earthquake?"

Le Papillon looked at him.

"Hmm... As much as I hate to admit it, you may have a point." The anarchist turned away, his goggles' glassy gaze lingering on the cyber-ape. "And as the saying goes, why have a dog...?"

"No!" the girl cried out in horror.

"Marvellous," the doctor grumbled, eyeing first the earthquake machine, then the balloon tethered to the radio mast, and lastly the dangling rope ladder.

Le Papillon held out his hand for the portable control unit.

"If I wasn't being handsomely paid..."

"But you are," Le Papillon cut in, "so pass me that remote."

CHAPTER TWENTY-ONE

Agent Provocateur

THE THRUMMING VIBRATIONS within the iron-girder structure of the Eiffel Tower had ceased.

Ulysses stopped. He had passed the second tier platform and was now heading towards the intermediate platform. He had got so used to the constant low level vibrations that it was more of shock to him when they stopped than the destruction of the Paris Opera House had been the night before. It had him wondering if there was something worse still to come.

After several tense moments, during which nothing more terrible came to pass, Ulysses shook himself from his stunned reverie and set off again with a burst of renewed energy, taking the stairs two at a time. All that mattered now was that he made it to the top as quickly as he could.

What he wouldn't have done for the lift to be working, he thought, as he continued ever upwards. His knees were starting to ache, his heart was thumping in his chest and he was panting for breath. He was aware of the bullet wound in his shoulder again too, feeling the stitches pull as he exerted himself, using the hand rails to help pull himself up the cast-iron stairs. Adrenalin and the knowledge that time was running out allowed him to tap into hitherto unknown reserves of energy on his way to the top.

As he jogged on up the stairs, Ulysses considered the very real possibility that he was already too late to save the day. The damage had already been done. Central Paris had been laid waste, homes, public buildings and glorious monuments that had stood for centuries brought crashing to the ground, now just so many millions of tons of rubble lying under a pall of dust and smoke.

As if the destruction of the city hadn't claimed enough lives already, fires had broken out around the centre, and burst water mains and damage to the embankments of the Seine had resulted in widespread flooding.

The City of Lights had been transformed into a City of the Damned, and there was nothing Ulysses could do to change that, despite the fact that he had broken the very laws of time and space to change the world – his world – for what he hoped would be the better.

There was one niggling doubt that lingered at the back of Ulysses' mind and refused to go away. He could not recall hearing anything about the Paris earthquake before setting off for the Moon. A disaster on such an apocalyptic scale would surely have made the news across the Channel.

Was he really back in time in his own timeline, or had he somehow crossed over into another version of the world he knew? Or, if he hadn't crossed into another mirror world, had his actions since arriving in Paris somehow helped bring Le Papillon's plans to fruition?

He had told himself that the needs of the many surely should outweigh the needs of the one, when it came to Cadence Bettencourt's fate, and yet his actions since escaping the gendarmes in Montmartre had been motivated by nothing more than his own selfish desire, no matter how much he might try to pretend otherwise.

Was he, in truth, too late to change Emilia's fate anyway? Was it already written in the stars? And if this was an alternate timeline, he had to consider the possibility that in this reality he might not even have a relationship with Emilia to save in the first place. At that thought, his steps began to slow.

No, he couldn't start thinking like that. If he had indeed turned time on its head and challenged destiny for her sake, then he had to see things through to the end, otherwise all his endeavours would have been for naught. If Paris had died because of him, then he should damn well make sure it had died for a reason!

A sound from above him shook him from his musings; the crash of metal on metal getting louder all the time. Something was coming, clattering and bouncing down the zigzagging stairs towards him.

And then he saw it, shadows strobing through the open portions of the iron staircase above his head as something heavy barrelled towards him.

Ulysses contemplated turning and running, before admitting to himself that the tumbling object would surely catch up with him in the end.

No, his best bet was to stay precisely where he was.

The object rounded the turn with a hollow crash. It was a metal drum, bouncing down the steps as it spun, picking up speed again now that it was past the turn.

Ulysses braced. The barrel bounced off a step and crashed down directly in front of him. Ulysses launched himself into the air, up and over the barrel as it rolled beneath him. He landed two steps further up from where he had been standing before.

As the barrel continued to crash its way down the stairs towards the secondary viewing platform, Ulysses resumed his climb. Another crash echoed from above him, and another. This wasn't over yet, not by a long shot.

Ulysses hesitated. Remaining where he was would probably give him the best chance of avoiding any other barrels coming his way. But then who knew how many more barrels there may be, and of course the longer he delayed, the greater the chance Le Papillon and his accomplice had to get away.

Ulysses took the next flight of stairs two at a time, reaching the turn to the next flight just as a barrel caught up with him. Using the handrails to help him again, Ulysses pulled himself up so that his feet were balanced on the rail, his arms braced against an iron pillar as he stretched his body across the stairs. The barrel bowled past beneath him and on down the tower.

Not wanting to waste any more time, Ulysses jumped from the handrail onto the next flight of stairs, his landing sending a reverberating clang through the ironwork just as another metal cylinder bowled into view.

Gripping the bannisters, Ulysses readied himself to jump again. As he was tensing, the barrel hit the very edge of an iron step and was sent spinning into the air.

Ulysses pulled himself low, throwing his arms up over his head. He could just see the barrel hurtling towards him at the periphery of his vision. Its shadow fell across him as it came down. Fearing the worst, he punched upwards with both arms, catching the edge of the rotating drum with his fists and altering its trajectory, ensuring that it didn't come crashing down on top of him. For the price of a few bruised knuckles, he had saved his skull.

With three barrels avoided so far, the adrenalin flowing freely again through his body and dousing the lactic burn in his legs, he resumed his ascent of the Eiffel Tower.

THE ROAR OF the primate made Ulysses freeze, his heart racing, the bullet wound in his shoulder throbbing.

He wasn't that far from the top of the tower, and at first he had taken the crashing sounds coming from above to be more barrels hurtling towards him. But the animal bellow had instantly dispelled any such thoughts. The ape was still very much alive and just as angry, and he was about to face the demented cyborg-monster once more, armed with nothing more than a pistol, his natural charm and charisma, and his God-given good looks.

But what other choice did he have? He couldn't shimmy up the side of the Eiffel Tower like the ape. Could he?

Ulysses dismissed the idea as nothing more than a foolish notion, a consequence of his exhausted, over-wrought mind, as prone it seemed to fits of madness as it was flashes of inspiration. Instead, his footsteps suddenly as heavy as those of a condemned man climbing the scaffold, the dandy set off up the next flight of stairs.

Above, he could see the bottom of the deactivated elevator stuck at the apex of the tower; beneath it, a nine-hundred-foot drop to the ground.

With a resounding clang, the ape dropped onto the landing above him, the shock of its landing making Ulysses grab for the handrails either side of him.

Their eyes met – his single right eye and the silverback's beady black marble gaze.

It stood there in all its terrible, mechanically-enhanced glory. Biceps bunched, thick toes curling around the leading edge of a step. The electrodes implanted in its skull crackled with coruscating energy as the ape raised its arms. In each huge hand it gripped the rims of two more barrels.

Ulysses glanced about him. There was no point trying to run. And if the animal decided to throw its missiles at him, no manner of dramatic athletics was going to be able to save him.

"Your move," Ulysses growled.

The ape snorted, nostrils flaring, black rubbery lips creasing in a grumpy pout. With a roar of bestial anger, it sent the last of the barrels at Ulysses.

"HE'S DEAD? YOU'RE sure of it?"

The ape said nothing but returned Le Papillon's goggle-eyed gaze with the same angry black stare it had given the British agent.

"What am I even doing talking to a monkey?" Le Papillon added under his breath.

There was no sign of a body, and the ape would have seen and pursued the dandy if he'd managed to double back down the stairs.

"All right, I'm satisfied. The bastard's dead. Let's go."

Without a second thought for the dead man, the anarchist returned to the top of the tower, the hulking cyber-ape knuckling its way back up after him.

ULYSSES QUICKSILVER LET out his pent-up breath. He stayed where he was for a moment, hanging from the bottom of the frozen elevator, arms and legs wrapped around the steel bars. The breeze blew in his hair as he waited for his thundering pulse to return to a steadier pace.

He'd taken a big risk, but then desperate situations and all that...

His ruse had relied on the ape's view being obscured by the tumbling barrels, and that the gorilla wouldn't realise that the dandy's death-defying leap to safety had been anything other than a death plunge, down through the middle of the tower.

But the risk had paid off in the end, and he had regained the element of surprise.

Ulysses gingerly extricated his legs from under the lift, hanging over the nine-hundred-foot drop for a moment before swinging himself across to the more secure position of a maintenance ladder. The only issue that remained was how best to turn the situation to his advantage.

"HOW LONG?" LE Papillon asked bluntly as he returned to the uppermost viewing deck, ignoring the sobbing of the girl bound to the girder.

Moreau paused as he struggled to climb the rope ladder to the balloon whilst manhandling a curiously-shaped piece of the Earthquake Machine.

"With help," the doctor grunted breathlessly with a nod of the head towards the gorilla, "not long now. Otherwise..."

"It's time we were gone from here. Paris bores me. I want to depart as quickly as possible. I have a meeting to attend elsewhere."

"Really?"

Le Papillon spun round, unable to hide the gasp of genuine surprise that escaped the vent of the mask covering his mouth.

The dandy was standing at the edge of the platform, the pistol in his hand trained on the anarchist.

"You! But you're..."

"Oh, no, I'm not. I'm still very much alive! I'm like a cat, me. I've got nine lives."

"Well I'd say you've used up a fair number of them by now," Le Papillon countered. "And you know what did for the cat, don't you? And you've been so very curious, haven't you, Mr Quicksilver?"

The anarchist began to raise the remote control still clutched in one white-gloved hand as the ape turned to face the interloper.

"Don't," the dandy growled, the knuckle of his index finger whitening as he increased the pressure on the trigger.

Le Papillon lowered the hand holding the remote.

"Time's up, Leroux. You're not going anywhere."

"Is that so?" the anarchist countered, his voice as cold and as sharp as an ice pick. "You really think you can stop me now? Do you not think that I would have prepared for every possible eventuality, leaving nothing to chance?"

"Not every eventuality. You didn't factor my escaping the death you had planned for me, did you?"

"You're too late. What are you going to do? Paris isn't doomed – it's already dead!"

"I'm Time's Arrow. I can't ever be too late."

It was only the action of a micro-second, but the dandy's glance at the girl gave him away.

"Oh, I see. The fate of one girl matters more to you than all of Paris, does it?"

"Right at this moment, yes," Quicksilver replied with icy calm, his gun never wavering from its target. "Or to put it another way, you have to be able to come to terms with the things you cannot change and yet have the courage to change the things you can."

"I see," the butterfly-collector said, not moving an inch. And then, directing his words at his accomplice, "Untie the girl."

"What? But –"

"Just do it!"

For a moment no one said anything, as the doctor descended the ladder, placing the piece of technology he had been carrying on the ground and beginning to loosen the knots securing the girl to the tower.

"You know this thing responds to verbal commands as well, don't you?"

"What?" The dandy suddenly looked startled, his previously calm demeanour cracking at last.

"Ishmael," Le Papillon said, a wry smile taking shape beneath his mask. The ape looked at him. "Grab the girl."

Obediently, the ape seized the girl in one huge hand. Cadence gave a scream.

"And now, Monsieur Quicksilver," the anarchist went on, "I give you a choice. You can either finish what you came here to do and stop me, motivated by some misguided desire for revenge, or you can save the girl."

He could see by the look on the dandy's face that he had uncovered the fool's weakness.

"So, Mr Quicksilver, what's it to be? Me, or the girl?"

CHAPTER TWENTY-TWO

Beauty and the Beast

ULYSSES HAD NO choice.

With a scream of frustrated rage he took aim at Le Papillon as the anarchist dashed for cover, even as the gorilla came for him.

The gunshot's report was amplified by the echoing ironwork of the tower. The bullet ricocheted from a girder as Le Papillon ducked for cover behind the lift housing.

And then the silverback was in front of Ulysses, its gaping maw open in another roar, the blunt enamel chisels of its teeth on show, giving Ulysses an idea of what the ape had in mind for him.

Cadence Bettencourt cried out as the beast swung her about in its huge right hand. She was still alive, at least. Ulysses guessed that however Le Papillon's accomplice had re-wired the ape's brain, it responded very literally to instructions. The anarchist hadn't told the animal to kill the girl, so she wasn't dead – yet.

Ulysses turned the gun on the cyborg ape even as it brought its left arm around across its body in a powerful back-handed swipe. But before he could pull the trigger, the weapon was sent flying from his hand by a blow that left his fingers stinging with pain. The gun vanished over the edge of the tower, clattering and clanging its way down the stairs.

"*Merde!*" Ulysses cursed, stumbling backwards.

The silverback bounded forward. But it had fallen for Ulysses' bluff, the dandy ducking under its massive outstretched arm and dashing across the platform after the fleeing anarchist.

"Get up the ladder! We need to go!" Le Papillon hissed, already clambering up the swaying rope ladder himself.

"But what about the bloody machine?" Dr Montague Moreau said.

"Forget the bloody machine!"

"But it was you who wanted to take it with us."

"I know what I said, but the plan has changed."

Moreau muttered something under his breath as he bundled several pieces of the dismembered machine into his arms and attempted his own ascent of the rope ladder one-handed.

"What did you say?" Le Papillon hissed.

"I said, the girl was right."

"What?"

"No plan escapes contact with the enemy."

Le Papillon said nothing but re-doubled his efforts to reach the basket, and yet struggling to keep hold of the remote control still in his left hand as he did so.

Moreau had somehow set it to 'automatic' – the anarchist didn't understand the ins and outs of it, but then that was why he had involved Dr Montague Moreau in his enterprise in the first place – but he hadn't wanted to relinquish his hold of it just yet. The cyber-ape – or Ishmael, as Moreau insisted on calling it – had proved too useful and resilient a weapon to simply discard just yet. When it had dealt with the dandy once and for all, it could re-join them.

As the two men climbed, the rope-ladder twisting and swaying wildly, the anchored balloon drifted over them, pulling the ladder taught. Le Papillon and Moreau suddenly found themselves attempting to climb up the underside of a ladder now stretched out sharply from the vertical.

Finding himself with nothing between him and the devastated Parc du Champ-du-Mars a thousand feet below, Le Papillon panicked and tightened his grip on the ladder. The remote control slipped from his grasp in the process.

Below him, Moreau gave a cry of dismay as he watched the cunning box of tricks tumble through the air.

For the time being at least, the cyber-ape was lost to them.

ULYSSES DODGED ANOTHER swipe of the gorilla's arm, diving across the platform and ending up next to the jumble of equipment left behind by the fleeing anarchists. Lying amongst the wreckage of the disassembled Earthquake Machine was a length of copper pipe. It was the closest thing to a weapon Ulysses could see.

Barking in annoyance, the enraged ape swung at the dandy again. There was a resounding clang as the pipe now gripped in Ulysses' hands connected with one of the animal's bionic augmetics.

Ulysses recoiled, stumbling backwards as the juddering force of his blow reverberated up his arms and through his body, eliciting renewed spasms of pain from the bullet wound in his shoulder.

The gorilla had been seriously disabled by having to keep a hold of Cadence with one hand and it was a disadvantage Ulysses was determined to capitalise upon. He doubted he would have had a hope against the beast otherwise. And yet for as long as their struggle continued, Cadence was always going to be in jeopardy.

Her screams and cries of alarm had been silenced and Ulysses didn't even know if she was still conscious. He couldn't let this continue any longer. Besides, the longer the battle went on, the closer the terrorists got to escaping unpunished.

As the silverback moved in for the kill, Ulysses leapt into the air and swung again. This time the copper connected with the electrodes implanted into the ape's skull. A disharmonious chord rang out, like a chorus of mismatched tuning forks.

The ape opened its mouth wide in a silent scream of unimaginable agony, its beady eyes screwed tight shut against the pain, and let go of the girl. Cadence landed on the platform and remained where she fell, in a motionless heap.

"Cadence!" Ulysses shouted.

The woman answered him with a muffled groan.

"Cadence! You have to get up!"

The crumpled body moved.

"Get out of the way!"

On hands and knees now, her auburn tresses tumbling about her head and hiding her face from view, she crawled across the grilled deck to the relative safety of the lift housing.

Having done as much as he could for the girl for the time being, Ulysses turned his attention back to the ape. The only hope either he or Cadence had of being truly out of harm's way was if he somehow found a way to stop the brute once and for all. He doubted that a length of copper piping alone was going to do it, but for the time being it was all he had to hand.

Ulysses swung the pipe at the ape again, but this time the savage beast was ready for him, a huge hand plucking his improvised weapon out of the air and sending it spinning over the edge of the platform.

Rising up on its hind-legs, the cyborg gave another monstrous roar and beat its chest with its massive, pile-driver fists.

Ulysses' mind was racing as fast as his pulse. Unarmed, he was nonetheless not completely defenceless against the adapted animal, not as long as he kept his wits about him. Even as he was watching the beast, trying to judge what its next move might be, he was also checking out his surroundings, seeing how he might turn his environment against the gorilla.

Trying to trick the ape into taking a wild plunge over the edge of the tower seemed like a pointless exercise. He doubted the ape would fall for it. Despite all the cranial surgery the primate had clearly had to endure, the various procedures it had undergone didn't seem to have dulled its natural instincts, or the speed of its reactions.

Pieces of discarded machinery lay about the platform, mainly around the entrance to the sabotaged elevator. Perhaps he could find something else from amongst the debris that he could turn into a weapon.

And then there was Cadence Bettencourt.

"Cadence!" he shouted, as the ape advanced, its splayed toes gripping the deck.

He tried again. "Cadence!"

The silverback sprang. Ulysses launched himself at its feet. The beast came down on the spot where he had been standing a moment before.

Ulysses performed a tidily executed forward roll, miraculously ending up back on his feet, and then sprinted for the protective corner of the top of the elevator shaft.

"Cadence!"

"What… What can I do?" came the young woman's groggy response.

"Anything! Whatever you can!" Ulysses gasped as the flung himself out of the way as the ape hefted a metal component in one hand, as if it was nothing more than a pebble, and hurled it in his direction. The object disintegrated with a sharp metal *clang* as it smashed into the lift housing. "Otherwise this isn't going to end well – for either of us!"

"Are you in?" Le Papillon asked. He didn't even bother to look round as he fired the burners.

Taking the grunted exhalation and crash of ordinateur parts and audio equipment landing at his feet as a yes, he opened the gas valves even further, the balloon's envelope swelling as he did so.

The anarchist had considered not waiting for the good doctor, of course, but he had been concerned that he might still have need of the man's technological skills, since he had been forced to leave most of the Earthquake Machine behind.

If he was to ensure safe asylum when he reached his intended destination, he wanted to make sure that he had every asset he could to hand to ensure the continued protection of his employer.

"Pull up the anchor and let's away from here," he ordered his accomplice.

"What about the ladder?" the doctor panted.

"Lose it."

ALWAYS TRY TO turn an enemy's strength against him, was what Ulysses' fencing tutor at Eton had impressed upon his students. Memories of the old gym hall came to mind now, along with the ghost of an aroma of floor polish and stale sweat.

He wasn't sure Master Murray would have included silverback gorillas among the list of enemies his favoured pupil might have to face in years to come, but strategy and cunning was all Ulysses had to rely on now, and he was going to need to use every trick in his arsenal if he was to somehow stop the adapted ape once and for all, and still save the day.

The ape was possessed of a brutal animal intelligence that was made up of cunning and instinct more than anything else. But Ulysses was possessed of a highly developed cunning streak too. The two of them, man and ape, weren't that distantly related in evolutionary terms as Professor Galapagos' and Professor Crichton's research had demonstrated.

The savage animal was becoming more and more frustrated with Ulysses with every attack he evaded. It had nowhere else to go and no other conflicting commands coming from its controllers, and so its sole purpose had become to beat the dandy into submission. But Ulysses could use that to his advantage.

The gorilla raised its massive fists above its head and brought them down hard on the deck of the platform, the metal gauntlets sheathing its forearms buckling the metal plates as Ulysses side-stepped out of the way.

The ape tensed, but the gauntlets had become wedged in the damaged deck plates. It growled, pulling harder, great slabs of muscle bunching as it struggled to free itself.

In that moment, Ulysses leapt, landing on the ape's right arm and from there, pulling himself up onto the animal's shoulder using handfuls of matted fur to aid his ascent. The raging beast intensified its efforts still further, tugging its fists free of the floor at last, the action only serving to help Ulysses on his way as it raised its arms in instinctive fury.

As he found himself tumbling forwards over the ape's back, Ulysses grabbed at the thick metal collar mounted over the transmitter bolted between the animal's shoulders. He clung on with desperate fingers as his legs slid down the silver furred back and he ended up hanging from the monster's shoulders.

As he kicked and jerked to keep clear of the ape's grasping fingers, he scoured the electrodes screwed into its skull, seeing if there were any exposed cables that he could disconnect.

A thrumming bass note – like some sort of electronic interference played at loud volume – shook the top of the tower.

From his precarious position, turning his head this way and that, Ulysses tried to focus on the source of the sound, fearing for a moment that the Earthquake Machine had been reactivated.

The ape recovered first. Strong fingers closed around the dandy's ankle and pulled hard. Ulysses cried out in pain and surprise as his fingers slipped from the smooth metal of the animal's chrome collar. And then he was flying through the air.

In that moment one thought flashed through his mind – not where might he land, whether he would end up going over the edge, or what the ape might do to him should he survive – but what would happen to his dear, darling Emilia without him there to save her.

He landed painfully on his back and slid across the deck, before being arrested by the balustrade that ran around its edge.

Blinking himself back from the verge of unconscious, Ulysses saw the gorilla knuckling towards him, its face wrenched into a pained grimace. It was only then that the dandy registered that the discordant noise had changed pitch.

When the animal was only a few feet from him it stopped altogether. The ape's face was a knot of nervous tics and twitches.

The note changed again.

The ape screamed – a horrible sound borne of pain, rage and base animal fear – and its eyes blazed red.

The animal stumbled forwards, clutching at its skull and the implanted metal probes. The bellowing roar of pain continued as the primate tugged at the thick electrodes, even as arcs of electrical discharge encircled its head in a crown of scintillating blue sparks.

Its crashing, half-falling, half-stumbling footsteps brought it ever closer, forcing Ulysses to drag himself out of the way of the hulking brute.

And then, at the edge of the platform, before the barrier built to keep sightseers safe, the cyber-ape stopped. Its face went slack and Ulysses found himself unable to tear his gaze from the distant look in the beast's eyes. In that instant, for the first time since encountering the gorilla atop the roofs of Montmartre, he felt pity for the animal.

As Ulysses stared into the gorilla's unblinking eyes, the furious light in those obsidian orbs faded. The ape's arms went slack and the huge, bionically-enhanced animal toppled forwards.

Unbalanced by its heavy augmetics the silverback slipped headfirst off the platform and commenced its long, silent fall to the ground, a thousand feet below.

Ulysses turned from observing the ape's death-plunge and stared dumbly at the dishevelled Cadence Bettencourt, and the device in her hands. It looked like a cross between a loud-hailer and a Martian ray gun.

"What did you do?"

"Well it was quite simply really." Cadence held up the box of tricks. "I used this to broadcast a resonating feedback loop tuned to the precise resonance frequency of the electrodes in the ape's skull and then turned up the gain."

"In layman's terms?"

"I melted its brain."

Ulysses continued to stare at her in stunned disbelief.

"It was the electrodes resonating inside it's skull that killed it, disrupting the neural pathways of the brain. Of course, the vibration of the electrodes would have also effectively liquefied the soft tissue of its brain."

"No, you're wrong." Ulysses said, peering back over the edge of the tower. He could just make out the ape's corpse spread-eagled on the broken ground below. "It wasn't the resonating electrodes. 'Twas Beauty killed the beast."

For a moment neither of them said a word, the only sound the keening of the wind and the furious roar of gas-burners firing.

"Leroux!" Ulysses suddenly shouted, looking to the radio mast above but seeing no balloon tethered there.

"What do we do now?" Cadence said, watching the anarchist's balloon disappearing into the haze of dust and smoke hanging over the city.

"We go after him."

Cadence fixed him with a penetrating stare, pupils dilating in excitement, a smile creasing her lips.

"Is the bike still flightworthy?"

"Come and take a look for yourself," Ulysses said, meeting her smile with a broad grin of his own. "Only trouble is, you know what the parking's like in central Paris," he added, making for the stairs.

"No," Cadence said, "but I'm beginning to get a pretty good idea." And with that she set off after him.

"READY?' CADENCE ASKED, as she lowered her goggles and revved the throttle.

"Whenever you are," Ulysses replied, settling himself on the padded seat of the steam-velocipede behind her. He was just glad to be able to have a bit of a sit-down for a minute or two.

"Ready!" the robo-parrot screeched from its pannier behind both them.

"Then... How do you English put it?" Cadence thought for a moment. "*Chocks away? Tally-ho?*"

"*Chocks away* will do just fi –" But Ulysses didn't get to finish his sentence, as the sudden launch snatched the breath from his lungs and the very words from his mouth.

With a squeal of tyres, and a scream of engine noise, the velocipede hurtled forwards.

As Cadence drove it straight at the far side of the platform, the speedometer powered up to the crucial forty-four-miles-an-hour mark, and the bike took off, a synthesised squawk of "Tally-ho!" ringing from the iron rafters of the Eiffel Tower.

CHAPTER TWENTY-THREE

Off The Rails

"There they are!" Ulysses shouted needlessly over the roar of the wind.

"I know!" Cadence shouted back over her shoulder, her eyes hidden behind the reflecting lenses of her flying goggles. "I can see it too."

"I can see it too!" parroted the robo-bird, its brass wings flapping in excitement.

Paris wasn't even a speck on the southern horizon any more. From this high altitude, Ulysses could just make out the sparkle of sunlight on the waters of the Channel far ahead of them. While a thousand feet below, the patchwork pattern of French fields, dark green patches of woodland, and the winding course of a railway line hurried past beneath them. A hundred yards directly in front of them was Leroux's balloon, sailing towards the coast ahead of the prevailing southerly wind.

The sun was climbing towards its zenith and it was turning out to be a very pleasant late spring day – the weather in total contrast to the disaster that had struck Paris and that both Ulysses and Cadence had managed to live through.

Despite his attention being focused on the escaping anarchist, Ulysses could still appreciate the beauty and the wonder of the view he was afforded. Of course he had enjoyed toy-town vistas such as this one before, having travelled via dirigible to most corners of the globe, but riding on the back of the flying bike – without several inches of reinforced glass to protect him – lent an added sensation of closeness to his surroundings.

"I don't suppose you thought about attaching parachutes when you were busy putting this little run-around of yours together, did you?" Ulysses asked.

"What?" Cadence called back, over the howling of the wind in their ears.

"It doesn't matter!"

The balloon – with all its additions, including canvas sails, steering rudder mechanism, and basket-mounted rocket-boosters – was only five hundred yards away now.

When he and Cadence had set off from the primary viewing platform of the Eiffel Tower, Ulysses hadn't given much thought to what he would do once they caught up with the villains. All that had mattered at the time was catching up with them, and some vague sense of seeing justice served.

Or was it revenge? Revenge for what they had done to Cadence's uncle, and the cavalier approach they had taken to the lives of others – even what they had done to the gorilla, by turning it into simply another weapon in their selfish arsenal.

A shrill steamy whistle from below had Ulysses peering down again. Beneath them, the Paris to London Express chuffed closer and closer. Clearly the train had left Paris before the Earthquake Machine had been activated.

"There they are!" the parrot squawked, returning Ulysses' attention to the balloon.

"How far now?" he shouted into the wind.

"Three hundred yards and closing," the bike's pilot replied.

Ulysses saw the gas-fired rocket boosters flame before he heard the hot roar of them firing. The basket jerked forwards, the balloon envelope taking a moment to catch up, and then the whole was moving away from the velocipede at an increasing rate of knots.

"They're getting away!" Ulysses exclaimed helplessly from the back of the bike.

"They're getting away!" the parrot squawked.

"I know! I can still see!" Cadence retorted.

Ulysses hated not being in control. He would never have described himself as a control freak, but his current helplessness was exposing him as a terrible backseat driver.

"But they won't be for long."

Cadence shifted her grip on the throttle, her thumb hovering over the red button.

"Hang on to something!" she shouted, and ignited the velocipede's turbo boost.

Ulysses grabbed hold of Cadence, wrapping his arms tight about her waist as the bike rocketed forwards. It ate up the distance between them and the balloon, the inflated envelope rapidly filling Ulysses' field of view.

"That's more like it!" Ulysses thrilled.

"I know, but it burns fuel like there's no tomorrow." Cadence shouted.

They were so close now he could hear the terrorists' cries of alarm rising from below.

"Pull up! Pull up!" the parrot demanded as Cadence closed on the balloon. "Can you get me over the top?" Ulysses called.

"Yes," the pilot replied, "but why?"

"Well… It's the parachute situation I mentioned earlier."

"What parachutes?"

"Precisely."

"I was in a hurry," Cadence threw back. "I had a British agent to save from certain cyber-ape-induced death! Remember?"

"I remember," Ulysses muttered.

Cadence grunted and gunned the throttle, adjusting the angle of the ailerons and setting the velocipede into a slow climb.

The stitched canvas of the balloon, the envelope taut with mooring lines, hove into position below them.

And then the turbo boost sputtered and died.

"What happened?" Ulysses froze, half out of the saddle, his hands on Cadence's shoulders.

"It can't be possible!" the young woman gasped.

"What?" the dandy pressed.

"We're almost out of fuel. But how can that be?"

"Um, I might have made use of the turbo boost myself whilst engaged in my bid to rescue you," Ulysses explained apologetically. "How long have we got?"

He could see that the balloon was already starting to pull away from them, the inflated canvas, the ropes and lines passing out of reach underneath the bike.

"Actually, don't bother answering that." His view of the balloon had begun to be replaced by the distant meadows and forests of Nord Pas De Calais.

Standing on the seat behind her, his hands on her shoulders to balance himself, Ulysses leaned forward. Cadence turning in surprise, curious to see what he was doing.

"Thanks for everything," he said in her ear and, as she opened her mouth to respond, kissed her. Breaking contact, he turned his attention to the balloon drifting out of reach.

"Here goes nothing!" the parrot squawked, and Ulysses jumped.

"THEY'RE RETREATING!" MOREAU exclaimed.

"Are you sure?" Leroux was beside him in an instant. The mask was gone now, the need for anonymity having long passed, his pale blond hair whipping about the top of his head in the downdraft from the burners.

"I'm sure. Look!" The doctor pointed.

Sure enough, there was the steam-powered flying velocipede the silverback had chased through the bustling streets of Paris.

"What are they doing? Is this some kind of trick?" As someone who planned every detail of every scheme down to the last detail, Le Papillon didn't believe in chance and so was suspicious to the last. "Why would they do that? Why would they fall back when they're so close?"

"We're a long way from Paris," Moreau said, his tone suggesting that the answer should be obvious to anyone, "and there's no such thing as a limitless power supply; so I'm guessing they're running low on fuel."

"As simple as that?"

"As simple as that."

"So what will happen to them now?"

"Well if the girl's any kind of a pilot she'll probably glide her contraption down to the ground. If not, then their descent will be much faster and the landing one they're less likely to walk away from."

"Nothing's as simple as that."

"Why can't it be, just for once?" Moreau sighed. "We're almost at the coast. No one has a hope of catching us now."

"Aha! No! Look!" Le Papillon shouted in triumph, pointing at the receding bike as it banked left, breaking off its pursuit. "Quicksilver's gone!" And then his tone of triumph became one of annoyance as realisation dawned. "Which means he's..."

There was the whizzing sound of something sliding down a rope at speed, and then the slack crown line went taut as a figure swung into view from beyond the curve of the balloon envelope above them.

"On the balloon," the dandy adventurer finished for him as he swung himself into the basket, planting both feet squarely in the middle of the anarchist's chest, sending him flying.

ULYSSES LANDED HARD in the bottom of the basket, setting the balloon rocking. At the same time, Leroux landed in a crumpled heap on the other side of the basket.

Adrenalin masking the dull ache of his various injuries, Ulysses grabbed hold of a rope and used it to pull himself to his feet as Le Papillon came at him. From somewhere up above came the hiss of hot air escaping the canvas envelope.

Ulysses ducked the man's clumsy swipe and came up under him, lifting him off his feet and sending him crashing down on the wicker floor of the basket.

But the butterfly-collector was already on his feet again, an expression of undiluted fury on his face, the balloon's anchor in his hands. Ulysses took a step backwards as the enraged man adjusted his grip on the heavy iron grapple, ready to hurl it at Ulysses.

The dandy suddenly found himself remembering the last time he had been inside a hot air balloon. How long ago had it been? Two years? Longer? Travelling in time really messed with your sense of its passing. What he did recall was that on that occasion, things hadn't ended well.

Below them the Paris to London Express whistled loudly, closer than before. The balloon was losing height, and fast.

With a grunt of effort, Leroux heaved the anchor in Ulysses' direction. Taking a step forward, Ulysses caught the swinging anchor in his right hand. He gave a gasp of pain as the weight of it pulled at his shoulder, but used its momentum to swing him round as he landed a punch that sent Leroux crashing into the bottom of the basket again.

And as he swung the punch, he let go of the anchor, the grapple sailing over the edge of the basket, its tethering rope unspooling wildly after it.

The train whistled again, louder still.

Stepping back from the floored villains, Ulysses dared a glance over the edge of the basket. He could see the roofs of the carriages speeding past beneath and the blur of the track beyond.

The train whistled a third time. What was the fuss? he wondered.

The railway track approaching the coast, fields giving way to a cluster of buildings, the station, a myriad platforms, the sparkle of the morning sun on the calm sea beyond – and between them the gaping black mouth of Isambard Kingdom Brunel's Trans-Channel Tunnel.

The last time Ulysses had passed this way was when had ridden the train through the tunnel himself on his way home to Magna Britannia, after being presumed dead for a year and a half.

The basket suddenly lurched, so much so that Ulysses almost found himself tipped out. The two villains groaned as they tumbled backwards across the bottom of the basket.

The dandy clung on as the speeding balloon matched the speed of the hurtling train, the basket tilted sharply. The anchor line was stretched taut between the balloon and the rear of guardsman's carriage, where the iron grapple had snagged around the handrail.

This being the express, the train showed no signs of slowing down as it approached the station. Passing straight through, it ate up the yards – not miles now – that remained between them and the mouth of the tunnel.

The balloon was no longer losing height and Ulysses didn't like to imagine what would happen when it collided with the heavily-reinforced tunnel mouth.

Perhaps if he could cut the rope...

He looked around the basket. He saw a couple of rucksacks and sand-bags hung from hooks in the leather-covered rim, but there was no sign of an axe or even a knife that he could use to cut through the tether. Behind him, Leroux stirred.

That left only one option, as far as Ulysses was concerned.

Whipping off his belt, placing the leather strap over the taut mooring rope, Ulysses pulled it into a tight loop, before looping it around both his wrists, and then jumped.

The train's whistle suddenly deafening, drowning out the sound of the wind in his ears and the whizz of scorched leather on rope, Ulysses slid down the length of the anchor line, tumbling into the back of the guard's van just as it entered the mouth of the Trans-Channel Tunnel.

Picking himself up, he opened the door at the rear of the train and threw himself through, the door slamming shut again behind him.

Putting a hand to the bundle of papers stuffed into his jacket pocket, a wry smile forming on his face, an exhausted and dishevelled Ulysses Quicksilver set off for First Class.

BEHIND HIM, AS the Paris to London Express disappeared underground, the balloon collided with the tunnel mouth. Its burner housing crumpled and buckled. Gas canisters ruptured, and the canvas envelope was consumed by a ball of angry orange fire as the fuel cylinders exploded.

CHAPTER TWENTY-FOUR

One-Way Ticket to Hell

THE ATTENDANT PEERED down his nose at the ragged man with an eye-patch sitting in the well-upholstered seat in First Class, noting the way his filthy hands had already marked the pristine white coverings on the arm-rests with barely-disguised disgust. But before he could open his mouth to say anything and have the vagabond ejected from the train, the man took a ticket from a pocket of his soiled jacket and handed it over. "I think you'll find everything's in order," he said with a smile.

First Class wasn't busy – it certainly hadn't been hard for Ulysses to find a seat – but that didn't alter the fact that the attendant would clearly have much rather seen the dishevelled dandy ejected from the train than allowed him to remain in this carriage a moment longer. And yet, faced with the insurmountable evidence of the paper-work in front of him, it seemed that the attendant couldn't argue against Ulysses' right to do just that.

The express rattled on its way through the darkness under the sea as the man took what seemed to Ulysses an inordinate amount of time checking his papers. For a moment the dandy even began to wonder whether the falsified documents were really as convincing as he had believed them to be.

"Very good, sir," the attendant said at last, looking like he had just swallowed a wasp. "Enjoy your journey."

The steward turned to go.

"Are you still serving breakfast?"

"Breakfast, sir?" The scowl was still in place. Nothing was going to shift that look of disgust from his face.

"Yes, you know. The meal that comes between supper and lunch."

"I suppose I can check for you, sir, if you would like."

"I would like," Ulysses replied, smiling through the grime and blood. "A couple of croissants will do." The attendant turned to go again. "Oh, and a copy of *The Times* if you can find one."

Without another word, the steward set off for the dining carriage with what could have been described as grateful haste.

Ulysses raised an arm and gave his jacket a sniff. He did smell a little potent. There was probably a shower somewhere on board for use by First Class passengers. He would have to ask the attendant when he came back with Ulysses' newspaper and croissants. But there wasn't any rush. In fact, Ulysses thought as he rested his head against the cushioned rest of his seat, he probably had time to catch forty winks before having to do anything else at all.

Letting his shoulders relax, he felt the tension ooze out of them, and was soon asleep.

ULYSSES WOKE WITH a jolt. The dream – a phantasmagoria involving a giant ape and a hot air balloon – faded in an instant.

He looked around him, momentarily disorientated. In the next moment it all came back to him; he was aboard the Paris-London Express and heading for good old Blighty at last. But what had woken him?

He sat forward in his seat, gripping the armrests tightly, casting his senses about him to try to work out what it was his subconscious had spotted but that he was still missing.

"Your croissants, sir."

The attendant was suddenly there again, placing a china plate bearing two twists of pastry, a folded linen napkin, silver-plated butter knife, miniature pat of butter and tiny pot of apricot jam on the table cloth in front of him.

"And your paper."

A copy of yesterday's *Times* was carefully inserted into the rack on the wall between the darkened windows of the carriage.

"Are we speeding up?" Ulysses asked.

"Through the tunnel, sir?" he snorted, as if to say, *Don't be ridiculous, you one-eyed idiot.* Ulysses felt he was lucky the steward couldn't call for the men in white coats for as long as they were still on board the train.

"There are very strict rules regarding how fast the train can travel through the Trans-Channel Tunnel, sir. You know, in case of derailments."

"That's what I thought," Ulysses said, getting to his feet.

"Sir, there is nothing to worry about, I can assure you." The attendant sounded almost agitated now. The other First Class passengers were starting to peer in their direction, curious to know what all the fuss was about. Sour expressions were accompanied by a succession of tuts and a bout of aggravated huffing.

"Don't worry," Ulysses said, picking up the butter knife and hiding the blade in the palm of his hand, a guilty looked in his uncovered eye. "I'll sort it."

Ignoring the attendant's plaintive cries of "Would sir please return to his seat?" Ulysses headed for the front of the train.

IT DIDN'T TAKE him long to reach the forward guard's van and, having left the passenger carriages behind, make his way through the service carriage to the train's tender.

Opening the door from the guard's van he entered the howling darkness of the Trans-Channel Tunnel itself. Above him, caged hazard lights hurtled past at terrific speed, while smoking oil lamps upon the train itself threw fleeting shadows and a haze of yellow light across the curving walls and roof.

Unlike most locomotives, the train's tender was contained within its own carriage, allowing engine personnel to travel from the engine to other parts of the train with ease. Ulysses stepped from the guard's van to the tender compartment, just as the train sped up with a powerful lurch.

Steadying himself with a hand against a rail, he crossed over, and then stopped to settle his nerves and catch his breath, realising that his heart was racing once more. Whatever tiredness he might have been feeling had been dispelled by his renewed sense of alarm.

What could be wrong? he wondered as he advanced along the corridor that ran the length of the tender. But of course, deep down, he already knew the answer to that question.

But how could Leroux have survived the destruction of the balloon? He had been down on his hands and knees in the bottom of the basket. Besides, no one had followed the dandy down the taut anchor-line-cum-death-slide, of that he was certain. Wasn't he?

There had to be another explanation. Perhaps the driver of the train had been taken ill – a heart attack or a stroke maybe – and fallen against the controls, causing the train to speed up.

Ulysses was almost at the engine now, ears straining to hear anything over the chuffing of the locomotive as it hurtled on its way under the seabed.

It was then that he stumbled upon the body. He could only see the corpse's legs sticking out from a narrow alcove, where the driver and boilerman no doubt took their breaks. The rest of the body was covered by a bundle of what looked like parachute silk.

Of course! Ulysses cursed himself for an idiot. When he had been searching for a knife, or something suitable with which to cut the anchor line, the rucksacks he had only half been aware of must have been packed with a parachute each.

The silk showed signs of scorching, where debris from the explosion had fallen on it and burned through, but it had clearly worked well enough.

Leaving the body behind, he took a deep breath and stepped through the adjoining doorway from the tender box into the cabin of the hurtling engine.

The figure crouched over the locomotive's controls snapped his head round. Ulysses gasped.

"Well, well, well. If it isn't the cat," Le Papillon managed before his speech was subsumed by a bout of savage coughing.

So, the anarchist had survived the balloon's destruction after all. A part of Ulysses' being thrilled at that piece of knowledge. He looked forward to relishing the look on the anarchist's face when he realised that justice would be served, that Time's Arrow had caught up with him at last and would make him pay properly for his heinous crimes.

Leroux might have escaped death, but he hadn't come away from the exploding balloon unscathed. He was still dressed in his legionnaire's uniform, although it was now torn and singed in numerous places, the left epaulette hanging by a thread, the jacket hanging open at the front, half its buttons missing.

He still wore the gloves too, although they were no longer white. But there was no sign of his goggled gas-mask, and he had suffered as a result.

His face was a mess of bloody blisters. Much of his white-gold hair was missing: the top of his scalp was a seared dome of twisted pink flesh, the rest scorched black. Over the smells of engine oil, burning coal and sooty smoke, Ulysses' nose twitched at the acrid stench of burnt human hair. The man was clearly finding it hard to breathe.

But, Ulysses considered, it was no less than he deserved.

"So," Valerius Leroux wheezed, "how many lives do you have left now?

"More than you, I'll warrant," the dandy replied, his tone as cold as the rage inside him was hot.

The butterfly-collector's body was wracked by another painful bout of coughing. "Maybe so," he managed at last. "But I shall recover. When I am done with you I shall disappear, and when I am recovered I shall be reborn. Like the butterfly emerging from the chrysalis."

"But where can you go?" Ulysses' grip on the knife hidden in his hand tightened.

"Oh, you'd be surprised. And when I get there I shall be welcomed with open arms."

"Then why not just go there? I believed you to be dead. Why not stay that way? I wouldn't have been any the wiser."

The anarchist's blistered face twisted into a grimace of rage and hatred.

"What, and leave things unresolved between us?"

The lepidopterist's hand was on the accelerator handle. Knowing little about the operation of locomotives, Ulysses searched desperately for the brake.

When he spotted it at last, a knot of ice formed in the pit of his stomach. He was no engineer, but he knew it was no longer going to be possible to stop the speeding express.

At this rate, travelling at this speed, as soon as the train exited from Brunel's Trans-Channel Tunnel on the English side, the first bend it reached would cause it to jump the rails, the resulting crash causing the deaths of God alone knew how many more innocent victims.

"So you would sacrifice everyone on board this train – and many others – to satisfy your desire for revenge?" Ulysses growled.

"And you wouldn't?"

"What are you talking about?" Ulysses snapped, feeling his face flush with heat. "I'm nothing like you!"

"Aren't you?" Leroux said smiling darkly.

"Was that the driver I almost tripped over back there?"

"No," the lepidopterist laughed, "I think that was the boilerman."

"That was the boilerman? So what happened to the driver?"

"He got off at the last stop."

"There wasn't a last stop."

"There was for him."

"You're nothing but a common murderer, aren't you?"

"I can assure you, there is nothing common about me!" Leroux hissed vehemently.

"Why, then?" It was all Ulysses could think to say in the face of the man's raging psychoses.

Leroux smiled through the burning pain. "Why not?"

Ulysses slipped the hilt of the knife into his hand. The blade gleaming in the flickering orange lights of the tunnel.

His nemesis didn't appear to be armed, even though he had clearly managed to do away with the driver and boilerman without much trouble. But knives and the like... that wasn't his style, was it? Le Papillon preferred to employ other things as weapons for dramatic effect; the gorilla, the pipe organ under the Paris Opera House, the Eiffel Tower. And now, the Paris to London Express.

Taking a deep breath, Ulysses turned his back on the gasping Leroux and walked away from the cabin.

"What?" he heard Leroux spit. "Is that it? You're just giving up?" The butterfly-collector sounded almost disappointed.

Ulysses kept walking. He passed the body of the boilerman buried beneath its silken shroud, only stopping when he was at the rear of the tender compartment, the sooty wind whipping his hair and making his eye water.

He looked down at the thickly greased coupling mechanism locking the locomotive and its tender to the rest of the train. Crouching down, gripping a handrail for support with his left hand, he set about uncoupling the train.

"Hey! What are you doing?"

The attendant from earlier was at the door of the guard's van.

There was a dull metal *clonk* and the locomotive separated from the rest of train.

"Saving your life!" Ulysses called back over the chuffing noise of the engine. "I suggest you pull the emergency brake!"

Freed of the additional weight, the engine was already pulling away from the uncoupled carriages.

Ulysses watched the disconnected train slowly disappear as the darkness of the tunnel swallowed it up. When he could make out the yellow glow of the carriage windows no longer, he stepped back inside the tender compartment.

It was time to finish this.

* * *

"WHAT?"

The expression on the anarchist's face said it all.

"But I thought…"

"You thought wrong," Ulysses said. "I have denied you your final victory. The passengers are safe. There's only you and me now."

Ulysses went for him then, the tortured terrorist raising his hands in a futile effort to fend off the blows that came thick and fast.

Once his hands had been bloodied enough, his knuckles raw and dripping, the dandy stepped back.

He still might not win Most Dapper Dan of the Year, in his current state, but his chances were a darn sight better now than the butterfly-collector's.

"Why?" Le Papillon gasped through broken teeth, a gruel of blood and saliva dribbling from his mouth.

"Because every artist needs an audience to appreciate his work," Ulysses replied, taking something from his trouser pocket.

The metal bracelets rattled in his hand as he advanced on the terrorist. There were no bludgeoning blows this time, but Leroux was too weak to resist him as he snapped one of the bracelets shut around the man's right wrist and closed the other end of the handcuffs securely about the accelerator handle.

Ulysses reached over the beaten man, and pushed harder on the accelerator control.

"What are you doing?" Le Papillon gasped, peering at Ulysses through bruised and bloodied eyes.

There was a fire in the gentleman adventurer's one remaining eye as he regarded the murderer of Paris, his face set like stone.

Bending down, he put his mouth to Leroux's ear.

"What does it look like?" he hissed.

"What? You're insane!"

"Scream if you want to go faster."

As the hurtling flight of the locomotive increased in velocity, Ulysses returned to the tender box compartment.

When he returned to the driver's cabin, less than a minute later, the parachute harness was strapped tight across his chest, the parachute itself folded loosely over one arm.

The terrorist's horrified expression said it all.

"We're nothing alike, you and I," the dandy said, holding out the butter knife towards the vanquished Leroux. He could see a light at the end of the tunnel.

"What do you mean?" the other whispered weakly.

"You didn't give us a chance. You left us to die atop the Eiffel Tower. But I'm different. I'm going to give you a chance."

The knife landed at the man's feet, within reach of his left hand. Its blunt edge gleamed dully in the English sunlight penetrating the tunnel.

And with that Ulysses Quicksilver turned and left Le Papillon to face his fate alone.

STANDING AT THE rear of the locomotive, the wind whipping at his hair and clothes, nothing but the empty track before him, Ulysses suddenly found himself bathed in bright sunshine as the engine leapt from the dark confines of the Trans-Channel Tunnel.

Leroux's screams merged with the white noise of the wind whistling in his ears.

How did the saying go? It certainly felt like the sun was shining on the righteous at that moment.

Body tensed, in expectation of the inevitable, the dandy cast the bundle of parachute silk into the air.

The wind caught it immediately, unfurling it and filling the canopy in an instant. Ulysses Quicksilver was yanked clear of the train and into the sky.

A moment after that, the locomotive hit a curve in the track and jumped the rails. Spinning onto its side, it careened into a siding and into the back of a line of aggregate trucks, pushing them ahead of it as it ploughed across the tracks, throwing a cascade of sparks from its iron hull.

Having been pulled high into the air by the opening parachute, Ulysses began to descend again. From his elevated position, he watched the locomotive's progress as it powered into the back of an oil truck, as the engine sleeve suffered some catastrophic failure. The truck crumpled like a paper bag, a myriad hot sparks igniting the fuel it contained. The resulting fireball was even more impressive than the one that had consumed the balloon.

Ulysses smiled, even as he winced against the light and heat of the rising cloud of oily smoke and greasy orange flame, coming down hard on his knees as the parachute deposited him on the gravel at the side of the track.

Time's Arrow could not be denied. Justice had been served. Fate had been satisfied. Le Papillon, the murderer of the Paris, was dead.

Ulysses Quicksilver was home, and Destiny awaited.

EPILOGUE

Future Perfect

LONDINIUM MAXIMUM. THE sight of the unmistakeable smog-shrouded skyline, the clatter of the Overground, the putrid lingering stink of the sluggish Thames, the tang of pollution at the back of his throat, he drank it all in. Ulysses Quicksilver smiled. It was good to be home.

He hadn't realised how much he had missed old the place. But then in the past few days he'd hardly had time to think about anything much, other than how to get out of France and back to Blighty. And now that he had returned to the bosom of Magna Britannia, he could at last devote his energies to preventing the woman he loved from ever embarking upon her ill-fated trip to the Moon, and his younger self from the torture and torment he had been forced to endure, one way or another, over the last three months or more.

From his vantage point, atop the hill in Greenwich Park, in the shadow of the Royal Observatory, he was presented with an unparalleled view of the Syzygy Industries facility.

Only seven miles or so across London, his younger self was probably at home right now, sharing a glass of cognac with his brother Barty as the two of them pored over the days papers.

Barty! His one remaining eye blurred and he was forced to wipe the tears away with the back of his hand.

He hadn't thought about his errant sibling in… how long was it?

He had been so caught up with his own worries, he hadn't even considered that he might yet be able to save his younger brother too.

And Nimrod would be there.

The memory of his devoted butler and valet brought fresh tears.

But he couldn't return home yet. If he turned up on his own doorstep in this state, asking to speak with his younger self, that would cause more problems than it solved, of that he was certain.

No, he couldn't risk jeopardising everything now. Time's Arrow had to be subtler than that.

Having had time to reason things out, he realised now that it wasn't enough to simply stop his beloved from boarding the Apollo XIII at Heathrow. He had to stop Wormwood and Shurin, and the others, and make sure that their plan could never come to fruition in any form.

Sabotage, he thought as he scanned the forest of pipework and manufactory barns of the cavorite works; that was the way to go.

He smiled at that and gave a half chuckle.

Sabotage had been Le Papillon's way. To think that the anarchist had inspired him! The meticulous planning and masterminding, like playing a game of chess from behind the scenes, moving the pieces into place without anyone realising they were ever playing against him.

Ulysses laughed. It was a sinister, mirthless sound. Perhaps they were more alike than he had first wanted to admit.

He looked down at his feet. He was straddling the metal bar that marked the Prime Meridian. It was here that time in the British Empire – in fact, all time across the world and beyond – effectively 'began.'

Here time was 'made,' determined. And it was here that Time's Arrow had landed at last.

A plan began to form. But as it took shape, so the problems began to surface from the slough of his despond.

There was too much that he needed before he could even attempt to put a plan into action, but in his current condition – separated from his resources, his influence and his friends – he was going to have to find new allies to help him.

Something flitting through the darkness from the eaves of Flamsteed House behind him distracted him momentarily. It was a bat, hunting moths in the dusky evening gloom.

And then a thought came to him. He knew just who to ask.

Time was of the essence, and it was time he called in a favour.

Smiling to himself, Ulysses set off down the hill, a veritable spring in his step.

"How is the arm, doctor?"

Montague Moreau looked from the huge man squeezed into the chair behind the large mahogany desk, to the neat sling strapped across his chest, to the old woman standing in the corner of the room, carpet bag in hand, and then finally back at his ruggedly handsome host.

"It is better, thank you," he answered in stumbling English.

"Good, good," the other said, his tone suggesting he didn't care a jot how Moreau was feeling. "I'm so glad."

For several long moments, the only sounds that disturbed the office were the ticking of the battalion of clocks that covered the wall behind the desk, each set to a different time zone somewhere in the world, and beyond – London, Paris, St Petersburg, New York, Hong Kong, Atlantic City, Pacifica, Tranquillity, New Sidonia – and the scratching of the man's fountain pen as he put his name to a typed letter.

"Where am I?"

"Tell me, doctor, was Quicksilver in Paris the whole time?" the man asked, not looking up, but adding his signature to another official-looking document.

"What? What do you mean, the whole time?"

"Before, during and after the earthquake?"

"Er... Yes."

Moreau was confused. Who was this man and what was his

interest in the British agent? Quicksilver was the last person he had expected to find himself having to talk about. What about Le Papillon? What about what they had done to Paris?

The man's unresponsive silence only made it worse.

"Ishmael first ran into him after the Pascal killing."

"Interesting." Still the man didn't look up.

"How did I come to be here?"

He remembered parachuting onto the train, barely in time. He remembered waiting for the Magna Britannian authorities to rescue him and the other passengers from the uncoupled carriages stuck in the Trans-Channel Tunnel. But after disembarking at St Pancras, his memory was... hazy.

"When was the last time you saw him?"

"Quicksilver?" Moreau glanced at the old woman again. The wizened crone had not moved or spoken once since escorting him into the curious, artefact-filled office. "Um... After he jumped from the balloon. Before Le Papillon and I parachuted onto the train."

The man added his autograph to another formal looking piece of paper. He was clearly a very busy and important man.

"What is this place?"

The man looked up at last, put the lid on his pen, place the pen on the blotting pad on the desk, and leaned back in his chair, which creaked in response.

The man wasn't overweight, but he was huge. He looked not unlike a wrestler who bought his clothes bespoke from an exclusive Savile Row tailor.

He turned on a smile and just as quickly turned it off again.

Carefully placing the pile of signed documents in a polished mahogany out-tray, the man opened a drawer and took out a sheaf of papers barely contained within a cut card folder. Undoing the string that held everything together, the man placed the folder on the desk, pushing it towards Moreau.

"Tell me, doctor" – the man flicked the folder open to reveal a bundle of blueprints and detailed anatomical drawings – "what do you make of this little lot?"

Unable to help himself, Moreau leant forwards and picked

up the first piece of paper that came to hand, his eyes widening in wonder as he examined the intricately annotated illustration.

It looked like some impossible amalgam of ape, crab and shark, surmounted by a leering human head that was connected to the nightmarish body by an elongated neck.

"Is this for real?"

The man's smile switched on for a brief moment. He picked up the pen again. "I could make use of a man of your talents," he said, rolling the pen between his fingers.

Moreau looked up from the freakish anatomical study and into the other's flinty gaze.

"Dr Moreau," the man said, "I'd like to make you an offer; an offer of employment. Do you think you might be interested at all?"

Moreau held the man's gaze. It wasn't really as if he had a choice, but the grotesque image on the paper in his hand intrigued him... excited him even. Just when it had seemed like everything was coming to an end, suddenly he had a glorious future ahead of him.

Montague Moreau smiled.

"When do I start?"

But at my back I always hear
Time's winged chariot hurrying near...

– Andrew Marvell, To His Coy Mistress, 1681

I never think of the future. It comes soon enough.

– Albert Einstein, 1930

THE END

JONATHAN GREEN is a writer of speculative fiction, with more than forty books to his name. He is the creator of Abaddon Books' *Pax Britannia* steampunk universe, and *Time's Arrow* is his eighth novel set within that world.

He has written for such diverse properties as *Doctor Who*, *Star Wars: The Clone Wars*, *Sonic the Hedgehog*, *Teenage Mutant Ninja Turtles* and *Moshi Monsters*, but – outside of the steampunk milieu – he is probably best known for his contributions to the *Fighting Fantasy* range of adventure gamebooks and numerous Black Library publications, which draw inspiration from the table top war-gaming systems of *Warhammer* and *Warhammer 40,000*.

He currently divides his time between West London and rural Wiltshire. To find out more about his latest projects visit WWW.JONATHANGREENAUTHOR.COM.

AUTHOR'S NOTE

THE BOOK YOU hold in your hands is, I believe, the first of its kind. It was initially published in three parts, in ebook form (from 2011 to 2012), before being collected in this paperback edition.

What makes it so unusual – and, I believe, unique – is that the readers actively helped determine the course of the story. After part one, *Red-Handed*, was released, readers voted online as to how they would like the story to continue. I then wrote part two, *Black Swan*, the narrative being influenced by the majority decision. After *Black Swan* was released, readers were encouraged to have their say again, and based on the outcome I finally wrote part three, *White Noise*.

The challenge, during all this, was to write a story that when collected as one novel, read like it had been written as one novel right from the start, and was not just a collection of novellas. Whether I succeeded or not is for you to decide.

Personally I am very pleased with what we have achieved with *Time's Arrow*. I'm not using 'we' here as Queen Victoria might either, for this project involved all sorts of open-minded individuals saying "Yes" to me at various stages along the way and without whom the ebook experiment would never have got off the ground. So, a few thank yous are required...

Firstly, to Jonathan Oliver, editor-in-chief of Abaddon and Solaris Books and Wielder of the Red Pen, for being so enthused by the whole Pax Britannia concept in the first place and latterly so keen to make this project a success. Secondly, to David Moore, desk editor, master ebook maker and Keeper of the Elements of Style, for turning my fusty Word documents into much prettier, Victorian-flavoured zeros and ones, as well as writing the tantalizing copy that made people want to have their say. And thirdly to Ben Smith, book publishing manager and Custodian of the Spreadsheets, who ultimately made sure everything happened on time so that it could happen at all.

One of the most exciting things for me about this project was that because there were three ebooks, Simon Parr – daring designer and pixel painter extraordinaire – ending up producing three covers for what was really just the one book. I know I am biased but I would have to say that they are among his best work to date. So thank you, Simon!

This might sound corny, but a big thank you to the readers who downloaded each part of the adventure in ebook form and voted on how the story should develop. If they hadn't thrown themselves into the experiment it wouldn't have worked – simple as that.

Lastly, thanks are due to David Bradley and Richard Edwards of SFX Magazine for allowing the interview that follows this 'brief' author's note (and which first appeared online in its entirety at www.sfx.co.uk) to be reproduced here.

But before I go, I would just like to point out that Matt Zitron (who gets a blink-and-you'll-miss-it-mention in Chapter Seven "The Scarlet Pimpernel Returns") is the name of a real person and appears in this book courtesy of the Genre for Japan charity auction, which took place in April 2011, in support of the Red Cross efforts in the aftermath of the Japan Earthquake. The character appearing under Matt's name is, of course, wholly fictional (and also appears in Al Ewing's Pax Britannia novel *Pax Omega*). Thanks to Matt's sterling fund-raising efforts, *Time's Arrow* is dedicated to his son Isaac.

Jonathan Green, Wiltshire, MMXII

THE *SFX* INTERVIEW

EVER WISHED YOU could have a little more input into the books you read? With *Time's Arrow*, the eighth Ulysses Quicksilver novel in Abaddon's Pax Britannia series, author Jonathan Green is making the storytelling a collaborative affair. Taking the "Choose your own adventure" principle of *Fighting Fantasy* and playing it out on a much larger scale, the first instalment of *Time's Arrow*, *Red-Handed* is now available as an ebook, and it ends with a cliffhanger. How the story continues will depend on the results of a vote to decide what happens next – so the rest of the novel is in your hands. We had a chat with Green to find out a little more about the project...

Have you enjoyed experimenting with the novel format?

It's certainly exciting to feel that we're doing something with the established novel format that's not been done for a long time. *Time's Arrow* partly came out of the way that Dickens would write his books piecemeal, and influenced by the popularity of certain characters among his readership. I feel that with this project we're truly taking steampunk literature back to its Victorian roots.

You've written *Fighting Fantasy* novels before. How has the writing of this compared? Have you approached it in a similar way?

There is a crossover element and the idea was certainly inspired by the fact that I have written so many gamebooks – and not just for the Fighting Fantasy range either. I've written gamebooks featuring *Doctor Who* and *Sonic The Hedgehog*, as well as characters from the *Star Wars* universe. I'm currently working on my thirteenth gamebook, which takes the grim darkness of the 41st millennium as its setting as it's for Games Workshop's publishing imprint Black Library. And I've recently had my first gamebook app, *Temple Of The Spider God*, published by Tin Man Games for the iDevice of your choice.

However, in general I have approached *Time's Arrow* as I would approach the writing of any other novel. The big difference is that I don't know how the story is really going to progress until the votes have been counted and verified. And for someone who plans his books in minute detail before he ever starts writing them, that's the challenging bit.

Is it odd writing a novel when you don't know how exactly it's going to end – and knowing you're not in full control?

Absolutely! I wouldn't describe myself as a control freak but when it comes to creating a plot and a whole world within a novel, I suppose that's exactly what I am. I believe that detailed chapter breakdowns are what have prevented me from ever suffering a case of writer's block. This time it's going to be the pressure of the deadline that's going to have to keep me going!

Would the different versions of the story be radically different?

The protagonist Ulysses Quicksilver starts the novel in a particular place and I know where he needs to end up at the end of *Time's Arrow*, but everything in between…? That could vary enormously. We'll just have to wait and see what the public decide.

Was there much debate over where to put the "choice" points, or did they grow organically out of the story?

My *Pax Britannia* novels have generally followed a familiar Three Act format so that seemed like the sensible way to go with *Time's Arrow*. And I always like to end each part on a cliffhanger anyway to keep people hooked and wanting to read more. Of course I'm hoping that when the story is read as a whole, the section breaks will appear to have grown organically from the story itself.

Would you be interested in doing other versions of the novel where the other choices were made?

To be honest, probably not. When people ask me which of the books I've written is my favourite, the answer's always the same: it's the next one. That's what excites and inspires me, applying the whole creative process to tease out a tale where before there wasn't one.

Going back to a story I'm done with and writing an alternative version... that doesn't sound like quite so much fun. I want to know where the characters and storyline are going next, not where they might have been if things had worked out differently.

Do you think you'll be tempted to change anything when all of the chapters are put together as a full book, or will they stay as they were?

I don't want to change anything once the story's done, otherwise I'll feel like I've cheated people. If you want the readership to be invested in a project such as this, at the end of the day you have to give them what they asked for, otherwise it will feel like you've conned them.

For good or for ill, what appears in the three ebooks will be what appears in print (bar any typos that are spotted in the meantime).

Is it something you'd like to try again?

Yes, I think I would. It's too early to say if this is the model Abaddon would want to follow with the *Pax Britannia* range in the future. But it would be fun to continue in a similar vein if it's what people want and they respond with enthusiasm to *Time's Arrow*. Maybe it could become a trademark of mine...

Interview by Richard Edwards
November 2011